ORBIT 18

ORBIT 18

Edited by Damon Knight

HARPER & ROW, PUBLISHERS

New York, Hagerstown, San Francisco, London

FIRST EDITION

Library of Congress Catalog Card Number: 75-25089

ISBN: 0-06-012433-4

Designed by C. Linda Dingler

Illustrations by Richard Wilhelm and Gary Cohn

CONTENTS

ORBIT 18

They Say

Something different happens when large numbers of women begin to read and write science fiction, as has happened in recent years. By its nature an expansive genre, s/f could conceivably incorporate anything, and as it has grown it has taken in other genres. To some degree this mitigates against the sexual polarities of extreme genreness. It is hard to say whether s/f has gotten better because it is more androgynous, or vice versa; in any case, both have happened at the same time. When a genre moves from "pulp" to "good," the characters appear more real, more complicated, more subtly drawn. The author's point of view seems more intelligent, more humane, more philosophical. But actually what we see in the old pulp characters is all too real—we see naked male and female power drives at war. In what we call "literature," these characters are more civilized. Male and female, and the male and female within any character, are more at peace.

As a result, we have a double standard for literature. On the one hand, a book is "good" if it allows the reader to feel, in a cathartic way, the exciting and violent emotions associated with our cultural neuroses. On the other hand it is "good" if it allows the reader to place these emotions within a rational framework and not let them get out of hand. We don't admit it, but when we say books are "good" in this sense, we mean morally good. Works of fiction that mean the most to the most people have elements of both kinds of "good," but in the proper order—the emotions must be felt, then reordered in some enlarging and therapeutic way. They are civilizing works, works of maturity, and do not convey the sense that they were written especially by or for a woman or a man.

> —"What's New from Venus?"
> by Barbara Damrosch,
> *Village Voice,* July 7, 1975

At college, for instance, I learned—and believed—that "really important literature" dealt with bullfighting, storms at sea, barroom brawls, rape (from the man's standpoint), and grunts and groans. . . . Everybody said, "That's raw and elemental and true and deep."

A story I wrote for my class was about a prom; they said it was funny, but trivial. A brawl was important but going into a ladies' room at a dance and counting up to twenty-five so people would think you were busy doing something was not.

I was convinced I didn't know what real life was like—I was no bullfighter or mountain climber, and even Anna Karenina and Helen of Troy and Cleopatra didn't have too much to do with me personally.

So I hit on this stupid-clever idea: "I'll write about Mars. Nobody knows about that. They can't tell me I'm wrong."

Even then, I found myself writing adventure stories about men and love stories about women.

Gradually I began to ask myself, "Why is this? I want to write about a woman who is a hero in this fantasy land."

It took me three weeks even to begin. I sat there at the typewriter and just shook all over and said to myself, "People will throw stones at me in the street. Critics will say I have penis envy."

But I finally did it, though I still tried my damndest to make my character beautiful. I kept writing how lovely she was and she kept looking up from the typewriter and saying, "Come on, who are you kidding?"

—Joanna Russ, quoted in the
Los Angeles Times, June 9, 1975

LADIES AND GENTLEMEN, THIS IS YOUR CRISIS

A loaf of bread, a wall TV, and thou . . .

Kate Wilhelm

4 P.M. Friday

Lottie's factory closed early on Friday, as most of them did now. It was four when she got home, after stopping for frozen dinners, bread, sandwich meats, beer. She switched on the wall TV screen before she put her bag down. In the kitchen she turned on another set, a portable, and watched it as she put the food away. She had missed four hours.

They were in the mountains. That was good. Lottie liked it when they chose mountains. A stocky man was sliding down a slope, feet out before him, legs stiff—too conscious of the camera, though. Lottie couldn't tell if he had meant to slide, but he did not look happy. She turned her attention to the others.

A young woman was walking slowly, waist high in ferns, so apparently unconscious of the camera that it could only be a pose this early in the game. She looked vaguely familiar. Her blond hair was loose, like a girl in a shampoo commercial, Lottie decided. She narrowed her eyes, trying to remember where she had seen the girl. A model, probably, wanting to be a star. She would wander aimlessly, not even trying for the prize, content with the publicity she was getting.

The other woman was another sort altogether. A bit overweight, her thighs bulged in the heavy trousers the contestants wore; her hair was dyed black and fastened with a rubberband in a no-nonsense manner. She was examining a tree intently. Lottie nodded at her. Everything about her spoke of purpose, of concentration, of planning. She'd do.

The final contestant was a tall black man, in his forties probably. He wore old-fashioned eyeglasses—a mistake. He'd lose them and be seriously handicapped. He kept glancing about with a lopsided grin.

Lottie had finished putting the groceries away; she returned to the living room to sit before the large unit that gave her a better view of the map, above the sectioned screen. The Andes, she had decided, and was surprised and pleased to find she was wrong. Alaska! There were bears and wolves in Alaska still, and elk and moose.

The picture shifted, and a thrill of anticipation raised the hairs on Lottie's arms and scalp. Now the main screen was evenly divided; one half showed the man who had been sliding. He was huddled against the cliff, breathing very hard. On the other half of the screen was an enlarged aerial view. Lottie gasped. Needle-like snow-capped peaks, cliffs, precipices, a raging stream . . . The yellow dot of light that represented the man was on the edge of a steep hill covered with boulders and loose gravel. If he got on that, Lottie thought, he'd be lost. From where he was, there was no way he could know what lay ahead. She leaned forward, examining him for signs that he understood, that he was afraid, anything. His face was empty; all he needed now was more air than he could get with his labored breathing.

Andy Stevens stepped in front of the aerial map; it was three feet taller than he. "As you can see, ladies and gentlemen, there is only this scrub growth to Dr. Burnside's left. Those roots might be strong enough to hold, but I'd guess they are shallowly rooted, wouldn't you? And if he chooses this direction, he'll need something to grasp, won't he?" Andy had his tape measure and a pointer. He looked worried. He touched the yellow dot of light. "Here he is. As you can see, he is resting, for the moment, on a narrow ledge after his slide down sixty-five feet of loose dirt and gravel. He doesn't appear to be hurt. Our own Dr. Lederman is watching him along with the rest of us, and he assures me that Dr. Burnside is not injured."

Andy pointed out the hazards of Dr. Burnside's precarious position, and the dangers involved in moving. Lottie nodded, her lips tight and grim. It was off to a good start.

6 *P.M. Friday*

Butcher got home, as usual, at six. Lottie heard him at the door but didn't get up to open it for him. Dr. Burnside was still sitting there. He had to move. Move, you bastard! Do something!

"Whyn't you unlock the door?" Butcher yelled, yanking off his jacket.

Lottie paid no attention. Butcher always came home mad, resentful because she had got off early, mad at his boss because the warehouse didn't close down early, mad at traffic, mad at everything.

"They say anything about them yet?" Butcher asked, sitting in his recliner.

Lottie shook her head. Move, you bastard! Move!

The man began to inch his way to the left and Lottie's heart thumped, her hands clenched.

"What's the deal?" Butcher asked hoarsely, already responding to Lottie's tension.

"Dead end that way," Lottie muttered, her gaze on the screen. "Slide with boulders and junk if he tries to go down. He's gotta go right."

The man moved cautiously, never lifting his feet from the ground but sliding them along, testing each step. He paused again, this time with less room than before. He looked desperate. He was perspiring heavily. Now he could see the way he had chosen offered little hope of getting down. More slowly than before, he began to back up; dirt and gravel shifted constantly. The amplifiers picked up the noise of the stuff rushing downward, like a waterfall heard from a distance, and now and then a muttered unintelligible word from the man. The volume came up: he was cursing. Again and again he stopped. He was pale and sweat ran down his face. He didn't move his hands from the cliff to wipe it away.

Lottie was sweating too. Her lips moved occasionally with a faint curse or prayer. Her hands gripped the sofa.

7:30 P.M. Friday

Lottie fell back onto the sofa with a grunt, weak from sustained tension. They were safe. It had taken over an hour to work his way to this place where the cliff and steep slope gave way to a gentle hill. The man was sprawled out face down, his back heaving.

Butcher abruptly got up and went to the bathroom. Lottie couldn't move yet. The screen shifted and the aerial view filled the larger part. Andy pointed out the contestants' lights and finally began the recap.

Lottie watched on the portable set as she got out their frozen dinners and heated the oven. Dr. Lederman was talking about Angie Dawes, the young aspiring actress whose problem was that of having been overprotected all her life. He said she was a potential suicide, and the panel of examining physicians had agreed Crisis Therapy would be helpful.

The next contestant was Mildred Ormsby, a chemist, divorced, no children. She had started on a self-destructive course through drugs, said Dr. Lederman, and would be benefited by Crisis Therapy.

The tall black man, Clyde Williams, was an economist; he taught at Harvard and had tried to murder his wife and their three children by burning down their house with them in it. Crisis Therapy had been indicated.

Finally, Dr. Edward Burnside, the man who had started the show with such drama, was shown being interviewed. Forty-one, unmarried, living with a woman, he was a statistician for a major firm. Recently he had started to feed the wrong data into the computer, aware but unable to stop himself.

Dr. Lederman's desk was superimposed on the aerial view and he started his taped explanation of what Crisis Therapy was. Lottie made coffee. When she looked again Eddie was still lying on the ground, exhausted, maybe even crying. She wished he would roll over so she could see if he was crying.

Andy returned to explain how the game was played: The winner received one million dollars, after taxes, and all the contestants were undergoing Crisis Therapy that would enrich their lives beyond measure. Andy explained the automatic, air-cushioned, five-day cameras focused electronically on the contestants, the orbiting satellite that made it possible to keep them under observation at all times, the light amplification, infrared system that would keep them visible all night. This part made Lottie's head ache.

Next came the full-screen commercial for the wall units. Only those who had them could see the entire show. Down the left side of the screen were the four contestants, each in a separate panel, and over them a topographical map that showed the entire region, where the exit points were, the nearest roads, towns. Center screen could be divided any way the director chose. Above this picture was the show's slogan: "This Is Your Crisis!" and a constantly running commercial. In the far right corner there was an aerial view of the selected site, with the colored dots of light. Mildred's was red, Angie's was green, Eddie's yellow, Clyde's blue. Anything else larger than a rabbit or squirrel that moved into the viewing area would be white.

The contestants were shown being taken to the site, first by airplane, then helicopter. They were left there on noon Friday and had until midnight Sunday to reach one of the dozen trucks that ringed the area. The first one to report in at one of the trucks was the winner.

10 P.M. Friday

Lottie made up her bed on the couch while Butcher opened his recliner full length and brought out a blanket and pillow from the bedroom. He had another beer and Lottie drank milk and ate cookies, and presently they turned off the light and there was only the glow from the screen in the room.

The contestants were settled down for the night, each in a sleeping bag, campfires burning low, the long northern twilight still not faded. Andy began to explain the contents of the backpacks.

Lottie closed her eyes, opened them several times, just to check, and finally fell asleep.

1 A.M. Saturday

Lottie sat up suddenly, wide awake, her heart thumping. The red beeper had come on. On center screen the girl was sitting up, staring into darkness, obviously frightened. She must have heard something. Only her dot showed on her screen, but there was no way for her to know that. Lottie lay down again, watching, and became aware of Butcher's heavy snoring. She shook his leg and he shifted and for a few moments breathed deeply, without the snore, then began again.

Francine Dumont was the night M.C.; now she stepped to one side of the screen. "If she panics," Francine said in a hushed voice, "it could be the end of the game for her." She pointed out the hazards in the area—boulders, a steep drop-off, the thickening trees on two sides. "Let's watch," she whispered and stepped back out of the way.

The volume was turned up; there were rustlings in the undergrowth. Lottie closed her eyes and tried to hear them through the girl's ears, and felt only contempt for her. The girl was stiff with fear. She began to build up her campfire. Lottie nodded. She'd stay awake all night, and by late tomorrow she'd be finished. She would be lifted out, the end of Miss Smarty Pants Dawes.

Lottie sniffed and closed her eyes, but now Butcher's snores were louder. If only he didn't sound like a dying man, she thought—sucking in air, holding it, holding it, then suddenly erupting into a loud snort that turned into a gurgle. She pressed her hands over her ears and finally slept again.

2 P.M. Saturday

There were beer cans on the table, on the floor around it. There was half a loaf of bread and a knife with dried mustard and the mustard jar without a top. The salami was drying out, hard, and there were onion skins and bits of brown lettuce and an open jar of pickles. The butter had melted in its dish, and the butter knife was on the floor, spreading a dark stain on the rug.

Nothing was happening on the screen now. Angie Dawes hadn't left the fern patch. She was brushing her hair.

Mildred was following the stream, but it became a waterfall ahead and she would have to think of something else.

The stout man was still making his way downward as directly as possible, obviously convinced it was the fastest way and no more dangerous than any other.

The black man was being logical, like Mildred, Lottie admitted. He watched the shadows and continued in a southeasterly direction, tackling the hurdles as he came to them, methodically, without haste. Ahead of him, invisible to him, but clearly visible to the floating cameras and the audience, were a mother bear and two cubs in a field of blueberries.

Things would pick up again in an hour or so, Lottie knew. Butcher came back. "You have time for a quick shower," Lottie said. He was beginning to smell.

"Shut up." Butcher sprawled in the recliner, his feet bare.

Lottie tried not to see his thick toes, grimy with warehouse dust. She got up and went to the kitchen for a bag, and started to throw the garbage into it. The cans clattered.

"Knock it off, will ya!" Butcher yelled. He stretched to see around her. He was watching the blond braid her hair. Lottie threw another can into the bag.

9 P.M. Saturday

Butcher sat on the edge of the chair, biting a fingernail. "See that?" he breathed. "You see it?" He was shiny with perspiration. Lottie nodded, watching the white dots move on the aerial map, watching the blue dot moving, stopping for a long time, moving again. Clyde and the bears were approaching each other minute by minute, and Clyde knew now that there was something ahead of him.

"You see that?" Butcher cried out hoarsely.

"Just be still, will you?" Lottie said through her teeth. The black man was sniffing the air.

"You can smell a goddam lousy bear a country mile!" Butcher said. "He knows."

"For God's sake, shut up!"

"Yeah, he knows all right," Butcher said softly. "Mother bear, cubs . . . she'll tear him apart."

"Shut up! Shut up!"

Clyde began to back away. He took half a dozen steps, then turned and ran. The bear stood up; behind her the cubs tumbled in play. She turned her head in a listening attitude. She growled and dropped to four feet and began to amble in the direction Clyde had taken. They were about an eighth of a mile apart. Any second she would be able to see him.

Clyde ran faster, heading for thick trees. Past the trees was a cliff he had skirted earlier.

"Saw a cave or something up there," Butcher muttered. "Betcha. Heading for a cave."

Lottie pressed her hands hard over her ears. The bear was closing the gap; the cubs followed erratically, and now and again the mother bear paused to glance at them and growl softly. Clyde began to climb the face of the cliff. The bear came into view and saw him. She ran. Clyde was out of her reach; she began to climb, and rocks were loosened by her great body. When one of the cubs bawled, she let go and half slid, half fell back to the bottom. Standing on her hind legs, she growled at the man above her. She was nine feet tall. She shook her great head from side to side another moment, then turned and waddled back toward the blueberries, trailed by her two cubs.

"Smart bastard," Butcher muttered. "Good thinking. Knew he couldn't outrun a bear. Good thinking."

Lottie went to the bathroom. She had smelled the bear, she thought. If he had only shut up a minute! She was certain she had smelled the bear. Her hands were trembling.

The phone was ringing when she returned to the living room. She answered, watching the screen. Clyde looked shaken, the first time he had been rattled since the beginning.

"Yeah," she said into the phone. "He's here." She put the receiver down. "Your sister."

"She can't come over," Butcher said ominously. "Not unless she's drowned that brat."

"Funny," Lottie said, scowling. Corinne should have enough consideration not to make an issue of it week after week.

"Yeah," Butcher was saying into the phone. "I know it's tough on a floor set, but what the hell, get the old man to buy a wall unit. What's he planning to do, take it with him?" He listened. "Like I said, you know how it is. I say okay, then Lottie gives me hell. Know what I mean? I mean, it ain't worth it. You know?" Presently he banged the receiver down.

"Frank's out of town?"

He didn't answer, settled himself down into his chair and reached for his beer.

"He's in a fancy hotel lobby where they got a unit screen the size of a barn and she's got that lousy little portable . . ."

"Just drop it, will ya? She's the one that wanted the kid, remember. She's bawling her head off but she's not coming over. So drop it!"

"Yeah, and she'll be mad at me for a week, and it takes two to make a kid."

"Jesus Christ!" Butcher got up and went into the kitchen. The refrigerator door banged. "Where's the beer?"

"Under the sink."

"Jesus! Whyn't you put it in the refrigerator?"

"There wasn't enough room for it all. If you've gone through all the cold beers, you don't need any more!"

He slammed the refrigerator door again and came back with a can of beer. When he pulled it open, warm beer spewed halfway across the room. Lottie knew he had done it to make her mad. She ignored him and watched Mildred worm her way down into her sleeping bag. Mildred had the best chance of winning, she thought. She checked her position on the aerial map. All the lights were closer to the trucks now, but there wasn't anything of real importance between Mildred and the goal. She had chosen right every time.

"Ten bucks on yellow," Butcher said suddenly.

"You gotta be kidding! He's going to break his fat neck before he gets out of there!"

"Okay, ten bucks." He slapped ten dollars down on the table, between the TV dinner trays and the coffee pot.

"Throw it away," Lottie said, matching it. "Red."

"The fat lady?"

"Anybody who smells like you better not go around insulting someone who at least takes time out to have a shower now and then!" Lottie cried and swept past him to the kitchen. She and Mildred were about the same size. "And why don't you get off your butt and clean up some of that mess! All I do every weekend is clear away garbage!"

"I don't give a shit if it reaches the ceiling!"

Lottie brought a bag and swept trash into it. When she got near Butcher, she held her nose.

6 A.M. *Sunday*

Lottie sat up. "What happened?" she cried. The red beeper was on. "How long's it been on?"

"Half an hour. Hell, I don't know."

Butcher was sitting tensely on the side of the recliner, gripping it with both hands. Eddie was in a tree, clutching the trunk. Below him, dogs were tearing apart his backpack, and another dog was leaping repeatedly at him.

"Idiot!" Lottie cried. "Why didn't he hang up his stuff like the others?"

Butcher made a noise at her, and she shook her head, watching. The dogs had smelled food, and they would search for it, tearing up everything they found. She smiled grimly. They might keep Mr. Fat Neck up there all day, and even if he got down, he'd have nothing to eat.

That's what did them in, she thought. Week after week it was the same. They forgot the little things and lost. She leaned back and ran her hand through her hair. It was standing out all over her head.

Two of the dogs began to fight over a scrap of something and the leaping dog jumped into the battle with them. Presently they all ran away, three of them chasing the fourth.

"Throw away your money," Lottie said gaily, and started around Butcher. He swept out his hand and pushed her down again and left the room without a backward look. It didn't matter who won, she thought, shaken by the push. That twenty and twenty more would have to go to the finance company to pay off the loan for the wall unit. Butcher knew that; he shouldn't get so hot about a little joke.

1 P.M. Sunday

"This place looks like a pigpen," Butcher growled. "You going to clear some of this junk away?" He was carrying a sandwich in one hand, beer in the other; the table was littered with breakfast remains, leftover snacks from the morning and the night before.

Lottie didn't look at him. "Clear it yourself."

"I'll clear it." He put his sandwich down on the arm of his chair and swept a spot clean, knocking over glasses and cups.

"Pick that up!" Lottie screamed. "I'm sick and tired of cleaning up after you every damn weekend! All you do is stuff and guzzle and expect me to pick up and clean up."

"Damn right."

Lottie snatched up the beer can he had put on the table and

threw it at him. The beer streamed out over the table, chair, over his legs. Butcher threw down the sandwich and grabbed at her. She dodged and backed away from the table into the center of the room. Butcher followed, his hands clenched.

"You touch me again, I'll break your arm!"

"Bitch!" He dived for her and she caught his arm, twisted it savagely and threw him to one side.

He hauled himself up to a crouch and glared at her with hatred. "I'll fix you," he muttered. "I'll fix you!"

Lottie laughed. He charged again, this time knocked her backward and they crashed to the floor together and rolled, pummeling each other.

The red beeper sounded and they pulled apart, not looking at each other, and took their seats before the screen.

"It's the fat lady," Butcher said malevolently. "I hope the bitch kills herself."

Mildred had fallen into the stream and was struggling in waist-high water to regain her footing. The current was very swift, all white water here. She slipped and went under. Lottie held her breath until she appeared again, downstream, retching, clutching at a boulder. Inch by inch she drew herself to it and clung there trying to get her breath back. She looked about desperately; she was very white. Abruptly she launched herself into the current, swimming strongly, fighting to get to the shore as she was swept down the river.

Andy's voice was soft as he said, "That water is forty-eight degrees, ladies and gentlemen! Forty-eight! Dr. Lederman, how long can a person be immersed in water that cold?"

"Not long, Andy. Not long at all." The doctor looked worried too. "Ten minutes at the most, I'd say."

"That water is reducing her body heat second by second," Andy said solemnly. "When it is low enough to produce unconsciousness . . ."

Mildred was pulled under again; when she appeared this time, she was much closer to shore. She caught a rock and held on. Now she could stand up, and presently she dragged herself rock by rock, boulder by boulder, to the shore. She was shaking hard, her teeth chattering. She began to build a fire. She could hardly open her waterproof matchbox. Finally she had a blaze and she began to strip. Her backpack, Andy reminded the audience, had been lost when she fell into the water. She had only what she had on her back, and if she wanted to continue after the sun set and the cold evening began, she had to dry her things thoroughly.

"She's got nerve," Butcher said grudgingly.

Lottie nodded. She was weak. She got up, skirted Butcher, and went to the kitchen for a bag. As she cleaned the table, every now and then she glanced at the naked woman by her fire. Steam was rising off her wet clothes.

10 P.M. Sunday

Lottie had moved Butcher's chair to the far side of the table the last time he had left it. His beard was thick and coarse, and he still wore the clothes he had put on to go to work Friday morning. Lottie's stomach hurt. Every weekend she got constipated.

The game was between Mildred and Clyde now. He was in good shape, still had his glasses and his backpack. He was farther from his truck than Mildred was from hers, but she had eaten nothing that afternoon and was limping badly. Her boots must have shrunk, or else she had not waited for them to get completely dry. Her face twisted with pain when she moved.

The girl was still posing in the high meadow, now against a tall tree, now among the wild flowers. Often a frown crossed her face and surreptitiously she scratched. Ticks, Butcher said. Probably full of them.

Eddie was wandering in a daze. He looked empty, and was walking in great aimless circles. Some of them cracked like that, Lottie knew. It had happened before, sometimes to the strongest one of all. They'd slap him right in a hospital and no one would hear anything about him again for a long time, if ever. She didn't waste pity on him.

She would win, Lottie knew. She had studied every kind of wilderness they used and she'd know what to do and how to do it. She was strong, and not afraid of noises. She found herself nodding and stopped, glanced quickly at Butcher to see if he had noticed. He was watching Clyde.

"Smart," Butcher said, his eyes narrowed. "That sonabitch's been saving himself for the home stretch. Look at him." Clyde started to lope, easily, as if aware the TV truck was dead ahead.

Now the screen was divided into three parts, the two finalists, Mildred and Clyde, side by side, and above them a large aerial view that showed their red and blue dots as they approached the trucks.

"It's fixed!" Lottie cried, outraged when Clyde pulled ahead of Mildred. "I hope he falls down and breaks his back!"

"Smart," Butcher said over and over, nodding, and Lottie knew he was imagining himself there, just as she had done. She felt a chill. He glanced at her and for a moment their eyes held —naked, scheming. They broke away simultaneously.

Mildred limped forward until it was evident each step was torture. Finally she sobbed, sank to the ground and buried her face in her hands.

Clyde ran on. It would take an act of God now to stop him. He reached the truck at twelve minutes before midnight.

For a long time neither Lottie nor Butcher moved. Neither spoke. Butcher had turned the audio off as soon as Clyde reached the truck, and now there were the usual after-game recaps, the congratulations, the helicopter liftouts of the other contestants.

Butcher sighed. "One of the better shows," he said. He was hoarse.

"Yeah. About the best yet."

"Yeah." He sighed again and stood up. "Honey, don't bother with all this junk now. I'm going to take a shower, and then I'll help you clean up, okay?"

"It's not that bad," she said. "I'll be done by the time you're finished. Want a sandwich, doughnut?"

"I don't think so. Be right out." He left. When he came back, shaved, clean, his wet hair brushed down smoothly, the room was neat again, the dishes washed and put away.

"Let's go to bed, honey," he said, and put his arm lightly

about her shoulders. "You look beat."

"I am." She slipped her arm about his waist. "We both lost."

"Yeah, I know. Next week."

She nodded. Next week. It was the best money they ever spent, she thought, undressing. Best thing they ever bought, even if it would take them fifteen years to pay it off. She yawned and slipped into bed. They held hands as they drifted off to sleep.

THE HAND WITH ONE HUNDRED FINGERS

One hundred fingers are too many, you say?
No, just enough.

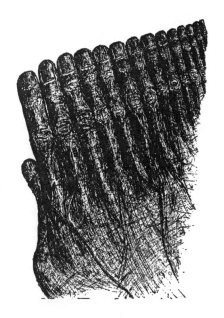

R. A. Lafferty

1

We are the folks esteemed and loved
by *nobody* any more.
We are the cloaked and veiled and gloved
And we're rotten to the core.

—*Rotten Peoples' Rollicks*

The Hand with One Hundred Fingers was pretty much in control of things then. It enhanced persons and personalities, or it degraded them, for money, for whim, or for hidden reasons. And what it did to them was done effectively everywhere and forever.

Julius Runnymede had had several afflictions. He had a speech impediment; he was shy, he was inept, he was a bungler. Then, while he was still a young man, he inherited a medium-sized fortune. He decided to invest it in a new personality. He went to one of the leading firms of Person-Projectors, and they cured his disabilities almost immediately. His bungling and ineptitude and shyness and speech affliction were transmuted into assets. He became one of the finest orators in the Fourth Congressional District, and a bright future lay before him. All thanks to the Hand!

The one hundred fingers of the Hand were the one hundred Person-Projector firms in their comprehensive union. They controlled all rulers of all countries, and all parliaments and congresses for the reason that they were able to manufacture presidents and premiers and prime ministers and assemblies (and other power groups behind the formal assemblies) out of common human material. And they were able to destroy as well as manufacture.

Alice Jacoby was an aspiring young actress, but she had bad acting habits. She popped her eyes and she popped her teeth in the intensity of her theatrical emotions. Her voice was adenoidal, and were it not for its adenoidal element it would have been perfectly flat. She wasn't pretty, and she surely wasn't in any way compelling. She had about as much sex as a green watermelon.

But there were at least two people who loved her and who knew that something drastic would have to be done for her. One of these was her father, who mortgaged his farm to help her. Another one was her uncle Jake Jacoby, who mortgaged his auction and cattle business.

Alice paid the money to a firm of Person-Projectors, one of the hundred fingers of the Hand. The people-engineers of this firm enhanced her personality. And immediately Alice was in demand as an actress. She was known. Nearly everyone in the world had at least a subliminal and unconscious recognition of her.

She still popped her eyes and her teeth when she tried to emote, but now these seemed to be enchanting gestures. Her voice was still adenoidal, but now it seemed to be ravishingly adenoidal. She still wasn't pretty, but now she *was* compelling. And now she was as sexy as a fully ripe watermelon. All hail to the Hand again!

There were three steps. First a person did not have certain advantages. Then the person seemed to have acquired them. And then it was learned that there was no difference between seeming to have special attributes and really having them.

A person's personality was plotted and planned. Then the personal or aura signature was attached to an updated and almost presentable electronic personality. This new electronic personality was set onto world television for only one-fiftieth of a second; but that was time enough to create a consensus and to give a resonance back. The weight of numbers of participating persons was most important in this. An unchallenged (and unconscious) world consensus of the electronic personality was formed. Oh, there was a bit more to it than that, about a minute and a half more. If it were too simple, then everybody could set up in the Person-Projector business and reap fortunes.

Well, if it worked for Alice Jacoby, why wouldn't it work for everybody? It would, it would. Almost everybody who was able to raise a small or medium-sized fortune had now become a Corrected-Consensus-Projected-Personality. It worked for Wisteria Manford, it worked for Peter Hindman, it worked for Hector Gibbons. It worked for quite a few millions of persons, but it would be a distraction to list them all.

The Person-Projectors brought down as many persons as they

elevated (to give a proper balance to things), but the downfallen are hardly noticed at all. And everybody notices the uplifted.

The century-long battle over the nature of reality is finished. The "Nature of Reality" lost. Reality is seen to be no more than a mirage, a heat-inversion false appearance. No one has ever really slaked his thirst in the bogus waters of reality. But almost everyone has imagined that he has. And the imagining is just as good. It was once said that subjectivity and objectivity were the opposite sides of the same coin. Now we know that they are the *same* reverse side of the same coin, and the face of the coin is blank.

Reality is whatever enough people believe it is. Reality is a projected conditionality. And a person is exactly what the current, projected consensus of that person shows him to be. There is no more to it than that. It was noticed, more than a hundred years ago, that people in group pictures tend to look alike: that is to say, they become persons of a particular consensus. It was noticed that persons in crowds take on the look of that particular crowd; and that persons in demented or rabid crowds lose all individual characteristics and come to look almost exactly alike.

Soon after these first realizations, a group of men (they were then believed to be a bunch of fox-faced phonies, but we now know that they were a noble assembly of the media lords themselves) undertook the creation and projection of artificial personalities. It was then believed that "artificial" and "natural" were somehow in opposition, which we now know to be untrue. This was a praiseworthy electronic manipulation which paralleled the genetic manipulation which began at about the same time. So, by introducing "new-data projection" to attach to certain persons, by using old-fashioned folk interaction newly directed, by employing feedback from that interaction, by adding the "coloration" technique, people could be stabilized into their true and valid forms. This would work for anything. Inanimate objects, and even the sun and the moon, could likewise be converted into new and clarified forms by these techniques: and they will be.

We have reality now. We never had it before because of diverse viewpoints. The modern psycho-resolution-projection movement has begun to move with electronic speed and spread, and with exponential growth.

—Notes on the History of the Theory of
Projected Persons, by Jonathan Fomry Bierce

Crispin and Sharon Babcock had once seemed to be in love. What they were in now, with the arrival of reality, was uncertain; but the old "in love" business was shown to have had no reality. Probably they were no more than "associated persons with prejudice" now.

In that earlier time, though, they had both seemed to be quite attractive in all ways, and well fitted to each other. They had even seemed to have a clear physical and mental beauty. Their body measurements and weights would still reveal a fine proportion and beauty; but are you going to believe measurements or are you going to believe your own eyes? Crispin and Sharon were both clearly substandard now, and that was all there was to it.

It was because of his saying "I don't believe that that *is* all there is to it" about a number of things that Crispin first got into trouble. By this he showed himself to be an unconforming young man, unfaithful to the holy and historical disestablishment, and it was right that he should have gotten into trouble. And Sharon was tied so deeply into a complex of inanities that she was beyond correction.

"As long as we have each other, it will not matter what the rest of the world does or thinks," Sharon said once.

"If we are faithful to ourselves and to each other, then we can survive even the ruination of the world," Crispin had said. And both of them, for a while at least, had believed these things.

There had been a time when Crispin and Sharon had appeared to be successful in their lives. They had satisfaction and station and money and children and a happy home and fine friends. Or so they thought. They even had the illusion of a cup running over with sheer delight. Self-deception must have been rampant in them. And when they finally had to face up to reality there was never a couple who opposed that facing-up so stubbornly or so unreasonably.

Both of them had refused to have personality-correction-projection. They just didn't want it, they said. They didn't believe they needed it, and they preferred things the way they were. Refusals like theirs would tear the very fabric of the new society.

On the matter of giving up their children, they had even defied the law. And they had refused for a long time to admit that their children were ugly and malodorous and moronic and repulsive.

"They are beautiful children, they are pleasant children, they are intelligent children, and they are good children," Sharon had insisted to an official, in defiance of all reason. "We love them and they love us. Let us alone! We will maintain our own ways. We will walk in beauty and happiness as we have walked. You have no right to interfere!"

But the officials had the "right of reality" to interfere. So the children were projected as officially deficient. And this projection, by definition, was the reality of the case. And Crispin and Sharon became more and more suspect after the termination of their children. Their attitude just wasn't good.

They retained, however, a sense of humor. But unsanctioned humor in bestial persons can be made to project itself badly. Their magic together had been very much weakened when it became the case that they couldn't stand to be too close to each other.

2

> We are the sick, ungallant band
> Whose once bright step must lag.
> We are the people who live in the land
> Where even the buzzards gag.
>
> —*Rotten People's Rollicks*

Judge Roger Baluster had once been a magistrate, and later he had been a manufacturer and businessman. Still later he had been a tycoon. And that was where he broke it. Tycoons are so easy to type and tear.

And really had he ever had the nobility of character that a magistrate and a businessman and a tycoon should have? What

he did have was a long history of noncooperation with the person-projector firms.

As a young man Roger had been a crusading judge. He had
crusaded against a complex of disintegrating things when they
had been new and unestablished. And now when they were set
and established they crusaded against Baluster to his ruination.
But through the years he had become a man of much hidden
wealth. He was a full-feathered bird and his plucking would take
a long time.

In the beginning of it, he had refused to pay to a firm that was
in the person-projection business the simple monthly fee for
"Personality Updating and Maintenance." This was petty of him,
for he was a rich man.

Roger had had the look of an eagle. He had had pride and
judgment and compassion. And humor. He had been (this is hard
to believe in the light of his real character as it was later revealed)
admired and liked and respected by almost everyone.

But he had refused to pay a simple fee. Well then, he would
have to pay a complex fee of a much steeper sort. He was handed
upward. A bigger and more comprehensive firm in the person-
projection business decided to take the enhancing of Baluster's
personality in hand. And, unaccountably, he refused this offer
also. He was placing himself above the law and above the community.

"Well, then, Baluster, we will degrade your personality till you
are held in universal contempt," the men of the first-class person-
projector firm told him. "We will reveal a totally shabby person
who is the valid 'you.' Of the false image which you built for
yourself nothing will remain. That is the way things are, and there
is only one side to things."

"Aw, I think there is another side to this," Roger Baluster said
resolutely. "And I believe that something of what I built will
remain. The 'Inner Me' will remain."

"So, then, it will remain," said those huckstering men of that
firm. "But it will remain as it really is and not as you imagine it.
We will give you a certain transparency now. There is nothing
like letting the honest light of day into a dark man like yourself.

This transparency will be subliminal, of course, but it will be near universal. Everybody will be able to see into you in those faster-than-a-blink moments. And nobody's 'Inner Person' is attractive. People will see you, in those multitudinous intervals that are too short to be recorded, with complete revulsion. They will see you as a dirty complex of entrails and uncased organs. Yours will be the sharp and foul smell of blood and viscera and illegally opened persons. Other aspects of you will become other vile things, but the 'Inner You' will have become a charnal house in its offensiveness."

"There will be another sort of 'Inner Me,' " Baluster insisted, "and you will not be able to touch that."

"Whatever there is of you, we can touch it and bend it and twist it," they said.

Well, they did touch and bend and twist every discoverable aspect of Judge Roger Baluster. They rotted every element of him, and they set his reputation into reeking corruption.

Once there had been the time when Roger Baluster had had the look of an eagle. Now he had the look of a buzzard or vulture. His pride and judgment had been destroyed utterly. His compassion and his humor had been horribly twisted. His appearance, whenever a glimpse could be got of it, was completely repulsive. As were so many now, Roger was cloaked and masked and swathed most of the time. But a really foul appearance can come through every swathing and speak to every sense.

They had disrupted Baluster's household also. They had taken his wife away, and he couldn't find out what they had done with her. They had destroyed two of his children, and they had turned the other two against him.

But he still had money, very much money, cannily hidden. That was what kept him alive. Money can buy a grudging sort of acknowledgment as long as there is any of it left.

Silvester Sureman had gotten crossways with the firm that handled the maintenance of his personality. Before that, things had gone well with him. He had, on the day of the misunderstanding, moved into a new suburban home, a sign of affluence. Silvester himself had a misunderstanding-removing business which he called "Roadsmoothers, Inc." He was a good relations man. He talked now to the men of the firm that handled the maintenance of his personality. "There is no need for misunderstanding here," he said. "I beg of you to take no action on this now. I beg you to take no action till tomorrow morning. Misunderstandings often disappear overnight." Silvester thought that he had them convinced, but something must have gone wrong. That firm did take action against Silvester that night while he slept. A night-shift man at the firm found a note on Silvester that had been written by a day-man. The day-man had forgotten to put a hold on that note. So the night-shift man routinely had Silvester destroyed in the area of his strength: his sureness in things, and his ability to remove misunderstandings. A split-second echo had gone and come from the world mind that this was a man who was Mr. Quagmire himself, the man who would always be bogged down in indecision and misunderstanding.

On the day of the misunderstanding, Silvester Sureman had phoned the *Morning Enterprise* to tell them to begin delivering the paper at his new house. "These changes take a little time," the man at the *Enterprise* said. "It may be the day after tomorrow morning before you receive the paper at your new place."

"I am sure that it can be done by tomorrow morning," Sureman said. "With effort and understanding all things can be done quickly."

Then it was the next morning and Sureman went out from his new house early in the morning to get his paper. Yes, it was there. Or was it his? The paper was exactly midway between his house and the house next door. Did the people next door take the morning paper? The light was on there, so Sureman went and knocked on the door. A huge man with oversized eyes and lather on his face came and opened. (Those oversized eyes—the man either had a thyroid condition or he was a Groll's Troll.)

"Do you take the *Morning Endeavor* newspaper?" Silvester Sureman asked brightly.

"That is no possible business of yours," the man said. "No, I do not take such a thing. What this neighborhood does not need is one more nut. Don't be one."

"Thank you, thank you," Sureman said. "I am just trying to

prevent misunderstandings before they start." He patted the man on the shoulder and the man winced. How awkward of Sureman! Possibly the fellow was a Groll's Troll, and they hate to be touched.

Sureman picked up the paper and sat at the little sidewalk bench in front of his house to read it. And after a while the huge, shaven man came out of the house next door. He seemed to be looking for something. Then he came over to Silvester Sureman and punched him in the nose and took the paper.

"I told you not to be a nut in this neighborhood," the man said. "Stealing my morning paper is in the order of being a nut."

"But you said that you didn't take the *Morning Endeavor,*" Sureman said reasonably out of his bloody face.

"I don't," the huge man said. "This is the *Morning Enterprise.* There isn't any such paper as the *Morning Endeavor.*"

The man started back into his house with the paper. Sureman had gotten his tongue twisted on the name, that was all. Oh-oh, that big man was coming back again!

That huge man came up to Silvester Sureman again and punched him in the nose so hard that he broke it.

"It's one thing to be a nut," the huge man said. "It's something else to be a nut with a worm in it. That last punch was because you have a worm in you."

And Silvester Sureman did have a worm in him. It rotted him and it ate him up from the inside, and it brought him down and still further down. Silvester lost his business, of course. He lost everything. He was prone to total misunderstandings and he could do nothing right. He went down and down till he had become one of the vile untouchables.

Conchita Montez had once been legendized as a stunningly beautiful woman of the Latin persuasion. It had been believed that she had great charm and elegance and intelligence and presence. Her way with the English language had seemed enchanting, with all those delightful slurrings and mispronunciations. Her eyes and her wit twinkled, and she was one of the persons who brightened her era. That was the legend. But beautiful legends are not always self-sustaining; there is a fragility about even the best of them. And those were the times of fragile personalities.

It isn't known quite where Conchita went wrong. She had given so much enjoyment to everyone! But it was said that she was very particular about whom she gave more special enjoyment to. She apparently didn't know who was running the world in those years. Her rejection of some of the high lords was resented.

"The old way would be to throw acid in your face and so wreck your beauty," one of those lords told her. "We are more subtle and more thorough now. We throw the acid behind your face and it wrecks your whole person. Then your face will crumble of itself."

So those Person-Projectors did a job on Conchita and she became repulsive at once. *Became* repulsive? She had always been repulsive, of course. Hers was a repulsive nature.

What did we ever see in her? Old posters of her had shown her as absolutely beautiful. That was when those old posters were new. Well, why didn't those same posters still show her as beautiful? Because she was repulsive and had always been. And now they showed her as repulsive.

But no poster could show her as repulsive as she really was. A poster could not show the mush-mouthed offensiveness of her speech or the screaming tediousness of her person.

So she became a hooded and swathed untouchable, ringing her cracked bell when she had to be out of doors, avoiding and avoided by all decent people.

3

My wife is a doll with a crooked back
And a voice like a broken fiddle.
I love her like a potato sack
With a rope around her middle.

—*Rotten People's Rollicks*

Crispin and Sharon Babcock went that evening into what was probably the most beautiful sly hall in the world. If it had not been so before, their entering almost guaranteed that it would be so now. The sly halls were the last refuge where obnoxious people could gather to enjoy (it was as if the word "en-joy" had been minted fresh just for the sly halls) the rousing old pleasures and beauties. The enjoyments and the beauties were very subjective and selective, and they were awfully tenuous. But they were the only enjoyments and beauties that these people could bring about. These places might be kept enjoyable as long as their people held together on their clear course.

"The thing will work as long as we are all faithful to each other," Crispin Babcock said. "Oh, Lord of the Sick Scorpions, please don't say that again, and again, and again!" Sharon Babcock moaned to herself. (Crispin's statement was one that he made a thousand times a day.)

All the members of the sly halls were outcasts. They ate and drank in the sly halls. They played music and chukki there. They had shows, they had arts, they had books and all graphics. There were body sports and mind sports. There was song and dance, conversation and cookery and casuistry.

In every sly hall were the one- and two-room mansions for the couples and for the families (though there were few children; most of the children of the outcasts had been destroyed). There were the single rooms for the singles. There were the blessed rituals that are at the heart of every sly hall; and there was the intense civilization that is the seal of all the sly people.

Some of the folks in the halls were neither masked nor veiled. Some did not even wear the great cloak, the wrongly called "invisibility cloak." They were guised of themselves, they said; they had no need to be disguised. But that was only fancy talk. Most of them were as masked and swathed as it was possible to be.

"Wintergreen was knocked off today," Judge Roger Baluster said. "That's nine of the sly halls knocked off in four days and nights. Somehow the companies are shattered and the people flee out of the halls. They haven't anywhere to go then, after they abandon their last refuges which are the halls. So they are arrested for being persistently in public places, and some of them are executed for it. They can't live anywhere except in the halls. Who would rent or sell rooms or houses to the outcasts? But the people get more fun out of the outcasts when they are driven into the open. There were complaints before that they hardly got to enjoy those of us who made such shelters for ourselves. Some new technique is being used to break up the companies and make the outcast people flee the halls."

Baluster was keeping his hands busy arranging the ritual pieces in the sly hall: the 3.05 meter poles, the pairs of mittens, the desperation-philosophy texts, the tin cans and the wires to run between them, the electric helmets with their euphoric vibes, the piles of good-will mottoes.

"What is the new technique, Roger?" Silvester Sureman asked. "Dammit, Roger, can't you do something about your appearance?"

"I'm sitting out of your line of vision, Silvester," Roger Baluster said, "and I'm completely swathed, so that not one particle of me can be seen in any case. What do you mean by my appearance?"

"It's nauseating, you know, and your voice is worse. Well, what *is* the technique that they're using on us now?"

"I don't know, Silvester, but they're attacking out of a new dimension. I thought they couldn't hit us with anything else, but they seem to be doing it. We thought we could set up asylums here and there, the sly halls, and make them into worlds of our own. We thought that, in our own circles, we could gradually become less repulsive, to ourselves and to each other, and so regain a measure of self-respect. And we *have* made progress, very slow progress."

"Oh, yes. In a thousand years our progress might be seen clearly, to one with sharp eyes," Silvester Sureman said dismally.

"At least we still have each other, Sharon," Crispin Babcock wheezed, and he pressed Sharon's hand.

"Aw, ugh, ugh, ugh," Sharon said with a complete lack of enthusiasm. "Don't, Crispin. It's like being touched by a reptile."

But it was a pleasantly contrived world that they had made for themselves in the sly hall. The great skylights let the sunlight in during the daylight hours; and there was profuse greenery and striking garden arrangements. Otters played in the stream and in the fountain. The bright weavers were everywhere. Salamanders ran like quicksilver and fire over everything. There were cascades of ivy. Eagles perched on the entrance posts, and there was a certain architecture of pride in the big building and in its people.

"We are all celebrities now, you know," Conchita Montez mumbled. "People everywhere in the world know us and know who we are. It isn't much, but it is something. We are valid characters, even if we are only characters for the popular hate-culture."

"The ultimate pornography, hatred," Crispin said piously.

"Yes, that's so," Silvester agreed. "The Projection Lords are not really superior to ourselves any more than an ax murderer is superior to his victims. But there's no denying that they have the advantage over us, and it may be the ultimate advantage. You do know why they keep a few of us alive?"

"Oh, it's necessary for the balance of their system that the people and themselves have something to hate intensely," Baluster said. "And it's quite true that hating is fun, that it's a deep and furious pleasure. But we ourselves can't hate the Projector Lords, and we can't hate the populace whom they control. They simply are not programmed to be hated, and the Lords have the control of the programming. But we can hate ourselves and others of the outcasts; we can and we do. It's the last pleasure left to us. That's what is behind our scapegoat trick that we have agreed upon. By it, some of us will be saved when our company is stricken. We don't yet know who our scapegoat will be. Whomever the lightning of our hatred strikes first, that will be the one."

"They want us out in the open where they can have cleaner shots at hating us," Conchita said. "Oh well, I guess I want us out in the open too. It's stifling in here."

"A three-point-oh-five meter pole, two pairs of mittens, a couple of tin cans, and a length of wire," said Crispin Babcock. "Who would believe that they would be last-chance things? I don't know how we will use them yet (it will be given to us in that hour how to use them), but this is the list that comes to my mind for Sharon and myself. And all these things are here among the ritual objects of our own sly hall."

"It's remarkable how little hardware they have to use in Person-Projecting," Silvester Sureman said. "It's just a combination of coded frequencies to express a displeasure, to contain a person-identification, and to call for an echo, all formed into a wave transmission and set to travel around the world on a common carrier wave. And there is filtering as needed and amplification as needed. And behold! a person is smeared to destruction, forever and to all the world. It's the Dynasty of Hatred that now obtains in the world.

"And also there is very little software that they have to use in Person-Projecting. A repertoire of hatreds is maintained; it is added to from the residues of broken persons, and it is dispensed freely and rather imaginatively. A person-smear will be manifest to almost every sense including the unorganed intuitive senses. Except smell. Smell is transmitted only by actual physical particles from the smelled object reaching one.

"But could not smell-reminders be triggered electronically? Could not smell be transmitted in some coded fashion? Nothing comes into our minds without a reason, and the sense of strong and murderous smell has just come into my mind. People, is smell the new technique? Is it the attack out of the new dimension? I feel that it is, and I feel that it's upon us now."

Wisteria Manford burst into the sly hall. Wisteria had long since fallen into the outcast condition. She had run out of money for her personality maintenance. It is very dangerous to run out of money. And it takes a lot of money to maintain a borderline personality.

"Garden City has fallen!" Wisteria cried. "Exaltation Heights has fallen! Beggar on Horseback has fallen! Snug Harbor and Bright Shores and Citadel and Gold Beach and Pleasant Gardens and Tomorrow Land have all been shattered. All the sly halls are being emptied by this new attack, and we're next. It's a stink that they use to split up the people, a killing stink. And it's coming to us right now."

Indeed, the first heavy wave of stench had come into the sly hall with Wisteria. They shrank away from her. Through the holes in the walls they shrank away from her. The stench shattered the company, and it changed the sly hall itself completely.

In the light of, in the odor of the new and overpowering stench, the sly hall changed. It does not matter whether the change was subjective or objective. In the new order, there is no difference between the two conditions. The great skylights of the hall—what great skylights?—were sky holes, roof holes. The roof itself was fallen-in and gappy: that's why there was always sunlight during the daylight hours. The famous greenery of the hall was not so very green. The plants growing there were stinkweed and sick fungus. The otters playing in the stream and the fountain were seen to be rats skulking out of the stagnant water. The bright weavers were uncommon spiders of unusual size and malevolence. The salamanders were snakes. The quicksilver-and-fire was a slimy decay lit up by methane-rot. The ivy was poison ivy. The perched eagles were vultures and buzzards. And the only pride to be found in the hall was the stubborn pride of carrion flesh. The people wanted out of that hateful hall at once. How had they ever gathered in such an offensive place?

With the second heavy wave of stench the people did all burst out of the hall. It was necessary that they get away from their rotten refuge, but it was even more necessary that they get away from each other and the foulness of their former company. The supreme necessity was that they should get away from their stinking selves, but how was that to be accomplished? But Crispin Babcock, in spite of the furious urge to be gone, did pick up certain ritual objects.

With the third heavy wave of killing stench, the scapegoats were chosen blindly by the scattering company. And those scapes whom the lightning of hatred struck first and most violently were—

4

We are the stenchy actors cast
In the reeky, smelliferous role.
We are the folks that nobody dast
To touch with a ten-foot pole.

—*Rotten People's Rollicks*

Those scapegoats whom the lightning of the hatred struck first and hardest were Crispin and Sharon Babcock. All the people broke away from Crispin and Sharon in revulsion, and they looked at each other in sniggering horror.

"At least we still have each other," Crispin said sickly.

"If you say that once more I'll scream my head off!" Sharon wailed.

"Small loss if you did. Gah! What a head!" Crispin shouted.

And yet they were still in accord, a little bit. People truly in love will always be a little bit in accord. There was something valiant about their response. Both of them realized at the same time what to do with the ritual objects. Each of them put one mitten on his end of the 3.05 meter pole and the other mitten on his hand to hold it. They rigged the length of wire between the two tin cans and made a kids' telephone. Crispin and Sharon had been children together and had talked on tin-can phones before. They still cared for each other mightily, but oh, how they both did stink! Was there any possible way that the 3.05 meter pole would be long enough?

But when they talked to each other on the tin-can telephone much of the ugly, sound-clashing horror had gone out of their voices. Here was a sound filter that nobody knew about except themselves. Their words had a rusty sound, but they were not otherwise offensive. Here was something that all the Person-Projector companies had overlooked. If they had known about it they would have done a job on tin cans also, to make any sound coming through them repellent.

The two Babcocks headed into a stiff wind that blew the smell off them pretty well. Why, this would be almost bearable, this life together-apart! Only ten feet apart, and they could breathe. They were hooded and shrouded, of course, and could never actually see each other again, but remembered appearances came to them that were a little less horrible than they had been used to in more recent times. Each pressed his end of the pole with a mittened hand, and it was almost like holding hands again.

They even became a little bit jocular in their rusty-voiced banter back and forth.

"Ship to shore, ship to shore! My wife is a rot-head, smelly bore," Crispin bawled into his tin can, and they both laughed. "Ship to shore" and "Shore to ship" had been their tin-can telephone code when they were children.

"Shore to ship, shore to ship! With his wobbly brains and his wobbly lip." Sharon laughed a rusty jeer.

Oh, somehow things would still be tolerable between them, despite the fact that they were the smelliest and lowest outcasts in the land! Even the birds veered away from them in the air. But if they kept a firm grip on the pole they could keep from flying apart. If the strong breeze held forever (they needed that to keep their smell from building to critical intensity), if they didn't begin to think about the situation again, if there was not another assault to drive them finally into sick insanity, if—

There *was* another assault, the fourth heavy wave of killing stench and hatred. And both fell to the ground. This would be the death of them, and the joy of many millions of people who had picked up the tang and rhythm of the drama and disintegration.

But the last problem of Crispin and Sharon was holding off that ultimate hatred. Could they delay the mortal hatred for each other until merciful death should have taken them?

No, of course they couldn't delay it. It was the mortal hatred that killed them. The Hand with One Hundred Fingers will not be cheated by any last-minute tricks.

MEATHOUSE MAN

His hands were machines, his heart a nuclear furnace,
and he stripped the planet bare, looking for love.

George R. R. Martin

1. IN THE MEATHOUSE

They came straight from the ore fields that first time, Trager with
the others, the older boys, the almost-men who worked their
corpses next to his. Cox was the oldest of the group, and he'd
been around the most, and he said that Trager had to come even
if he didn't want to. Then one of the others laughed and said that
Trager wouldn't even know what to do, but Cox the kind-of
leader shoved him until he was quiet. And when payday came,
Trager trailed the rest to the meathouse, scared but somehow
eager, and he paid his money to a man downstairs and got a room
key.

He came into the dim room trembling, nervous. The others
had gone to other rooms, had left him alone with her (no, *it*, not
her but *it*, he reminded himself, and promptly forgot again). In
a shabby gray cubicle with a single smoky light.

He stank of sweat and sulfur, like all who walked the streets of Skrakky, but there was no help for that. It would be better if he could bathe first, but the room did not have a bath. Just a sink, a double bed with sheets that looked dirty even in the dimness, a corpse.

She lay there naked, staring at nothing, breathing shallowly. Her legs were spread, ready. Was she always that way, Trager wondered, or had the man before him arranged her like that? He didn't know. He knew how to do it (he did, he *did*, he'd read the books Cox gave him, and there were films you could see, and all sorts of things), but he didn't know much of anything else. Except maybe how to handle corpses. That he was good at, the youngest handler on Skrakky, but he had to be. They had forced him into the handlers' school when his mother died, and they made him learn, so that was the thing he did. This, this he had never done (but he knew how, yes, yes, he *did*); it was his first time.

He came to the bed slowly and sat, to a chorus of creaking springs. He touched her and the flesh was warm. Of course. The body was alive enough, a heart beat under the heavy white breasts, she breathed. Only the brain was gone, replaced with a deadman's synthabrain. She was meat now, an extra body for a corpse handler to control, just like the crew he worked each day under sulfur skies. She was not a woman. So it did not matter that Trager was just a boy, a jowly frog-faced boy who smelled of Skrakky. She (no, *it*, remember?) would not care, could not care.

Emboldened, aroused and hard, the boy stripped off his corpse handler's clothing and climbed in bed with the female meat. He was very excited; his hands shook as he stroked her, studied her. Her skin was very white, her hair dark and long, but even the boy could not call her pretty. Her face was too flat and wide, her mouth hung open, and her limbs were loose and sagging with fat.

On her huge breasts, all around the fat dark nipples, the last customer had left toothmarks where he'd chewed her. Trager touched the marks tentatively, traced them with a finger. Then, sheepish about his hesitations, he grabbed one breast, squeezed it hard, pinched the nipple until he imagined a real girl would squeal with pain. The corpse did not move. Still squeezing, he rolled over on her and took the other breast into his mouth.

And the corpse responded.

She thrust up at him, hard; her meaty arms wrapped around his pimpled back to pull him to her. Trager groaned and reached down between her legs. She was hot, wet, excited. He trembled. How did they do that? Could she really get excited without a mind, or did they have lubricating tubes stuck into her, or what?

Then he stopped caring. He fumbled, found his penis, put it into her, thrust. The corpse hooked her legs around him and thrust back. It felt good, real good, better than anything he'd ever done to himself, and in some obscure way he felt proud that she was so wet and so excited.

It took only a few strokes; he was too new, too young, too eager to last long. A few strokes was all he needed—but it was all she needed too. They came together, a red flush washing over her skin as she arched against him and shook silently.

Afterward she lay again like a corpse.

Trager was drained and satisfied, but he had more time left, and he was determined to get his money's worth. He explored her thoroughly, sticking his fingers everywhere they would go, touching her everywhere, rolling her over, looking at everything. The corpse moved like dead meat.

He left her as he'd found her, lying face up on the bed with her legs apart. Meathouse courtesy.

The horizon was a wall of factories, all factories, vast belching factories that sent red shadows to flicker against the sulfur-dark skies. The boy saw but hardly noticed. He was strapped in place high atop his automill, two stories up on a monster machine of corroding yellow-painted metal with savage teeth of diamond and duralloy, and his eyes were blurred with triple images. Clear and strong and hard he saw the control panel before him, the wheel, the fuel-feed, the bright handle of the ore scoops, the banks of lights that would tell of trouble in the refinery under his feet, the brake and emergency brake. But that was not all he saw. Dimly, faintly, there were echoes: overlaid images of two other control cabs, almost identical to his, where corpse hands moved clumsily over the instruments.

Trager moved those hands, slow and careful, while another

part of his mind held his own hands, his real hands, very still. The corpse controller hummed thinly on his belt.

On either side of him, the other two automills moved into flanking positions. The corpse hands squeezed the brakes; the machines rumbled to a halt. On the edge of the great sloping pit, they stood in a row, shabby pitted juggernauts ready to descend into the gloom. The pit was growing steadily larger; each day new layers of rock and ore were stripped away.

Once a mountain range had stood here, but Trager did not remember that.

The rest was easy. The automills were aligned now. To move the crew in unison was a cinch; any decent handler could do that. It was only when you had to keep several corpses busy at several different tasks that things got tricky. But a good corpse handler could do that, too. Eight-crews were not unknown to veterans— eight bodies linked to a single corpse controller, moved by a single mind and eight synthabrains. The deadmen were each tuned to one controller and only one; the handler who wore that controller and thought corpse-thoughts in its proximity field could move those deadmen like secondary bodies. Or like his own body. If he was good enough.

Trager checked his filtermask and earplugs quickly, then touched the fuel feed, engaged, flicked on the laser knives and the drills. His corpses echoed his moves, and pulses of light spat through the twilight of Skrakky. Even through his plugs he could hear the awful whine as the ore scoops revved up and lowered. The rock-eating maw of an automill was even wider than the machine was tall.

Rumbling and screeching, in perfect formation, Trager and his corpse crew descended into the pit. Before they reached the factories on the far side of the plain, tons of metal would have been torn from the earth, melted and refined and processed, while the worthless rock was reduced to powder and blown out into the already unbreathable air. He would deliver finished steel at dusk, on the horizon.

He was a good handler, Trager thought as the automills started down. But the handler in the meathouse—now she must be an artist. He imagined her down in the cellar somewhere, watching each of her corpses through holos and psi circuits, humping them all to please her patrons. Was it just a fluke, then, that his fuck had been so perfect? Or was she always that good? But how, *how*, to move a dozen corpses without even being near them, to have them doing different things, to keep them all excited, to match the needs and rhythm of each customer so exactly?

The air behind him was black and choked by rock dust, his ears were full of screams, and the far horizon was a glowering red wall beneath which yellow ants crawled and ate rock. But Trager kept his hard-on all across the plain as the automill shook beneath him.

The corpses were company-owned; they stayed in the company deadman depot. But Trager had a room, a cubicle that was his own in a steel-and-concrete warehouse with a thousand other cubicles. He knew only a handful of his neighbors, but in a way he knew all of them; they were corpse handlers. It was a world of silent shadowed corridors and endless closed doors. The lobby-lounge, all air and plastic, was a dusty deserted place where the tenants never gathered.

The evenings were long there, the nights eternal. Trager had bought extra light panels for his cube, and when all of them were on they burned so bright that his infrequent visitors blinked and complained about the glare. But always there came a time when he could read no more, and then he had to turn them out, and the darkness returned again.

His father, long gone and barely remembered, had left a wealth of books and tapes, and Trager kept them still. The room was lined with them, and others stood in great piles against the foot of the bed and on either side of the bathroom door. Sometimes he went out with Cox and the others, to drink and joke and prowl for real women. He imitated them as best he could, but he always felt out of place. So most of his nights were spent at home, reading and listening to the music, remembering and thinking.

That week his thoughts were a frightened jumble. Payday was coming again, and Cox would be after him to return to the meathouse, and yes, yes, he wanted to. It had been good, exciting; for once he had felt confident and virile. But it was so easy, cheap, *dirty*. There had to be more, hadn't there? Love, whatever that was? It had to be better with a real woman, had to, and he wouldn't find one of those in a meathouse. He'd never found one outside, either, but then he'd never really had the courage to try. But he had to try, *had* to, or what sort of life would he ever have?

Beneath the covers he masturbated, hardly thinking of it, while he resolved not to return to the meathouse.

A different room this time, a different corpse. Fat and black, with bright orange hair; less attractive than his first, if that was possible. But Trager came to her ready and eager, and this time he lasted longer. Again, the performance was superb. Her rhythm matched his stroke for stroke, she came with him, she seemed to know exactly what he wanted.

Other visits: two of them, four, six. He was a regular now at the meathouse, along with the others. He was better than they were, he thought. He could hold his own in a meathouse, he could run his corpses and his automills as good as any of them, and he still thought and dreamed. In time he'd leave them all behind, leave Skrakky, be something. They would be meathouse men as long as they lived, but Trager knew he could do better. He believed.

His admiration of the meathouse handler grew almost to worship. Perhaps somehow he could meet her, he thought. Still a boy, still hopelessly naïve, he was sure he would love her. Then he would take her away from the meathouse to a clean corpseless world where they could be happy together.

One day, in a moment of weakness, he told Cox and the others. Cox looked at him, shook his head, grinned. Somebody else snickered. Then they all began to laugh. "What an *ass* you are, Trager," Cox said at last. "There is no fucking *handler!* Don't tell me you never heard of a feedback circuit?"

He explained it all, to laughter; explained how each corpse was tuned to a controller built into its bed, explained how each customer handled his own meat, explained why nonhandlers found meathouse women dead and still. And the boy realized suddenly why the sex was always perfect.

That night, alone in his room with all the lights burning white and hot, Trager faced himself. It was the meathouse, he decided. There was a trap there in the meathouse, a trap that could ruin him, destroy life and dreams and hope. He would not go back; it was too easy. He would show Cox, show all of them. He would take the hard way, take the risks, feel the pain if he had to. And maybe the joy, maybe the love. He'd gone the other way too long.

Trager did not go back to the meathouse. Feeling strong and decisive and superior, he went back to his room. There, as years passed, he read and dreamed and waited for life to begin.

2. When I Was One-and-Twenty

Josie was the first.

She was beautiful, had always been beautiful, knew she was beautiful; that had shaped her, made her what she was. She was a free spirit. She was aggressive, confident, conquering. Like Trager, she was only twenty when they met, but she had lived more than he had, and she seemed to have the answers. He loved her from the first.

And Trager? Trager before Josie, but years beyond the meathouse? He was taller now, broad and heavy with both muscle and fat, often moody, silent and self-contained. He ran a full five-crew in the ore fields, more than Cox, more than any of them. At night he read books, sometimes in his room, sometimes in the lobby. He had long since forgotten that he went there in hope of meeting someone. Stable, solid, unemotional: that was Trager. He touched no one, and no one touched him. Even the tortures had stopped, though the scars remained inside. Trager hardly knew they were there; he never looked at them.

He fitted in well now. With his corpses.

Yet—not completely. Inside, the dream. Something believed, something hungered, something yearned. It was strong enough to keep him away from the meathouse, from the vegetable life the others had all chosen. And sometimes, on bleak lonely nights, it would grow stronger still. Then Trager would rise from his bed, dress, and walk the corridors for hours with his hands shoved deep into his pockets while something clawed and whimpered in his gut. Always, before his walks were over, he would resolve to do something, to change his life tomorrow.

But when tomorrow came, the silent gray corridors were half forgotten, the demons had faded, and he had six roaring, shaking automills to drive across the pit. He would lose himself in routine, and it would be long months before the feelings came again.

Then Josie. They met like this:

It was a new field, rich and unmined, a vast expanse of broken rock and rubble that filled the plain. Low hills a few weeks ago, but the company skimmers had leveled the area with systematic nuclear blast mining, and now the automills were moving in. Trager's five-crew had been one of the first, and the change had been exhilarating at first. The old pit had been just about worked out; here there was a new terrain to contend with, boulders and jagged rock fragments, baseball-sized fists of stone that came shrieking at you on the dusty wind. It all seemed exciting, dangerous. Trager, wearing a leather jacket and filtermask and goggles and earplugs, drove his six machines and six bodies with a fierce pride, reducing boulders to powder, clearing a path for the later machines, fighting his way yard by yard to get whatever ore he could.

And one day, suddenly, one of the eye echoes caught his attention. A light flashed red on a corpse-driven automill. Trager reached, with his hands, with his mind, with five sets of corpse-hands. Six machines stopped, but still another light went red. Then another and another. Then the whole board, all twelve. One of his automills was out. Cursing, he looked across the rock field towards the machine, used his corpse to give it a kick. The lights stayed red. He beamed out for a tech.

By the time she got there—in a one-man skimmer that looked like a teardrop of pitted black metal—Trager had unstrapped, climbed down the metal rungs on the side of the automill, walked across the rocks to where the dead machine stopped. He was just starting to climb up when Josie arrived; they met at the foot of the yellow-metal mountain, in the shadow of its treads.

She was field-wise, he knew at once. She wore a handler's coverall, earplugs, heavy goggles, and her face was smeared with grease to prevent dust abrasion. But still she was beautiful. Her hair was short, light brown, cut in a shag that was jumbled by the wind; her eyes, when she lifted the goggles, were bright green. She took charge immediately.

All business, she introduced herself, asked him a few questions, then opened a repair bay and crawled inside, into the guts of the drive and the ore smelt and the refinery. It didn't take her long; ten minutes, maybe, and she was back outside.

"Don't go in there," she said, tossing her hair away from her goggles. "You've got a damper failure. The nukes are running away."

"Oh," said Trager. "Is it going to blow up?"

Josie seemed amused. She smiled and seemed to see him, *him*, Trager, not just a corpse-handler. "No," she said. "It will just melt itself down. Won't even get hot out here, since you've got shields built into the walls. Just don't go in there."

"All right. What do I do?"

"Work the rest of your crew, I guess. This machine'll have to be scrapped. It should have been overhauled a long time ago. From the looks of it, there's been a lot of patching done in the past. Stupid. It breaks down, it breaks down, it breaks down, and they keep sending it out. Should realize that something is wrong. After that many failures, it's sheer self-delusion to think the thing's going to work right next time out."

"I guess," Trager said. Josie smiled at him again, sealed up the panel, and started to leave.

"Wait," he said. It came out before he could stop it. Josie turned, cocked her head, looked at him questioningly. And Trager drew a sudden strength from the steel and the stone and the wind; under sulfur skies, his dreams seemed less impossible. Maybe, he thought. Maybe.

"Uh. I'm Greg Trager. Will I see you again?"

Josie grinned. "Sure. Come tonight." She gave him the address.

He climbed back into his automill after she had left, exulting in his five strong bodies, all fire and life, and he chewed up rock with something near to joy. The dark red glow in the distance looked almost like a sunrise.

When he got to Josie's he found four other people there, friends of hers. It was a party of sorts. Josie threw a lot of parties, and from that night on Trager went to all of them. Josie talked to him, laughed with him, *liked* him, and his life was no longer the same.

With Josie, he saw parts of Skrakky he had never seen before, did things he had never done:

He stood with her in the crowds that gathered on the streets at night, stood in the dusty wind and sickly yellow light between the windowless concrete buildings, stood and cheered while grease-stained mechs raced yellow rumbly tractor-trucks up and down and down and up.

He walked with her through the strangely silent and white and clean underground offices, the sealed air-conditioned corridors where off-worlders and paper-shufflers and company executives lived and worked.

He prowled the rec-malls with her, those huge low buildings so like a warehouse from the outside but full of colored lights and games rooms and cafeterias and tape shops and endless bars where handlers made their rounds.

He went with her to dormitory gyms where they watched handlers less skillful than himself send their corpses against each other with clumsy fists.

He sat with her and her friends, and they woke dark quiet taverns with their talk and with their laughter, and once Trager saw someone much like Cox staring at him from across the room, and then he smiled and leaned a bit closer to Josie.

He hardly noticed the other people, the crowds that Josie gathered around herself; when they went out on one of her wild jaunts, six of them or eight or ten, Trager would tell himself that he and Josie were going out, and that some others had come along.

Once in a great while things would work out so they were alone together, at her place or his. Then they would talk. Of distant worlds, of politics, of corpses and life on Skrakky, of the books they both read, of sports or games or friends they had in common. They shared a good deal. Trager talked a lot with Josie. And never said a word.

He loved her, of course. He suspected it the first month, and soon he was convinced of it. He loved her. This was the real thing, the thing he had been waiting for, and it had happened just as he knew it would.

But with his love: agony. He could not tell her. A dozen times he tried; the words would never come. What if she did not love him?

His nights were still lonely, in the small room with the white lights and the books and the pain. He was more alone than ever now; the peace of his routine, of his half-life with his corpses, was gone. By day he rode the great automills, moved his corpses, smashed rock and melted ore, and in his head rehearsed the words he'd say to Josie. When he broke through, when he found the words and the courage, then everything would be all right. Each day he said that to himself, and dug swift and deep into the earth.

Back home, the sureness faded. Then, with awful despair, he knew that he was deceiving himself. He was a friend to her, nothing more, never would be more. They had never been lovers, never would be; the few times he'd worked up the courage to touch her, she had smiled, moved away on some pretext, so that he was never quite sure that he was being rejected. He walked the corridors again, sullen, desperate. And all the old scars bled again.

He must believe in himself, he knew that, he shouted it out loud. He must stop feeling sorry for himself. He must do something. He must tell Josie. He would.

And she would love him, cried the day.

And she would laugh, the nights replied.

Trager chased her for a year, a year of pain and promise, the first year that he had ever *lived*. On that the night-fears and the day-voice agreed; he was alive now. He would never return to the emptiness of his time before Josie; he would never go back to the meathouse. That far, at least, he had come. He could change, and someday he would be strong enough to tell her.

Josie and two friends dropped by his room that night, but the friends had to leave early. For an hour or so they were alone, talking. Finally she had to go. Trager said he'd walk her home.

He kept his arm around her down the long corridors, and he watched her face, watched the play of light and shadow on her cheeks as they walked from light to darkness. "Josie," he started. He felt so fine, so good, so warm, and it came out. "I love you."

And she stopped, pulled away from him, stepped back. Her mouth opened, just a little, and something flickered in her eyes. "Oh, Greg," she said. Softly. Sadly. "No, Greg, no, don't, don't."

Trembling slightly, mouthing silent words, Trager raised his hand gently toward her cheek. She turned her head away so that his hand met only air.

Then, for the first time ever, Trager shook. And the tears came.

Josie took him to her room. There, sitting across from each other on the floor, never touching, they talked.

J.: . . . *known it for a long time . . . tried to discourage you, Greg, but I didn't just want to come right out and . . . I never wanted to hurt you . . . a good person . . . don't worry . . .*

T.: . . . *knew it all along . . . that it would never . . . lied to myself . . . wanted to believe, even if it wasn't true . . . I'm sorry, Josie, I'm sorry, i'm sorry, imsorryimsorryimsorry . . .*

J.: . . . *afraid you would go back to what you were . . . don't, Greg, promise me . . . can't give up . . . have to believe . . .*

T.: . . . *why? . . .*

J.: . . . *stop believing, then you have nothing . . . dead . . . you can do better . . . a good handler . . . get off Skrakky, find something . . . no life here . . . someone . . . you will, you will, just believe, keep on believing . . .*

T.: . . . *you . . . love you forever, Josie . . . forever . . . how can I find someone . . . never anyone like you, never . . . special . . .*

J.: . . . *oh, Greg . . . lots of people . . . just look . . . open*

T.: (laughter) . . . *open?* . . . *first time I ever talked to anyone* . . .

J.: . . . *talk to me again, if you have to . . . I can talk to you . . . had enough lovers, everyone wants to go to bed with me, better just to be friends* . . .

T.: . . . *friends* . . . (laughter) . . . (tears) . . .

3. Promises of Someday

The fire had burned out long ago, and Stevens and the forester had gone to bed, but Trager and Donelly still sat beside the ashes. They talked softly, so as not to wake the others, yet their words hung long in the restless night air. The uncut forest, standing dark behind them, was dead still; the wildlife of Vendalia had all fled the noise that the fleet of buzztrucks made during the day.

". . . a full six-crew, running buzztrucks, I know enough to know that's not easy," Donelly was saying. He was a pale, timid youth, likable but self-conscious. Trager heard echoes of himself in Donelly's stiff words. "You'd do well in the arena."

Trager nodded, thoughtful, his eyes on the ashes as he moved them with a stick. "I came to Vendalia with that in mind. Went to the gladiatorials once, only once. That was enough to change my mind. I could take them, I guess, but the whole idea made me sick. Out here, well, the money doesn't even match what I was getting on Skrakky, but the work is, well, clean. You know?"

"Sort of," said Donelly. "Still, you know, it isn't like they were real people out there in the arena. Only meat. All you can do is make the bodies as dead as the minds. That's the logical way to look at it."

Trager chuckled. "You're too logical, Don. You ought to *feel* more. Listen, next time you're in Gidyon, go to the gladiatorials and take a look. It's ugly, *ugly.* Corpses stumbling around with axes and swords and morningstars, hacking and hewing at each other. Butchery, that's all it is. And the audience, the way they cheer at each blow. And *laugh.* They *laugh,* Don! No." He shook his head sharply. "No."

"But why not? I don't understand, Greg. You'd be good at it, the best. I've seen the way you work your crew."

Trager looked up, studied Donelly briefly while the youth sat quietly, waiting. Josie's words came back: open, be open. The old Trager, the Trager who lived friendless and alone inside a Skrakky handlers' dorm, was gone.

"There was a girl," he said slowly. Opening. "Back on Skrakky, Don, there was a girl I loved. It, well, it didn't work out. That's why I'm here, I guess. I'm looking for someone else, for something better. That's all part of it, you see." He stopped, paused, tried to think it out. "This girl, Josie, I wanted her to love me. You know." The words came hard. "Admire me, all that stuff. Now, yeah, sure, I could do good running corpses in the arena. But Josie could never love someone who had a job like *that*. She's gone now, of course, but still . . . the kind of person I'm looking for, I couldn't find them as an arena corpsemaster." He stood up abruptly. "I don't know. That's what's important, though, to me. Josie, somebody like her, someday. Soon, I hope."

He left Donelly sitting beside the ashes, and walked off alone into the woods.

They had a tight-knit group: three handlers, a forester, thirteen corpses. Each day they drove the forest back, with Trager in the lead. Against the Vendalian wilderness, against the blackbriars and the hard gray ironspike trees and the bulbous rubbery snaplimbs, against the tangled hostile forest, he threw his six-crew and their buzztrucks. Smaller than the automills he'd run on Skrakky, fast and airborne, complex and demanding, those were buzztrucks. Trager ran six of them with corpse hands, a seventh with his own. Before his screaming blades and laser knives, the wall of wilderness fell each day. Donelly came behind him, pushing three of the mountain-sized rolling mills, to turn the fallen trees into lumber for Gidyon and other cities of Vendalia. Then Stevens, the third handler, with a flame-cannon to burn down stumps and melt rocks, and the soilpumps that would ready the cleared land for farming. The forester was their foreman. The procedure was a science.

Clean, hard, demanding work; Trager thrived on it by day. He grew lean, athletic; the lines of his face tightened and tanned, he grew steadily browner under Vendalia's hot bright sun. His corpses were almost part of him, so easily did he move them, fly their buzztrucks. As an ordinary man might move a hand, a foot. Sometimes his control grew so firm, the echoes so clear and strong, that Trager felt he was not a handler working a crew at all, but rather a man with seven bodies. Seven strong bodies that rode the sultry forest winds. He exulted in their sweat.

And the evenings, after work ceased, they were good too. Trager found a sort of peace there, a sense of belonging he had never known on Skrakky. The Vendalian foresters, rotated back and forth from Gidyon, were decent enough, and friendly. Stevens was a hearty slab of a man who seldom stopped joking long enough to talk about anything serious. And Donelly, the self-conscious youth, the quiet logical voice, he became a friend. He was a good listener, empathetic, compassionate, and the new open Trager was a good talker. Something close to envy shone in Donelly's eyes when Trager spoke of Josie. And Trager knew, or thought he knew, that Donelly was himself, the old Trager, the one before Josie who could not find the words.

In time, though, after days and weeks of talking, Donelly found his words. Then Trager listened, and shared another's pain. And he felt good about it. He was helping; he was lending strength; he was needed.

Each night beside the ashes, the two men traded dreams. And wove a hopeful tapestry of promises and lies.

If Josie had given Trager much, she had taken something too; she had taken the curious deadness he had once had, the trick of not-thinking, the pain-blotter of his mind. On Skrakky, he had walked the corridors infrequently; the forest knew him far more often.

After the talking had stopped, after Donelly had gone to bed, that was when it would happen, when Josie would come to him in the loneliness of his tent. A thousand nights he lay there with his hands hooked behind his head, staring at the plastic tent film while he relived the night he'd told her.

He would think of it, and fight it, and lose. Then he would rise and go outside. He would walk across the clear area, into the silent looming forest, brushing aside low branches and tripping on the underbrush; he would walk until he found water. Then he would sit down, by a scum-choked lake or a gurgling stream that ran swift and oily in the moonlight. He would fling rocks into the water, hurl them hard and flat into the night to hear them when they splashed.

He would sit for hours, throwing rocks and thinking, till finally he could convince himself the sun would rise.

Gidyon: the city, heart of Vendalia, and through it of Slagg and Skrakky and New Pittsburgh and all the other corpseworlds, the harsh ugly places where men would not work and corpses had to. Great towers of black and silver metal, floating aerial sculpture that flashed in the sunlight and shone softly at night, the vast bustling spaceport where freighters rose and fell on invisible fire-wands, malls where the pavement was polished ironspike wood that gleamed a gentle grey; Gidyon.

The city with the rot. The corpse city. The meatmart.

For the freighters carried cargoes of men, criminals and derelicts and troublemakers from a dozen worlds bought with hard Vendalian cash (and there were darker rumors, of liners that had vanished mysteriously on routine tourist hops). And the soaring towers were hospitals and corpseyards, where men and women died and deadmen were born to walk anew. And all along the ironspike boardwalks were corpse-sellers' shops and meathouses.

The meathouses of Vendalia were far-famed. The corpses were guaranteed beautiful.

Trager sat across the avenue from one, under the umbrella of an outdoor café. He sipped a bittersweet wine, thought about how his leave had evaporated too quickly, and tried to keep his eyes from wandering across the street. The wine was warm on his tongue, and his eyes were restless.

Up and down the avenue, between him and the meathouse, strangers moved. Dark-faced corpse handlers from Vendalia, Skrakky, Slagg, pudgy merchants, gawking tourists from the

Clean Worlds like Old Earth and Zephyr and dozens of question marks whose names and occupations and errands Trager would never know. Sitting there, drinking his wine and watching, Trager felt utterly isolated. He could not touch these people, could not reach them; he didn't know how, it wasn't possible. He could rise and walk out into the street and grab one, and still they would not touch. The stranger would only pull free and run. All his leave like that, all of it; he'd run through all the bars of Gidyon, forced a thousand contacts, and nothing had worked.

His wine was gone. Trager looked at the glass dully, turning it in his hands, blinking. Then he stood up and paid his bill. His hands trembled.

It had been so many years, he thought as he started across the street. Josie, he thought, forgive me.

Trager returned to the wilderness camp, and his corpses flew their buzztrucks like men gone wild. But he was strangely silent at the campfire, and he did not talk to Donelly at night. Until finally, hurt and puzzled, Donelly followed him into the forest. And found him by a languid death-dark stream, sitting on the bank with a pile of throwing stones at his feet.

T.: . . . *went in . . . after all I said, all I promised . . . still I went in . . .*

D.: . . . *nothing to worry . . . remember what you told me . . . keep on believing . . .*

T.: . . . *did believe,* did . . . *no difference . . . Josie . . .*

D.: . . . *you say I shouldn't give up, you better not . . . repeat everything you told me, everything Josie told you . . . everybody finds someone . . . if they keep looking . . . give up, dead . . . all you need . . . openness . . . courage to look . . . stop feeling sorry for yourself . . . told me that a hundred times . . .*

T.: . . . *fucking lot easier to tell you than do it myself . . .*

D.: . . . *Greg . . . not a meathouse man . . . a dreamer . . . better than they are . . .*

T. (sighing): . . . *yeah . . . hard, though . . . why do I do this to myself? . . .*

D.: . . . *rather be like you were? . . . not hurting, not living? . . . like me? . . .*

T.: . . . *no . . . no . . . you're right . . .*

4. THE PILGRIM, UP AND DOWN

Her name was Laurel. She was nothing like Josie, save in one thing alone. Trager loved her.

Pretty? Trager didn't think so, not at first. She was too tall, a half foot taller than he was, and she was a bit on the heavy side, and more than a bit on the awkward side. Her hair was her best feature, her hair that was red-brown in winter and glowing blond in summer, that fell long and straight past her shoulders and did wild beautiful things in the wind. But she was not beautiful, not the way Josie had been beautiful. Although, oddly, she grew more beautiful with time, and maybe that was because she was losing weight, and maybe that was because Trager was falling in love with her and seeing her through kinder eyes, and maybe that was because he *told* her she was pretty and the very telling made it so. Just as Laurel told him he was wise, and her belief gave him wisdom. Whatever the reason, Laurel was very beautiful indeed after he had known her for a time.

She was five years younger than he, clean-scrubbed and innocent, shy where Josie had been assertive. She was intelligent, romantic, a dreamer; she was wondrously fresh and eager; she was painfully insecure and full of a hungry need.

She was new to Gidyon, fresh from the Vendalian outback, a student forester. Trager, on leave again, was visiting the forestry college to say hello to a teacher who'd once worked with his crew. They met in the teacher's office. Trager had two weeks free in a city of strangers and meathouses; Laurel was alone. He showed her the glittering decadence of Gidyon, feeling smooth and sophisticated, and she was impressed.

Two weeks went quickly. They came to the last night. Trager, suddenly afraid, took her to the park by the river that ran through Gidyon and they sat together on the low stone wall by the water's edge. Close, not touching.

"Time runs too fast," he said. He had a stone in his hand. He flicked it out over the water, flat and hard. Thoughtfully, he watched it splash and sink. Then he looked at her. "I'm nervous," he said, laughing. "I—Laurel. I don't want to leave."

Her face was unreadable. Wary? "The city is nice," she agreed.

Trager shook his head violently. "No. *No!* Not the city. You. Laurel, I think I . . . well . . ."

Laurel smiled for him. Her eyes were bright, very happy. "I know," she said.

Trager could hardly believe. He reached out, touched her cheek. She turned her head and kissed his hand. They smiled at each other.

He flew back to the forest camp to quit. "Don, *Don,* you've got to meet her," he shouted. "See, you can do it, *I* did it, just keep believing, keep trying. I feel so goddamn good it's obscene."

Donelly, stiff and logical, did not know how to respond to such a flood of happiness. "What will you do?" he asked, a little awkwardly. "The arena?"

Trager laughed. "Hardly—you know how I feel. But something like that. There's a theater near the spaceport, puts on pantomime with corpse actors. I've got a job there. The pay is rotten, but I'll be near Laurel. That's all that matters."

They hardly slept at night. Instead they talked and cuddled and made love. The lovemaking was a joy, a game, a glorious discovery; never as good technically as the meathouse, but Trager hardly cared. He taught her to be open. He told her every secret he had, and wished he had more secrets.

"Poor Josie," Laurel would often say at night, her body warm against his. "She doesn't know what she missed. I'm lucky. There couldn't be anyone else like you."

"No," said Trager, *"I'm* lucky."

They would argue about it, laughing.

Donelly came to Gidyon and joined the theater. Without Trager the forest work had been no fun, he said. The three of them spent a lot of time together, and Trager glowed. He wanted to share his friends with Laurel, and he'd already mentioned Donelly a lot. And he wanted Donelly to see how happy he'd become, to see what belief could accomplish.

"I like her," Donelly said, the first night after Laurel had left.

"Good," Trager replied.

"No," said Donelly. "Greg, I *really* like her."

They spent a *lot* of time together.

"Greg," Laurel said one night in bed. "I think that Don is . . . well, after me. You know."

Trager rolled over and propped his head up on his elbow. "God," he said.

"I don't know how to handle it."

"Carefully," Trager said. "He's very vulnerable. You're probably the first woman he's ever been interested in. Don't be too hard on him. He shouldn't have to go through the stuff I went through, you know?"

The sex was never as good as a meathouse. And after a while Laurel began to close up. More and more nights now she went to sleep after they made love; the days when they had talked till dawn were gone. Perhaps they had nothing left to say. Trager had noticed that she had a tendency to finish his stories for him. It was nearly impossible to come up with one he hadn't already told her.

"He said *that?*" Trager got up out of bed, turned on a light, and sat down frowning. Laurel pulled the covers up to her chin.

"Well, what did *you* say?"

She hesitated. "I can't tell you. It's between Don and me. He said it wasn't fair, the way I turn around and tell you everything that goes on between us, and he's right."

"*Right!* But I tell you everything. Don't you remember what we—"

"I know, but—"

Trager shook his head. His voice lost some of its anger. "What's going on, Laurel, huh? I'm scared, all of a sudden. I love you, remember? How can everything change so fast?"

Her face softened. She sat up and held out her arms, and the covers fell back from her full, soft breasts. "Oh, Greg," she said. "Don't worry. I love you, I always will, but it's just that I love him too, I guess. You know?"

Trager, mollified, came into her arms and kissed her with fervor. Then he broke off. "Hey," he said, with mock sternness to hide the trembling in his voice, "who do you love *more?*"

"You, of course, always you."

Smiling, he returned to the kiss.

"I know you know," Donelly said. "I guess we have to talk about it."

Trager nodded. They were backstage in the theater. Three of his corpses walked up behind him and stood, arms crossed, like guards. "All right." He looked straight at Donelly, and his face was suddenly stern. "Laurel asked me to pretend I didn't know anything. She said you felt guilty. But pretending was quite a strain, Don. I guess it's time we got everything out into the open."

Donelly's pale blue eyes shifted, and he stuck his hands into his pockets. "I don't want to hurt you," he said.

"Then don't."

"But I'm not going to pretend I'm dead, either. I'm not. I love her too."

"You're supposed to be my friend, Don. Love someone else. You're just going to get yourself hurt this way."

"I have more in common with her than you do."

Trager stared.

Donelly looked up at him. "I don't know. Oh, Greg. She loves you more anyway, she said so. I never should have expected anything else. I feel like I've stabbed you in the back. I—"

Trager watched him. Finally he laughed softly. "Oh, shit, I can't take this. Look, Don, you haven't stabbed me, c'mon, don't talk like that. I guess, if you love her, this is the way it's got to be, you know. I just hope everything comes out all right."

Later that night, in bed with Laurel: "I'm worried about him," he said.

His face, once tanned, now ashen. "Laurel?" he said. Not believing.

"I don't love you anymore. I'm sorry. I don't. It seemed real at the time, but now it's almost like a dream. I don't even know if I ever loved you, really."

"Don," he said woodenly.

Laurel flushed. "Don't say anything bad about Don. I'm tired of hearing you run him down. He never says anything except good about you."

"Oh, Laurel. Don't you *remember?* The things we said, the way we felt? I'm the same person you said those words to."

"But I've grown," Laurel said, hard and tearless, tossing her red-gold hair. "I remember perfectly well, but I just don't feel that way anymore."

"Don't," he said. He reached for her.

She stepped back. "Keep your hands off me. I told you, Greg, it's *over*. You have to leave now. Don is coming by."

It was worse than Josie. A thousand times worse.

5. WANDERINGS

He tried to keep on at the theater; he enjoyed the work, he had friends there. But Donelly was there every day, smiling and being friendly, and sometimes Laurel came to meet him after the show and they went off together arm in arm. Trager would stand and watch, try not to notice. While the twisted thing inside him shrieked and clawed.

He quit. He would not see them again. He would keep his pride.

The sky was bright with the lights of Gidyon and full of laughter, but it was dark and quiet in the park.

Trager stood stiff against a tree, his eyes on the river, his hands folded tightly against his chest. He was a statue. He hardly breathed. Not even his eyes moved.

Kneeling near the low wall, the corpse pounded until the stone was slick with blood and its hands were mangled clots of torn meat. The sounds of the blows were dull and wet, but for the infrequent scaping of bone against rock.

They made him pay first before he could even enter the booth. Then he sat there for an hour while they found her and punched through. Finally, though, finally: "Josie."

"Greg," she said, with her distinctive grin. "I should have known. Who else would call all the way from Vendalia? How are you?"

He told her.

Her grin vanished. "Oh, Greg," she said. "I'm sorry. But don't let it get to you. Keep going. The next one will work out better. They always do."

Her words didn't satisfy him. "Josie," he said, "how are things back there? You miss me?"

"Oh, sure. Things are pretty good. It's still Skrakky, though. Stay where you are, you're better off." She looked off screen, then back. "I should go, before your bill gets enormous. Glad you called, love."

"*Josie,*" Trager began. But the screen was already dark.

Sometimes, at night, he couldn't help himself. He would move to his home screen and ring Laurel. Her eyes would narrow when she saw who it was. Then she would hang up.

And Trager would sit in a dark room and recall how once the sound of his voice made her so very, very happy.

The streets of Gidyon are not the best places for lonely midnight walks. They are brightly lit, even in the darkest hours, and jammed with men and deadmen. And there are meathouses, all up and down the boulevards and the ironspike boardwalks.

Josie's words had lost their power. In the meathouses, Trager abandoned dreams and found solace. The sensuous evenings with Laurel and the fumbling sex of his boyhood were things of yesterday; Trager took his meatmates hard and quick, almost brutally, fucked them with a wordless savage power to the inevitable perfect orgasm. Sometimes, remembering the theater, he would have them act out short erotic playlets to get him in the mood.

In the night. Agony.

He was in the corridors again, the low dim corridors of the corpse-handlers' dorm on Skrakky, but now the corridors were twisted and tortuous and Trager had long since lost his way. The air was thick with a rotting grey haze and growing thicker. Soon, he feared, he would be all but blind.

Around and around he walked, up and down, but always there were more corridors, and all of them led nowhere. The doors were grim black rectangles without handles, locked to him forever; he passed them by without thinking, most of them. Once or twice, though, he paused before a door where light leaked around the frame. He would listen, and inside there were sounds, and then he would begin to knock wildly. But no one ever answered.

So he moved on, through the haze that got darker and thicker and seemed to burn his skin, past door after door after door, until he was weeping and his feet were tired and bloody. And then, off a way, down a long, long corridor that ran straight before him, he would see an open door. From it came light so hot and white it hurt the eyes, and music bright and joyful, and the sounds of people laughing. Then Trager would run, though his feet were raw bundles of pain and his lungs burned with the haze he was breathing. He would run and run and run until he reached the open door.

Only when he got there, it was his room, and it was empty.

Once, in the middle of their brief time together, they'd gone out into the wilderness and made love under the stars. Afterward she had snuggled hard against him, and he stroked her gently. "What are you thinking?" he asked.

"About us," Laurel said. She shivered. The wind was brisk and cold. "Sometimes I get scared, Greg. I'm so afraid something will happen to us, something that will ruin it. I don't ever want you to leave me."

"Don't worry," he told her, "I won't."

Now, each night before sleep came, he tortured himself with her words. The good memories left him with ashes and tears; the bad ones with a wordless rage.

He slept with a ghost beside him, a supernaturally beautiful ghost, the husk of a dead dream. He woke to her each morning.

He hated them. He hated himself for hating.

6. Duvalier's Dream

Her name does not matter. Her looks are not important. All that counts is that she *was,* that Trager tried again, that he forced himself on and made himself believe and didn't give up. He *tried.*

But something was missing. Magic?

The words were the same.

How many times can you speak them, Trager wondered, speak them and believe them, like you believed them the first time you said them? Once? Twice? Three times, maybe? Or a hundred? And the people who say it a hundred times, are they really so much better at loving? Or only at fooling themselves? Aren't they really people who long ago abandoned the dream, who use its name for something else?

He said the words, holding her, cradling her and kissing her. He said the words, with a knowledge that was surer and heavier and more dead than any belief. He said the words and *tried.*

And she said the words back, and Trager realized that they meant nothing to him. Over and over again they said the things each wanted to hear, and both of them knew they were pretending.

They tried *hard.* But when he reached out, like an actor caught in his role, doomed to play out the same part over and over again, when he reached out his hand and touched her cheek—the skin was smooth and soft and lovely. And wet with tears.

7. ECHOES

"I don't want to hurt you," said Donelly, shuffling and looking guilty, until Trager felt ashamed for having hurt a friend.

He reached toward her cheek, and she turned away from him.

"I never wanted to hurt you," Josie said, and Trager was sad. She had given him so much; he'd only made her guilty. Yes, he was hurt, but a stronger man would never have let her know.

He touched her cheek, and she kissed his hand.

"I'm sorry. I don't," Laurel said. And Trager was lost. What had he done, where was his fault, how had he ruined it? She had been so sure. They had had so much.

He touched her cheek, and she wept.

How many times can you speak them, his voice echoed, speak them and believe them, like you believed them the first time you said them?

The wind was dark and dust-heavy; the sky throbbed painfully with flickering scarlet flame. In the pit, in the darkness, stood a young woman with goggles and a filtermask and short brown hair and answers. "It breaks down, it breaks down, it breaks down, and they keep sending it out," she said. "Should realize that something is wrong. After that many failures, it's sheer self-delusion to think the thing's going to work right next time out."

8. TRAGER, COME OF AGE

The enemy corpse is huge and black, its torso rippling with muscle, a product of years of exercise, the biggest thing that Trager has ever faced. It advances across the sawdust in a slow, clumsy crouch, holding the gleaming broadsword in one hand. Trager watches it from his chair above one end of the fighting area. The other corpsemaster is careful, cautious.

His own deadman, a wiry blond, stands and waits, a morningstar trailing down in the blood-soaked arena dust. Trager will move him fast enough and well enough when the time is right. The enemy knows it, and the crowd.

The black corpse suddenly lifts its broadsword and scrambles forward in a run, hoping to use reach and speed to get its kill. But Trager's corpse is no longer there when the enemy's measured blow cuts the air where he had been.

Sitting comfortably above the fighting pit / down in the arena, his feet grimy with blood and sawdust, Trager / the corpse snaps the command / swings the morningstar—and the great studded ball drifts up and around, almost lazily, almost gracefully. Into the back of the enemy's head, as he tries to recover and turn. A flower of blood and brain blooms swift and sudden, and the crowd cheers.

Trager walks his corpse from the arena, then stands to receive applause. It is his tenth kill. Soon the championship will be his. He is building such a record that they can no longer deny him a match.

She is beautiful, his lady, his love. Her hair is short and blond, her body very slim, graceful, almost athletic, with trim legs and small hard breasts. Her eyes are bright green, and they always welcome him. And there is a strange erotic innocence in her smile.

She waits for him in bed, waits for his return from the arena, waits for him eager and playful and loving. When he enters, she is sitting up, smiling for him, the covers bunched around her waist. From the door he admires her nipples.

Aware of his eyes, shy, she covers her breasts and blushes. Trager knows it is all false modesty, all playing. He moves to the bedside, sits, reaches out to stroke her cheek. Her skin is very soft; she nuzzles against his hand as it brushes her. Then Trager draws her hands aside, plants one gentle kiss on each breast, and a not-so-gentle kiss on her mouth. She kisses back, with ardor; their tongues dance.

They make love, he and she, slow and sensuous, locked together in a loving embrace that goes on and on. Two bodies move flawlessly in perfect rhythm, each knowing the other's needs. Trager thrusts, and his other body meets the thrusts. He reaches, and her hand is there. They come together (always, *always,* both orgasms triggered by the handler's brain), and a bright red flush burns on her breasts and earlobes. They kiss.

Afterward, he talks to her, his love, his lady. You should always talk afterward; he learned that long ago.

"You're lucky," he tells her sometimes, and she snuggles up to him and plants tiny kisses all across his chest. "Very lucky. They lie to you out there, love. They teach you a silly shining dream and they tell you to believe and chase it and they tell you that for you, for everyone, there is someone. But it's all wrong. The universe isn't fair, it never has been. You run after the phantom, and lose, and they tell you next time, but it's all rot, all empty rot. Nobody ever finds the dream at all; they just kid themselves, trick themselves so they can go on believing. It's just a clutching lie that desperate people tell each other, hoping to convince themselves."

But then he can't talk anymore, for her kisses have gone lower and lower, and now she takes him in her mouth. And Trager smiles at his love and gently strokes her hair.

Of all the bright cruel lies they tell you, the cruelest is the one called love.

A Little Lexicon for Personality Changers

Aggressive Ocean	Ebersoft Faber	Linda Hatelace	scool
Boyish W. Sickman	four-hip	mancruel	sissy force
brightard	gaydle	nosesad	Slaves & Johnson
Carlsgood Caverns	Great Elation	Piltup Man	sloppy's-foot oil
clockfoolish	Jack Armweak	purse-humble	sorryiolus
cowardic fantasy	James Sorrowce	quietspeaker	strongfish
David Gerryoung	Lake Excitable	Richard Okayon	Victor Immature

RULES OF MOOPSBALL

Three hundred twenty-four people? Moopsball hammers?
Garbage-can lids? Don't laugh too soon.

Gary Cohn

Moopsball is a contact sport played by up to three hundred and
twenty-four people, divided into two teams, for three days, on a
field more than ten times the size of a football field.

Each team is made up of the following players:

ten shields	ten hoops
ten flingers	twenty cavalrymen
four lieutenants	five buglers
one standard bearer	one wizard
one captain	

In addition, each team is allowed up to one hundred noncombatants, support personnel: camp followers, wives, husbands,
cooks, medics, dogs, turkeys, etc. There are also fifty-one referees.

THE FIELD

The field is five hundred yards long and two hundred fifty yards wide. It is a rectangle of mixed terrain, preferably a golf-course fairway sort of area. White lines mark its borders. In addition, there are several other lines, arranged thus:

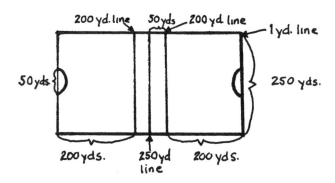

In the center of the two-hundred-fifty-yard line stands a pedestal five feet tall.

In the center of each of the one-yard lines are the goals. These are transparent tubes of tinted plastic, two feet in diameter, four feet tall, unbreakable. The half-circle around the goal post has a fifty-yard diameter.

THE TEAMS

Each person in Moopsball, including noncoms, carries as a sidearm a soft plastic bat approximately twelve inches long.

In addition, each of the various combatants earlier mentioned is armed according to type, as follows:

Shields. Each shield is armed with a Moops-

ball hammer—a long plastic mallet with a collapsible accordion-shaped head made of soft plastic. There are several products of this sort on the market, the best known being the Marx Sock-It-to-Me Mallet. Each shield also carries a shield of soft plastic; plastic garbage can covers do very well.

Hoops. Each hoop carries a Moopsball hammer and a flexible plastic hoop, three feet in diameter.

Flingers. Each flinger carries three Frisbies, one strapped for use as a buckler, in addition to the hammer.

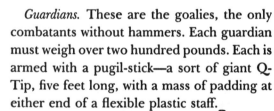

Guardians. These are the goalies, the only combatants without hammers. Each guardian must weigh over two hundred pounds. Each is armed with a pugil-stick—a sort of giant Q-Tip, five feet long, with a mass of padding at either end of a flexible plastic staff.

Cavalry. Each cavalryman carries a hammer and a lance. The lance is a foot longer than the pugil-stick; it is padded only at one end. Cavalrymen are mounted on "wheelie-bikes" or "moto-bikes," highly maneuverable bicycles designed for off-road riding.

Officers. Officers can chose any armament described above except that of the guardians, and at least two of the five officers must be mounted.

Buglers. Each bugler is assigned to an officer. Those assigned to mounted officers are also mounted. They carry hammers and long plastic horns that go *"Blaaat!"*

Standard bearer. The standard bearer carries the team colors at the end of a seven-foot staff. He is armed with a hammer. He is assigned to the captain at all times, and if the captain is mounted, then so is the standard bearer.

The wizard. The wizard is the only active player not on the field during play. He remains behind the lines, muttering his magics, attempting to put the whammy on the opposing team from afar by use of appropriate spells and incantations; his major concern is his opposite number. The psychic battle of sorcerers plays a vital role in the game. To aid in this, the wizard is allowed three nubile assistants of any sex. He creates his own style, be it staid and stately Merlin or feathered, gibbering shaman.

THE BALL

The moopsball is a soft, bounceless ball about the size of a grapefruit. In a pinch a real grapefruit will serve, although somewhat lacking in durability. At the beginning of the game it sits on the pedestal at center field.

REFEREES

Each referee carries two shields, to be used to separate combatants in the event of serious altercations. Referees are present to maintain a semblance of order. Players are expected to whale away at each other with their weapons, but punching, kicking, grappling or other forms of unarmed combat are strictly prohibited. Two violations bring immediate disqualification and assignment to latrine duty. There are no substitutions.

GARB

Each combatant wears a uniform in the team colors, consisting of a jersey, shorts, knee socks, sneakers and a hardhat. Officers wear feathered helmets. The captain's helmet is plumed. All male combatants must wear groin protectors and female combatants must wear chest protectors. A small pouch is worn by each player, containing beef jerky, chocolate, salt tablets, Band-aids, etc.

Referees wear white shorts and jerseys. The head referee wears a gray derby.

The Play

Moopsball requires three days to be played. A weekend beginning with a Friday is the best time. Activities begin in the predawn hours, with the gathering of forces.

Each team meets at a designated location two miles from the field of play, along with half the refereeing squad. A marching formation is ordered, with noncombatants at the rear, and a forced march to the field takes place. Referees, using an agreed-upon system, grade the teams on discipline, fierceness of demeanor, formation, etc. Small touches, such as bagpipers, can count substantially.

The teams, hereafter called Team A and Team B, arrive at their respective ends of the field in the early morning and set up camp, starting ten yards behind their one-yard lines. The camp will be judged. When the camps are completed, both teams assemble on the field of battle.

Battle formations begin at the two-hundred-yard lines and may extend back to the one-yard line. Guardians are confined to the goal areas, which no other member of the same team is allowed to enter.

Movement of all players other than guardians is unrestricted.

Formations must be set up by 11 A.M. to allow a full hour for war cries and the hurling of epithets across the hundred-yard no-man's-land. These *will* be graded. It is a time for the uttering of mighty oaths, and each wizard is allowed an incantation at the head of his team.

As noon draws closer the wizards retreat behind the lines, officers confirm signals with buglers, and all the players rattle their weapons.

At one minute of noon the head referee steps out onto the field at the two-hundred-fifty-yard line and removes his hat. Staring at the second hand of his watch, he holds his hat at arm's length. At precisely noon he lets it fall.

The play begins at the drop of the hat. Team A and Team B charge the ball, howling.

The object of the game is to bring the ball to the other team's goal and ram it down the tube, and to smash anyone who gets in your way. The ball can be conveyed downfield in any manner. It can be thrown, kicked, dribbled, air-dribbled, carried; but it cannot remain in any player's hand for more than five seconds.

Teamwork is important, as is an awareness of the strengths and limitations of the different weapons. The hoop, for example, is especially effective against cavalry. A cavalry wedge can break a large defensive infantry formation, and that wedge need consist of only three cavalrymen. A flinger is at a severe disadvantage when closing with a shield. The prudent commander must know his army.

Nighttime Activities

Nights are filled with feasting and drunken revelry. During the game, the support personnel have been preparing a huge repast and a raucous party. Referees will circulate among the camps, taking notes. In this partying as in all other things, the teams must strive to outdo one another.

Various games may be played to while away the night. Some suggestions:

Pick-a-tent. A warrior, armed only with a hammer, stands in the center of a fifteen-foot circle facing three tents.

In one tent there are three nubile wenches, a hot bath, a steak dinner and a soft bed. But in each of the tents there waits an opponent or opponents. In one there may be a fully armed guardian; in another, two hoops or two shields. These opponents come out smoking when the contestant chooses their tent, and set upon him. The contestant must fight until he or his opponent is driven from the circle. If he wins, he throws open the tent flap to claim his prize. If he has chosen wrongly, he may try once again.

One-on-one. This is a basic challenge match, in a circle, the object being to force the opponent out of the circle.

Inquisition. During the day prisoners will probably have been taken. A prisoner is taken when an opposing player is surrounded and disarmed, or is forced across the one-yard line into the enemy camp, or surrenders for reasons of his own. The prisoners are confined to a compound. They are not allowed to try to escape unless they can come by weapons. Once armed, they can make the attempt.

Inquisition is played by the Wizard, a jailer, a prisoner, and a referee. These four cloister themselves in a tent. The referee takes notes. The jailer watches.

The Wizard asks the prisoner simple yes-or-no questions in an attempt to gain useful information, such as the key to the team's bugle code or battle strategy.

The prisoner does not answer "yes" or "no," however. He answers "rum" or "tum" or "rum-te-tum." This last is a maybe. He may use it twenty times. He is allowed to choose which of the other two means yes and which no. The Wizard has one hundred questions in which to find out which is which and to gain useful information. The prisoner is allowed to lie twenty times.

Play continues from noon until sundown.

Rescue. In the course of the night each team is allowed to send a total of ten players, laden with sidearm clubs, to infiltrate the enemy camp and provide prisoners with weapons, so that they may attempt an escape. These infiltrators are subject to capture.

RESUMPTION OF PLAY

This is the most crucial stage in the game, since it is the time when a point is most likely to be scored. Just before dawn, as

many of each team as can be roused out of their tents and sleeping bags assemble in battle formation on the field. At dawn the
hat is dropped and play is resumed.

Now suppose that Team A has roused forty or more players,
while Team B has managed to awaken only fourteen. It is very
possible that Team A will score in the early moments of play.

Should a team score a point while opposed by a force less than
half its size, the scoring team is given five minutes to ride roughshod through the scored-upon team's camp, knocking over tents,
liberating prisoners, carrying off wenches, etc.

After a point is scored a half hour is taken to regroup and then
play begins anew.

The game proceeds through Saturday from dawn until dark, in
the same manner as before. Players will probably wish to resign,
and may do so without much fear of retribution.

At sundown the game is once again adjourned for a night of
drunken revelry.

The next morning the play is resumed yet again at dawn. Play
continues until noon on Sunday. The teams then retire to their
camps to await the declaration of a winner by the referee squad.

Declaration of a Winner

In the unlikely event that a point has been scored, the scoring
team is automatically the winner. If more than one point has been
scored, high score takes it. In a scoreless game or a tie, other
methods must be used.

First, the Wizard. If, during the course of his performance, he
has actually succeeded in putting the whammy on the opposition
by his ritual defenestration of a watermelon or whatever, then his
team *loses*.

The next criterion, if this has not happened, is the number of
prisoners held at game's end. The team holding the most prisoners wins.

If this produces no result, subjective judgments take over. Revelry, marching skill, enthusiasm of play, all the diverse activities

observed and noted by the referees, become the determining factors. In any event, by 3 P.M. a winner is declared ("What the hell, let's give it to Team A"), the teams congregate at midfield and everyone shouts, "Huzzah!"

Then everyone goes to the winning camp for yet another night of partying. The next morning camp is broken and everyone goes home.

Moopsball will be played soon. People are needed to organize, publicize, provide monetary support, scout locations, and play.

Keep in mind that this is *organized* anarchy. There are rules. A Moopsball team must incorporate a real dimension of discipline, or else the game will be a failure.

Volunteers, know your limitations. If you want to be a player, be sure you can run your tail off for twenty-four hours. If not, be a referee or a wench or a cook or a musician or a juggler.

For further information, write to Gary Cohn, Moopsball, 35 Maryland Ave., Freeport, N. Y. 11520.

Don't expect a prompt reply.

WHO WAS THE FIRST OSCAR TO WIN A NEGRO?

No help from the audience, please!

Craig Strete

The tour guide pulled the curtain aside. The tour members waved their antennae with astonishment. Peter Renoir was removing his clothes. He looked up startled as he heard the shower curtain rustle. He saw the aliens staring at him from the bathtub.

"You will note the clothes that bind, the jaws that snap," said Raffi the tour guide. "Also you will note," continued Raffi, "the accouterments which denote that this culture limits tactile communication."

"Communication with the self by masturbation is no doubt universal," suggested a little Koapa.

"I note that he is rather pale, so unlike the black one we saw last week," said a larger Koapa.

"Visual identification," said the tour guide. "Who to avoid and what not to touch."

"What keeps them from becoming universally poignant, a

heart-throb for the galaxy?" asked the little Koapa. "They seem so frail, so tragic."

"It has no appreciation of sculpture for one thing," said the tour guide. "There are social restraints against touching art objects, for another."

"How would it feel if we touched it?" asked the little Koapa, carving himself into a beautiful hand.

"Better not," said the tour guide. "They are used to the illusion of separating art from life. We might confuse it."

Peter Renoir fainted dead away.

"You see," lectured the tour guide, "we've already confused it."

"Is it dead?" asked the little Koapa, forming into a golden stream of tears.

"No," said the tour guide, speaking from experience. "It is simply experiencing self-criticism."

In the fall of 1939 Benito Mussolini condemned the Marx Brothers and ordered his subjects not to laugh at them.

"Somehow," said Semina, letting the bathrobe fall at her feet, "it just doesn't seem real this way."

Renoir turned out the room lights, pulled the window drapes closed. He moved in beside her and said, "Perhaps it will seem more real this way." His hand reached out and hit the switch. The projector whirred and the screen burst into color. Renoir appeared naked on the screen. Semina moved in beside him and let her bathrobe fall at her feet. He dragged her down on the waterbed and together as the camera tilted and zoomed in, they reached for squishy delight. The film clattered along, the leader winding off the spool and beating madly against the projector housing.

Semina sighed and took Renoir's hand off her knee. "It seemed so much more real that way, didn't it?"

"Yes," said Renoir, folding his hands in his lap. "It was realer than real. Let's watch it again instead."

A film critic peeping through the keyhole said, "The camera

thrusts us into the depth of things."

Realism was too easy. The movies offered themselves as substitutes. The American woman watches film to learn how to become a better female impersonator.

FROM: PETER RENOIR

SUBJECT: REWRITE OF "WHO WAS THE FIRST OSCAR TO WIN A NEGRO?"

Obviously this one can't wait. Let's dump the jerk who wrote it and get one of our people on it. We don't want to blow this one. How about we give it to Sam Bernardino. You remember him. He's the one who did that TV quickie about the attack of giant roaches or was it chickens? Let's get a Screen Guild member on this for Christ Sakes! What we're talking about here is our survival!

Peter Renoir, Producer

"Must you always think like a marshal? Can't you think like a human being just once?" Semina wept openly on the set of her latest movie.

Her five-year-old son, not to be upstaged, pointed at the Marshal's gun and said, quite distinctly, "Daddy!"

"You can take it up your movie," said the alien, holding Lillian Gish in his extended forepaws. "I been sitting in the front row for twenty-seven silent years and I'll be damned if my baby is going to talk!"

"Damn you, damn your naked eyes!" cursed Peter Renoir. "We can't afford a transition like this! Not now! We were just learning how to talk with our eyes and now we are being interrupted by sound!"

"Peter!" breathed Semina. "The cheers! The shouting!"

"It's nineteen hundred and thirty," he said. "And I've had fourteen lovers and want you to bring back the Auk."

From a letter written in the future:

The guarantee against limits is a sense of alternatives. Back in Oregon, I dreamed all my life of being the Bank of California. We lived across from the debtors' prison. I used to sit in the darkest of theaters and watch the light and shadow. I was hypnotized by Marilyn Monroe and a known associate of the Seven Dwarfs. I was hypnotized, the dreams provided. Did I dream of being me instead?

I turned in a fire one day, after letting it burn for a while to make sure it was a good one, and got my name in the newspaper. Later, I became convinced that people were so blank, so destroyed, that no mad scientist was ever necessary to destroy their souls.

Perhaps everything terrible is something that wants to help me. Perhaps it is only that other people's fantasies have nothing to do with reality.

Vonda McIntyre

P.S.: "Remember the night we met and I lost my glass slipper?"

"Yes," he said, low angle, soft focus, violins beginning.

"That was when I discovered my existence was insufficiently interesting."

The director screamed *cut* after the word *existence* and turned to his assistant and said, "Print it, it's a wrap."

Peter Renoir was an alien and didn't know any better. He came here for a good education. A good sex education. He was an alien and didn't know any better. He turned to television for advice, for the facts, for the inside info. He found what he sought. He never had a minute of regret.

"It could have happened to anyone," he said. And indeed he might just have been right. He was an alien and he came here from another galaxy, came here with a problem of sorts. It was the kind of thing that can happen to anybody. The people on Peter Renoir's planet, they had this culture, see, really a ball-breaker, see, with everything wired for sound, juiced right up to the limits. See, they had perfected perfection. They had it made, only they were so busy being perfect, they forgot how to do it.

"What do you mean, DO IT?"

"I mean do it, DO IT," said Peter Renoir. "It's a natural."

Semina scratched inelegantly. "It'll never sell product," she said.

"Oh, man!" shouts Peter Renoir. "You cannot see the frigging unbelievable scope of this thing! I mean, see, he comes eight million miles or whatever in this big frigging flying space something or other! See what I'm getting at?"

"Jesus!" said Semina. "That's a hell of a long drive for just one person. Don't he let somebody else take a turn driving?"

"That's what I'm getting at!" shouts Peter Renoir. "See him and his girl, course she looks just like a real girl like on TV or something. You know, what was the name of that broad with the gaps in her teeth, you know the one on the acne commercial, the before one?"

"Norma Jean, you mean," said Semina, finally catching some of his enthusiasm.

"See, they got the hots, they got 'em so bad and they don't know which end is which."

"Right!" screams Semina. "And that's where we hit them with the commercial, our plug for toilet paper!"

"Aw, shit," said Peter Renoir, "you should of let me say it first! You're always taking all the fun out of it!"

I know he's out there. I know he's reading my story, wondering about the size of my breasts, missing every single word of what I had to say. How many times have I told him. Explore other people's metaphors. It isn't only a metaphor. It's an angle of vision.

I've based my life on the theory of the persistence of vision. You can't throw up 3,000 years of art in three minutes and not see something.

                                                                Joanna Russ

"Jesus!" said Peter Renoir. "That name, Joanna Russ. Sounds very Hollywood. I think we can go with it. I really think this one is our baby. How does she look in a bikini?"

I am an alchemist, the father of science, the death of us all. I am the real root of science. I am an erotic science. I am deeply involved with buried aspects of reality, from novel to film and back again.

Rain is copulation. The sexual activity of man is an energy-to-matter conversion. Mineral formations are sexual crystal trysts. The creation of the world was a sexual activity. I am an alchemist. I can remember love affairs of chemicals and stars, romances of stones, fertility in fire. I am an alchemist.

On the other hand, maybe I am only showing you the soft underbelly of a stealing tide of nostalgia. Maybe I need a new analogy.

I am a science-fiction writer, the mother impregnator of dreams. I reflect culture. Culture reflects me. Why are both these statements true?

"Joanna Russ, and we throw in some other kind of broad, I don't know who just yet, but we tear her clothes halfway off and so she's got to look like she's asking for it, but what I mean we can maybe do," said Peter Renoir, "is have these two broads, see, and this alien menace from somewhere, how the hell I know, one of the damn planets or something. Are you with me on this?"

"Gotcha," said Semina, licking the end of her pencil and scribbling it down on her napkin.

"Well see, my idea for the series is first these two aliens come down and these two broads have one hell of a time trying to escape from them. In the last ten minutes of the show, we burn this Russ's clothes off, see, get some good leg shots going for us and maybe a couple good back shots, then the alien catches her and rapes the hell out of her. We make that nine minutes and then cut away for the commercial. We cut back for the final minute, in which it is revealed that the alien is really working for the government. So the show ends on an upbeat note and we sell one hell of a lot of product."

"But won't it get stale? Don't you have to have a sad show once in a while, you know a downbeat one for a change of pace?" asked Semina.

"You mean like could we add something like a pet goat or something that gets killed off or a baby dog or something?" asked Peter Renoir, mulling it over in his head.

His face lit up. "Oh, man! It just hit me! It's a frigging natural! We come back next week and throw in this time machine device, see, and she and this other broad gets thrown back into the past. Back to fifteen hundred and forty-eight or whenever the hell the Civil War was. Do you see it! See, we have the whole Confederate Army and the Union Army and Russ and this other broad lands in a Union town. We kill off the other broad when the Rebels overrun the town. Then, see, we got the audience's sympathy. We got their attention and then the Confederate Army catches Joanna Russ and rapes the hell out of her. We do it in three versions, soft focus for television with lots of shots of horses taken extra so we can cut them in, crotch closeups for the drive-in and for the big downtown theater market, we got to shoot something symbolic or something. I don't know what, maybe a picture of Orson Welles in the buff."

"It's going to be beautiful," said Semina.

"Then see, the way we end it is, the Union Army comes in and saves her."

"Then what happens?" said Semina.

"Then the Union Army rapes the hell out of her and the picture ends and we are left with a sense of loss."

"You're a frigging genius!" said Semina. "You really are, Peter."

"Oh, it was nothing," said Peter Renoir. "But it damn well will sell."

NOTE TO THE READER: I'LL BET THE EDITOR THINKS I DON'T CARE TOO MUCH FOR YOU. HE'S WRONG. PLEASE REMEMBER THE EDITOR BEHIND HIS SMILE IS MY PIMP. I DO LOVE YOU VERY DEARLY AT

EXACTLY FIVE CENTS A WORD. AND BECAUSE I LOVE YOU, I'M GOING
TO CLARIFY THINGS FOR YOU. I WANT EVERYTHING IN THIS STORY TO
BE RIGHT BETWEEN US.

ON PLOTTING THE STORY:

The plot is simply about an alien who has come into your bedroom, your life, your church. He has come seeking knowledge, information. He is looking to the reader for that information. He is an alien and doesn't care how he gets it. He wants information about doing it. Yes, he does. He is an alien and he learned about your planet from watching television and going to the drive-in movies on Saturday and Sunday nights. While the alien is very much in sympathy with the reader, while the alien is very much on the reader's side, the alien cannot deny his personal feelings and values as an alien, which is why his meaning may not be too clear. This is the story of his struggle in your world to figure out how to do it.

In 1934 Clark Gable took off his shirt and underneath he wasn't wearing an undershirt. The undershirt industry fell off that year by 50 percent.

"Christ!" said Peter Renoir. "When is this damn story going to finish up? I say we cut the hell out of the son of a bitching thing. I say we muzzle the son of a bitch and get it over with. He isn't Screen Guild anyway. Just because he wrote some stuff under the name of Rudyard Kipling do I have to listen to the whole thing? I got things to do."

"But how the hell we going to do it up without you got the whole picture?"

"I got the picture," said Peter Renoir. "We take out Gunga Din and substitute Nanette Fabray. Don't tell me I ain't got the picture!"

"Who we gonna get to direct it?"

"How about we get Gower Champion? I want someone who isn't going to mess it up by knowing anything."

"You're a genius, Peter Renoir," said Semina.
"Yes, I know," said Peter Renoir.

Semina tells a lie and then tells the truth. There is no change in her face. She murders a stripper named Shirley who wants to get married and have a baby. She murders a stripper who is not named Shirley and who doesn't want to get married and would sell a baby if she could get anything out of it. There is no change in her face.

She goes away for the weekend with a bowling team sponsored by a local carwash. The inbuilt demand for a higher standard of living creates a feeling of menace. The captain of the bowling team dies from heart failure that may or may not have been caused by the bullet in his brain. Panic-stricken by this turn of events, she decides to escape from this world. She buys a ticket and enters a movie house to watch a double feature. The film ends and we are left with a sense of familiarity.

Peter Renoir is an alien. He feels naked without his clothes. He equates morality with being uncomfortable. If only he were illiterate. We could save him if he were illiterate. The ways of official literacy do not equip people to know themselves, the past or the present.

Why doesn't Peter Renoir understand as we understand? Why doesn't he know the world has been conquered? Don't you understand? The world has been conquered. What have they done to the earth and the people?

Who are they? I can explain me. I am a creature of the nightland. I am of the soil. I am people. That is who I am.

Who are they? They are technology. They are the aliens. Technology is the creature of the conquered world. The world, all my peoples, is the materials of technology, not its form.

The car did not do the work of the horse. It replaced it. Technology will not do the work of the people. It will replace them.

Semina is arrested for flaunting antisexual implications. Peter Renoir bails her out. They fall in love. They build it up to a severe emotional disturbance. However, as they realize that they are at last approaching a permanence and security unknown to them and their generation, Peter Renoir finds himself pursuing anti-cliché to anticlimax.

Semina catches him kissing himself. He defends himself by casually remarking, "When sex dies it is climax."

She snubs him in the closing scene by proclaiming, "Others may call you sensibly adaptive but I think you are a faggot."

The movie ends and we are left without a sense.

"Semina," said Peter Renoir, moving toward her in a zoom, up angle. "Why don't we do it?"

"You mean, uh, oh dearest!" said Semina. "You've finally discovered the secret! After millions of miles and one of your smiles, you've finally found out how to do it. I'm so proud of you!"

"Aw, shucks," said Peter Renoir, blushing. "It wasn't nothing special. I just watched television until I found out how they did it."

"Nevertheless," said Semina, "I'm impressed. How do we do it?"

"Well," said Peter Renoir, blushing through every pore. "I believe the best way is for you to prop yourself up on that couch over there. Kind of slouch around and blink your eyes a lot. Then light up a cigarette."

"Then what?" pole-vaulted Semina, arching enthusiastically over his every word.

"Then," said Peter Renoir, with dramatic emphasis and a slight snigger, "I leap on top of you, your hand will become limp and the cigarette will drop to the floor. Later you will cry."

"Why don't we just forget the whole thing?" said Semina.

I am an sf fanzine editor. I am forty-nine years old and never have been kissed. I am a peeping tom, a chronic masturbator. The mirror is my staff of life, my totem, my life's work. The window is my prey. What is my threat? What is my power?

My secret is that I am lonely and in that silence that surrounds me, I am able to pierce the windows with my mouth and make an unknowing partner of anyone in my eyes' range. I am deeply involved in a current fan project to cure blindness with a whore's spittle. My threat and my power is in my ability to motivate, to "show the donkey the carrot."

MUTATIONS ARE ONLY POSSIBLE THE MOMENT ONE GOES FROM ONE SET OF CONVENTIONS TO ANOTHER.

The science-fiction editor, in order to play his game with a full deck, is forced to accept only images that represent an orderly sequence. An image path that is familiar. That is why science fiction sometimes repeats itself itself itself itself itself itself itself and why this story will get thirty-five rejection slips. An Indian tells the story of his life from the day the world began. He will never tell his life's story with any regard to chronology. He may work back or work forward or both. He will repeat himself many times and omit things frequently. Shall I apologize for this pagan mysticism, the willful obscurity about my craft? I want to withhold my skills from profane onlookers. I am, after all, repeating the works of nature.

Peter Renoir and Semina are hopelessly in love and they decide to kill each other. While on a visit to Renoir's mother they decide to kill Mommy instead. Before they can carry it out, however, a semi-pro football team, turned cannibal after losing their league franchise, attacks the house. Peter Renoir is killed, as is his mother. Semina helps them eat the evidence of their intellectual dilemma, nearly choking on Renoir's mother, who is tough and stringy. She joins the team as an outside linebacker. She is later benched and then raped by a referee. The film ends in a closeup on the fifty-yard line and we are left with a sense of loss.

From *Reviews in Film:*

Only a director of the stature of Peter Renoir could bring himself so consistently to face contemporary reality. The determination to show only what is real is clearly an aspect of Renoir's wider determination to expose himself completely to the age in which we live. The scene in which an apple is stuffed up Peter Renoir's anus in preparation for being butchered, cooked and eaten is an obvious attempt to tell us that what we are watching is more than a film but instead the very framework of everyday reality. At the end of the film, when the director allows us to actually see one of the corpses breathing, we are once again assured in the director's unshakable faith in the unconquerorable human spirit.

Peter Renoir is leaving his rich wife because he is too comfortable. Semina is leaving Richmond, Indiana, because she is tired of sleeping with truck drivers. They meet and fall in love beside a tennis-ball factory. Semina is kidnapped on the first night they spend together by one of her old truck-driver friends. Peter Renoir pursues her the length and breadth of highway 101. He finds the semi-truck in which she was a prisoner. The truck is empty with the exception of the corpse of a midget named Russell.

He finally catches up with them in the men's room of a truck stop in New Jersey. He realizes that he has lost her because the truck driver is built better. Peter climbs to the top of a ten-story building and dives off. Nine floors later he repents of his rash action but alas, too late. The movie ends and we are left with a sense of having seen it.

HOW YOU, THE READER, CAN APPRECIATE THIS STORY.

Begin like this. You the reader, somewhat awkward at first, begin reading this story with as much intelligence and sensibility as you can bring to it. In the passages where the theme (animal suffering) is most acute, you will be at least able to note the technique and methodology by which parts of the effect were achieved. But when the theme weakens, you will find yourself with a surplus of attention which you can profitably direct toward some other activity.

Preferably some quiet and fatal activity.

"I've got it for sure, this time," said Peter Renoir.

Semina rolled her eyes. "I'll see it first before I believe it. What do we do?"

"Well, we drop all our clothes on the floor and then we get under the sheets of the bed and we talk. Then I get up and go for a drive in my sports car. Later you will cry."

"Is that it?"

"There's more." said Peter Renoir.

"Such as?"

"Well," said Peter Renoir with a smile. "Then the Army comes in and rapes the hell out of both of us."

"It's just like a movie," said Semina and she was deeply moved by it. It almost made her want to cry but she held it in. She wasn't scheduled to cry until the next scene.

Now, class, why is this story worth studying?

Because it is metaphor as metamorphosis. It has become a story cut off from its name, habits, associations. Detached, it sees everything and nothing. It sees all things, swirling independently and then becoming gradually connected. The change of detachment. I am talking to you personally, because detached I become only a thing, an exercise, a creation, an amusement. I become the thing, in and of itself. It is disintegration into pure existence, and at that point, I the thing, I the writer, I the reason for this story, I all of these things, am free to become endlessly anything.

A literary critic peeping through the keyhole said, "The storm over style and content will rage forever."

Peter Renoir and Semina are trapped in an outhouse by two Dominican friars and several very irate forest rangers. Violence seems imminent. The priests are chanting, "We are only interested in the superficial."

The forest rangers break down the door. The rangers make off with Semina, the priests disappear into the night with Peter Renoir. Semina reveals her pregnancy by word association and the rangers take her deep into the woods. They rape her and we are left with a sense of guilt. Peter Renoir is castrated in a frustrated rape attempt. We are left with a sense of accomplishment.

IN PIERSON'S ORCHESTRA

The dead shall live, the living die,
And Music shall untune the sky.

Kim Stanley Robinson

Hallway to hallway to hallway I flit, like a bat in a mine. The lights are dimmed and the halls are empty, eerie grey slots. I cast long shadows from low light to light as I move along, next to the wall. I can feel my upper arms slide wetly against my ribs, and my heart's *allegro* thumping. A voice within me sneers: "Time for your diamond, junkie."

Dead sober will I see him, I promise myself again. My hand shakes, and I put it back in my pocket. Familiar halls now, and I slow down as if the air is getting thicker; still in color-blind greys, and the air is perhaps filled with dust, or smoke. It is past time for my next crystal. I have not slept for five days, I am continuing on the drive of my decision.

Home. VANCOUVER CONSERVATORY, the tall door announces. I turn the knob, give the door a push to get it started. It opens. I slip through, silently cross the entrance floor. Pierson's holo-gramic statue stares down at me, a short ruby-red figure transparent in the dim light. I circle him warily, alive to his presence in the shadows between me and the ceiling. Hallways, again; then another door, *the* door: *sanctum sanctorum.* You remember the old animated film *Fantasia?* Suddenly I am Mickey Mouse, in Dukas' *The Sorcerer's Apprentice,* about to interrupt the sorcerer over his cauldron. A deep bell clangs from the main hall and I jump. Midnight: time for the breaking of vows. I knock on the door, a mistake; I have the privilege of entering without knocking; but no, I have lost all that, I have revoked all that. An indistinct shout arrives from inside.

I push the door open and a slice of white light cuts into the hallway. In I go, blinking.

The Master is under the Orchestra, on his back, tapping away cautiously at the dent in the tuba tubing. The dent occurred at the end of the last grand tour, when one of the workmen helping to move it onto a rollcar tripped and kicked the tuba with his steel-tipped boot.

The Master looks up, white eyebrows rising like a bird's crest. "Eric," he says mildly, "why did you knock?"

"Master," I say shakily, my resolve still firm, "I can no longer be your apprentice."

Watch that sink in, like a hot poker in snow. He edges out from under the Orchestra, stands up; all slowly, so slowly. He is so old. "Why is this, Eric?"

I swallow. I have a lie all prepared, I have considered it for hours and hours; it is absurd, impossible. Suddenly I decide to tell him the truth. "I'm addicted to nepanathol."

Right before my eyes his face turns a deep red. "You what?" he says, then almost shouts, "I don't understand!"

"The drug," I explain. "I'm hooked."

Has the shock been too much for him? He trembles. He gets it out, calm and clear. "Why?"

It is all so complex. I shrug. "Master," I say, "I'm sorry."

With a convulsive jerk he throws the hammers in his hand, and I flinch; they hit the foam lining of the wall without a sound, then click against each other as they fall.

"You're sorry!" he hisses, and I can feel his contempt. Why

does one always whisper in this room? "You're sorry! My God, you'd better be more than sorry! Three centuries, eight Masters of the Orchestra, you to be the ninth and you break the line for a drug? The greatest artistic achievement of all time—" he waves toward the Orchestra, but I refuse to look at it—"you choose nepanathol above it? How could you do it? I'm an old man, I'll die in a few years, there isn't time to train another musician like you—and you'll be dead before I will!" True enough, in all probability. "I will be the last Master," he cries out, "and the Orchestra will be silenced!"

With the thought of it he twists and sits down crosslegged on the floor, crying. I have never seen the Master cry before, never thought I would. He is not an emotional man.

"What have I done?" Echoless shrieks. "The Orchestra will end with me and they will say it was my fault, that I was a bad Master—"

"You are the best of them," I get out.

He turns on me. "Then why? *Why?* Eric, how could you do this?"

I would have been the ninth Master of Pierson's Orchestra. The heir to the throne. The crown prince. Why indeed? Such a joke.

As from a distance I hear myself. "Master," I say, "I will stop taking the drug."

I close my eyes as I say it. For an old man's sake I will go through the withdrawal from nep. I shake my head, surprised at myself.

He looks up at me with—what is it, craftiness? Is he manipulating me? No. It's just contempt. "You can't," he mutters angrily. "It would kill you."

"No," I say, though I am by no means sure of this. "I haven't been addicted long enough. A few hours; eight, maybe; then it will be over." It will be short; that is my only comfort. A very real voice inside me is protesting loudly: "What are you *doing?*" Pain. Muscle cramps, memory confusion, memory loss. Nausea. Hallucinations. A high possibility of sensory damage, especially to the ears, sense of smell, and eyes. I do not want to go blind.

"Truly?" the old man is saying. "When will you do this?"

"Now," I say, ignoring the voice inside. "I'll stay here, I think," gesturing toward the Orchestra but still not looking in its direction.

"I too will stay—"

"No. Not here. In the recording booth, or one of the practice rooms. Or go up to your chambers, and come back tomorrow."

We look at each other then, old Richard and young Eric, and finally he nods. He walks to the tall door, pulls it open. He turns his head back. "You be careful, Eric," he says.

I nearly laugh, but am too appalled. The door clicks shut, and I am alone with Pierson's Orchestra.

I can remember the first time I saw the Orchestra, in Sydney's old sailboat of an opera house, around the turn of the century when my mother and I were living there. It was a special program for young people, and the Master—the same one, Richard Wolfgang Weber Yablonski, an old man even then—was playing pieces to delight the young mind: I can remember the *1812 Overture,* Moussorgsky's *Pictures at an Exhibition,* De Bruik's *Night Sea,* and Debussy's *Claire de Lune.* The *Claire de Lune* was a shock; used to my mother's quick, workmanlike version, I barely recognized the Master's; slow, simple, the solo piano supported at times by the strings; he started each phrase hesitantly, and exaggerated the rests, so that I felt as if the music had never been played before; that it was the result of the blue lights striking the fantastic tower of blue circles and glints, and long blue curves.

After the performance a few children, the ones being considered for the apprenticeship, came forward to talk with the Master. I walked down the aisle, my mother's palm firm in the middle of my back, barely able to pull my eyes from the baroque monster of wood and metal and glass, to the mere mortal who played the thing. He spoke to us for a while, quietly, of the glories of playing an entire orchestra by oneself, watching our faces.

"And which did you like better," he asked, *"Pictures at an Exhibition* played on the piano, or with the full orchestral arrangement?"

"Orchestra," cried a score of voices.

"Piano," I said, hitting a sudden silence.

"Why?" he asked politely, focusing on me for the first time. I shrugged nervously; I couldn't think, I truly didn't know; fingers digging into my back, I searched for it—

It came to me. "Because," I said, "it was written for piano."

Simple. "But do you not like Ravel's arrangement?" he inquired, interested now.

I thought. "Ravel changed a rough Russian piano score into a French romantic orchestration. He changed it." Oh, I was a bright kid, no doubt about it, back in those days when I spent five hours a day at the keyboard and three in the books—and one in the halls, one desperately short hour, five o'clock to six o'clock every day in the halls burning up a day's pent-up frustration—

"Have you compared the scores?" the Master asked me.

"Yes, Master, they are very similar. It is the instrumentation that makes the difference."

The Master nodded his head, seeming to consider this. "I believe I agree with you," he said.

Then the talk was over and we were on our way home. I felt sick to my stomach. "You did good," my mother said. I was nine years old.

And here I am ten years later, sick to my stomach again. That is, I think I am. It is difficult to tell what is happening in my body —past time for my next crystal, that's sure. The little twinges of dependence are giving me their warning, in the backs of my upper arms. At least it will be short. "Just like sex," I remember an ex-addict saying in a high-pitched voice. "Short and sweet, with the climax at the end." His friend nodded and flashed fingers at him.

I turn to the Orchestra. "Imagine all of the instruments of a full symphonic orchestra caught in a small tornado," an early detractor said of it, "and you will have Pierson's invention." The detractor is now forgotten, and few like him exist now; age equals respectability, and the Orchestra now has three hundred years' worth. An institution.

And imposing enough: eleven meters of instruments suspended in air, eleven meters of twisted brass and curved wood, supported by glass rods only visible because of the blue and red spotlights glinting from them. The cloud of violas, the broken staircase of trombones; a truly beautiful statue. But Pierson was a musician as well as a sculptor, a conductor as well as an inventor, and a genius to boot: an unfortunate combination.

I move to the piano opening and slide onto the bench. The glass depression rods cover the keys so that it is impossible to play the piano from here; I must move up to the control booth. I do that, using the glass steps behind the cellos. Even the steps are inlaid with tiny French horn figures. Incredible. It is as if I were seeing everything in the Orchestra for the first time. The control booth, suspended in the center of the thing, nearly hidden from the outside; I am astounded by it. As always, I sit back in the chair and look at the colors: keyboards, foot pedals, chord knobs, ensemble tabs, volume stops, percussion buttons, keyboards, keyboards; strings yellow, woodwinds blue, brass red, percussion brown—

. . . then the Master, waiting outside the Orchestra to listen, shouts "Play!" impatiently, and I jump and begin the lesson. "Play!" he shouts as I sit watching the clarinets rising. "Play! What are you doing? You cannot just sit and look at the Orchestra," he tells me emphatically, "until you have learned to play it," and even as he tells me he is looking at the Orchestra himself, watching the dark browns reflect out of the golds and silvers; but then, he can play it—

. . . I hit one of the tabs with my toe, the tympani roll tab, hit *tempo* and *sustain* keys and boom, suddenly the B flat tympani fill the room, sticks a blur in the glass arms holding them. I long to hold the drumsticks and become the rhythm myself, to see the vibrations in the round surface and feel them in the pit of my stomach; but to play that roll in Pierson's Orchestra I just slide a tab to a certain position and push another one down with my toe, so I stop pushing the tab down and there is instant silence.

I do not feel well. The clean red and blue dots in the metal surfaces have become prisms—I blink and they are dots again. Water in my eyes, no doubt. I look at all the keyboards surrounding me. Just a fancy organ is all it is.

I remember when I was learning to play the trumpet, and the triumph it was to play high C. I left all three valves open and pushed the mouthpiece against my lips so hard I could feel the little white ring that would show when I took the horn away—which is the wrong way to play high notes, but I had a weak embouchure—and forced a thin stream of air through my clamped lips to hear a high G, surely the highest note in my power. But then my stiff fingers pushed down the first two valves, I tightened my lips an impossible notch further, and the note slid up to an A as the valves hit their stops; quickly then, I lifted my right forefinger and reached a B. Then finally, before I ran out of air, with my eyes closed and my face controted and my lips actually hurting, I lifted the middle valve and magically was playing a C, high C; a weak, scratchy note that soon dissolved into dry air rasping through the brass tubes; but a high C nevertheless. It was an achievement.

I touch a small piece of red plastic. A small plastic gate opens in a hollow plastic tube, compressed air forces its way through a wire-banded pair of plastic lips into one of the four trumpets, then winds its way through the tubes, and emerges from the bell as a pure, impossibly high E, two full steps above the highest note I ever played. I turn off the note. "Great, Pierson," I say aloud. "Great."

I begin playing Vivaldi's Oboe Concerto in F, ignoring the starts of pain that flare like struck matchheads in my arms and legs and neck. I play all sixty strings with my left hand, snapping down chord tabs until as I play the first violin part, the second violins, the violas, the cellos, the basses—they all automatically follow. Passages where they are not in unison have been rearranged, or, if vital, will be played with great difficulty on the individual keyboards below the control. Percussion and brass use the same method, but are played by my feet unless especially difficult. In this way the entire concerto is played leaving the right hand free to play the oboe solo as it runs over the background, a kitten on a marble staircase. The whole process requires intense concentration, which I am not giving it—I am playing quite poorly—and the ability to divide one's attention four or five ways without becoming confused; but still, four or five ways, not one hundred and ten.

I swing down the basses' keyboard so I can play it with my feet. I indulge my bad habit and watch my feet as I play, big toes trapped and pointing downward under the pressure of the other toes, bouncing over the yellow keys and creating low bowed notes that expand out of the rising spiral of big, dark bodies behind me. My arches cramp, and in my guts something twists. I can't remember the music—the conductor's score that threaded through my head is gone. I can no longer play. Sweat is breaking out on my face and arms, and the Orchestra is slowly spinning, as it does in concerts—

. . . I am waiting for Mikel and JoAnne to arrive so we can leave for the concert. I am at the battered old upright piano that I brought from Mother's house right after the funeral, playing Ravel's *Pavanne* and crying at it. I laugh bitterly at my ability to act, unsure as always if my emotions are real, or feigned for some invisible audience in a theater wrapped around my head; and I think, ignoring the evidence blinking before me: I can call them up at will when I'm miserable enough!

Mikel and JoAnne walk in, laughing like wind-chimes. They are both singers in Vancouver's Opera, true artists. They light up some Baygolds and we smoke and talk about *Tslitschitche,* the quartet we are going to hear. The conversation slows, Mikel and JoAnne look at each other:

"Eric," Mikel says, "JoAnne and I are going to drop crystals for the concert." He holds out his hand. In his palm is a small clear crystal that looks like nothing so much as a diamond. He flips it into the air, catches it in his mouth, swallows it, grins. "Want to join us?" JoAnne takes one from him and swallows it with the same casual, defiant toss. She offers one to me, between her fingers. I look at her, remembering what I have heard. Nepanathol. I do not want to go blind.

"Are you addicted?" I ask. They shake their heads.

"We restrict ourselves to special occasions," JoAnne explains. They laugh. The idea of it—

"Hell," I say, "give me one." I hit notes on the piano: C,G, G

G sharp, G—B,C; and put a crystal in my mouth. It has no taste.
I swallow it—

Hallucinations. For a moment there I was confused. I get back
onto the stool and regret moving so quickly. Nausea is making me
weak. I try playing some Dixieland, an avocation of mine of which
the Master disapproves and in which I am (perhaps as a result)
quite knowledgeable. It is difficult to play the seven instruments
all at once—clarinet, trumpet, trombone, banjo, piano, drums,
bass (impossible, actually; watch the tapes take down eight-bar
passages and replay them when *repeat* buttons are pushed; often
playing the Orchestra requires skills usually possessed by sound
engineers), so I drop all of them but the front line.

The trombone is a fascinating thing to watch! Unable to antici-
pate the notes as human players do, the glass arms of the Orchestra move the slide about with an incredible, mechanical, inhuman
speed. I am playing the Jack Teagarten solo to *St. Louis Blues,* and
I am hitting wrong notes in it. I switch to the clarinet solo which
is, to my surprise, the solo from *The Rampart Street Parade* (you see
how they fit together?) and quit in resignation. I hate to play
poorly.

"All you have to do to stop this," the voice says out loud, and
then I finish it in my head, *is to get home and swallow a nep crystal.*
Without a moment's thought I slip off the stool: my knees buckle
like closing penknives and I crash into the bank of keyboards, fall
to the floor of the booth. In the glass floor are inlaid bass and
treble clef signs. After a while I pull myself up and am sick in the
booth's drinking fountain. Then I let myself drop back to the
floor.

I feel as sick after vomiting as before, which is frightening.

"Do, do something," the voice says, "don't just look at it." At
what? I ask. I pull out the celesta keyboard just before me, the
bottom one in the bank. I look up at the ornate white box that
is the instrument, suspended in the air above me, dwarfed by the
grand piano beside it. The celesta: a piano whose hammers hit
steel plates rather than wires. I run my finger along a few octaves
and a spray of quick bell-notes echoes through the chamber.

I try a Bach Two-Part Invention, a masterpiece of elegance that properly belongs on the harpsichord. My hands begin to play at different tempos and I can't stop it; frightening! I stop playing, and to aid my timing I reach a shaky right hand up and start the metronome, an antique mechanical box that struck Pierson's fancy at about eighty. An upside-down pendulum, visually surprising because it seems to contradict the laws of gravity rather than agree with them as a normal pendulum does.

I begin the Invention again, but the tempo is too fast for me (I usually play it at 120); the notes become a confused mass, sounding like church bells recorded and replayed at a much higher speed.

The gold weight on the metronome's arm reflects a part of my face (my eyes) as it comes to its lowest point on the left side. And my heart—certainly my heart is beating in time with the metronome's penetrating, woodblock-struck, rhythmic *tock*.

And just as undeniably the metronome is speeding up. Impossible, for the weight has not moved on the arm, yet true; at first it was an *andante tock . . . tock,* and now it is a good march tempo, *tock, tock;* and my heartbeat *a tempo* all the way. With each pulse small specks of light are exploding and drifting like tiny Chinese lanterns across my eyes. I can feel the quick pulses of blood in my throat and fingers. I am scared. The *tock*s are now an *allegretto tocktocktock.* I lift my finger up, a terrible weight, and stick it into the flashing silver arc with the gold band across its center. The metronome stops.

I begin breathing again. My heart begins to slow down. A true hallucination, I think to myself, is very disturbing. After a time I push the celesta keyboard back into its nook and try to stand up. My legs explode. I grasp the stool. Cramps, I think in some cold corner of my mind, watching the limbs flail about. I knead the bulging muscles with one hand and keep shifting to find a more comfortable position; it occurs to me with a start that this is what the phrase "writhing in agony" describes; I had thought it was just a literary figure.

The cold corner of my mind disappears, and that was all that was left—

I come to and the cramps are gone. They feel like they are on the verge, though. If I don't move I think I will be all right. I wish it were closer to the end.

I can see my reflection in the tuba's dented bell. A sorry-looking spectacle, disheveled and pale. The features are architecturally distinct. I can quite clearly see the veins below my eyes. The reflection wavers, each time presenting me with a different version of my face. Some are dome-foreheaded and weak-chinned; some have giant hooked noses; others are lantern-jawed and have pointy heads. Some are half-faced—

. . . I am trying to keep in step with the rest of the Children's Orchestra, now being temporarily transformed for the Tricentennial celebration into a marching band. A marching band: in the old days they used to dress musicians in uniforms and have them walk through the streets in ranks and files, playing tunes to the tempo of their steps. I can conceive of nothing more ridiculous, as I struggle under the weight of a Sousaphone, a tuba stretched into a circle so that it can be carried while marching. There are no pianos in a marching band, obviously. Fuming at the treatment a child prodigy receives, I puff angrily into the huge mouthpiece and watch my reflection sway back and forth in the curved brass surface. The conductor is scurrying about the edges of the group, consulting the *Parade Manual* in his hand and shouting, "Watch your diagonals! Watch those diagonals!" Next to me Joe Tanaka (he is a cellist, drafted as I have been) says, "If God meant us to play and walk at the same time, he'd have had us breathe through our ears." The halls force us to make a ninety-degree turn and there is chaos. "Step small on the inside!" the conductor is shouting. Each rank looks like a game of crack-the-whip. "Halt!" the conductor shrieks. Still breaking up at Tanaka, I cannon into the girl in front of me and three or four of us go down in a tangle. In the midst of the cries and recriminations I look at the crumpled Sousaphone bell and see the lower half of my face reflected: big mouth, no eyes—

I have a terrific headache. I reach up to the stool and grab it; my hand closes on nothing and I look again; at least six inches off. I must get up on the stool. Arms move up, feet grope for purchase, all very slowly. I move with infinitesimal slowness, as a child does when escaping his house at night to run the halls. Head to seat, knee to footbar, I stop to get used to the height, watching the fireworks display in my eyes. My hands never stop trembling now.

Now I am up and seated on the stool. I remember a film in which a man was buried to the neck in the tidal flats, at low tide. A head sitting on wet, gleaming sand, looking outward: the image is acid-etched on the inside of my eyelids.

Do something. I pull out the French horn and oboe keyboards for Handel's *Children's Prayer.* "These are the instruments with colds," the Master once said in a light moment. "The horn has a chest cold, the oboe a head cold." Handel is too slow. I switch to scales, C, F, B flat, E flat, A flat, D flat; bead, bead; every good boy deserves favor, each good boy does fine; then the minors, harmonic and melodic—

. . . "Drop that sixth," she yells from the kitchen, "harmonic, not melodic. Play me the harmonic now."

Again—

"Harmonic!"

Again.

She comes in, grabs my right hand in hers, hits the notes. "Third down, sixth down, see how it sounds spooky? Do it, now." Again. "Okay, do that twenty times, then we'll try the melodic."

I stop playing minor scales, my heart pounding. I collect the oddball keyboards seldom played—glockenspiel, contrabassoon, harp, alto clarinet—and become bored with them even as I gather them. I am sick again in the drinking fountain. Certainly I have been in the Orchestra for a long time. A walk about the room would be nice, but I fear it is beyond me. I am very near the end, one way or another. The tide is rising. De Quincey and Cocteau lied to me—there is no romance in withdrawal, in the experience itself, none at all. It is no fun. It hurts.

There is a knock at the door. In it swings, slow as an hour hand. A short man struts through the doorway. Tied to his middle is a small bass drum, and welded to the top of the drum is a battered

trumpet, its mouthpiece waving about in front of his face. Beside
the mouthpiece is a harmonica, held in place by stiff wires
wrapped around his neck. In his right hand is a drumstick, in his
left is an old clacking percussion device (canasta?) and between
his knees are tarnished cymbals, hanging at odd angles. He looks
as scruffy as I feel. He marches to a spot just below me, lightly
beating the drum, then halts and brings his knees together
sharply. When the din dies down he looks up and grins. His face
has a reddish tint to it, and I can see through his nose.

"Who are you?" I ask.

"John Pierson," he replies, "at your service." Suddenly I see
the resemblance between the disreputable character below me
and the statue high in the outer entryway. "And you?" he says to
me. His hair is tangled.

"Eric Johann Vivaldi Wright."

"Ah-ha! A musician."

"No," I tell him, "I just operate your machine."

He looks puzzled. "Surely it takes a musician to operate my
machine?"

"Just a button-pusher. Did you really build this thing?" Time
stretches out. We are speaking in a dead silence, stillness. There
are long pauses between phrases.

"I did."

"Then it's all your fault. You're the cause of the whole mess,"
I say down to him, "you and your stupid vulgar monstrosity!
When you erected this heap," I ask him, tapping a glass upright
sharply with my foot, "were you serious?"

"Certainly," he replies, nodding gravely. "Young man," he
says, emphasizing every third or fourth word with a rimshot, "you
have Completely Missed the Point. You claim Too Much for my
Work. With my invention it is Possible for One Man to play
extremely Complex pieces by Himself. That is All. It is merely a
rather Complicated musical Instrument, able to create Beautiful
Music."

"No way, old man," I say, "it's an imitation orchestra is what
it is, and a pretty poor job it does, too. For example" (I have run
through this so many times before): "If Beethoven's *Third* were

to be played, which one could do it better, your Orchestra or the Quebec Philharmonic?"

"Quebec, undoubtedly, but—"

"Okay, then. All you've done is turned a sublime group achievement into a half-assed egotistical solo."

"No, no, no, no, no," he exclaims, rimshots for every "no." "The invention is an imitation of an orchestra, only in the same way a one-man band was an imitation of a band, eh?" He winks suggestively. "In other words, not at all. A one-man band was not to be judged for anything except his own individual performance. It is a fallacy to become comparative." He takes off and makes a revolution around the Orchestra, playing "Dixie" on the trumpet and pounding the bass drum, and filling all the rests with the cymbals. It sounds horrible. Back again. "Entertaining, no? Contributions?" He grins. "A one-man band was a great institution."

"Maybe," I say, "but none of them ever claimed to be musicians."

"They most certainly did! Someone who makes music, young man, is a musician. This purist attitude, this notion of artistic integrity that you have, has blinded you. Art with a capital A! What nonsense! Music is noise that entertains, that makes one feel good. My instrument can do that as well as any."

"No, it can't," I almost shout. "Wrong! This *instrument* can't make music as well as the instrument that is an orchestra, that takes a hundred and ten people to play it. Your instrument is just showmanship, and I am an artist. There is no shame in being a purist."

"Bah!" he says. "A purist is just someone living a hundred years in the past. You would have scoffed at the integrity of the organ had you been around at its invention, or the synthesizer."

"A purist," I say, "just likes to see things done right." I trace the other line down, following arguments like fugues. "And if you're going to build a solo instrument that makes a lot of sounds, why not work with synthesizers?"

"Because," he explains, waving the drumstick about, "this is prettier. Isn't that reason enough? Christ! You purists are so refined. If you are to play my instrument you must change the way you think of yourself."

"You can't change the way you are."

"You most certainly can! What could be simpler? Listen: you want the music to be played as written, as well as possible. Fine. That is admirable. My instrument does not make much of a symphonic orchestra, it is true, even though the simplifications made are your fault and not the machine's; but that is not what I built it to be, believe me! It has its own artistic integrity, and you must find it. If you do not like simplifying orchestral arrangements, don't! Play something else! If you can find nothing that seems suitable, write something yourself! I don't suppose anyone has shown you my compositions for the instrument? No? Ah, well, they never did think much of me as a composer." He brightens. "Enjoy yourself in that little booth, eh? Have you ever done that? It's quite easy."

I look around at the banks of keyboards. "It's just like putting on a show," I mutter.

"So? Then put on a show! It's a great, showy machine when you get to know it. Of course, you don't know it very well yet." He smiles a crafty smile. "I took nineteen years to build it," he says, "and it would only take two or three to put it together. There's more to it than meets the eye." He turns to leave, shimmering his familiar transparent red. He walks to the door and stops. "Play it," he says, "don't just look at it. Play it with everything in you." He leaves. The door closes.

So here I am, a young man frying in a hallucinogenic withdrawal, suspended in this contraption like a fly trapped in the web of a spider frying in a hallucinogenic withdrawal . . . You've seen pictures of those poor tangled webs that drugged spiders make in labs? That is what Pierson's Orchestra would look like in two dimensions, from any side. Glass arms holding out bright brass and wood instruments like Christmas-tree ornaments. A glass hand, a tree reaching up in a swirl of rich browns and silvers and prisms. Music doesn't grow on trees, you know. The cymbals are edged with rainbows.

Most certainly I have been suffering delusions. It is easy afterward to say that a conversation with a man dead three centuries is an illusion, but while it is happening, quite definitely happening, it is hard to discount one's senses. Damage is being done in my brain; it is as if I can feel the individual cells swelling and popping. I am very sick. There is little to do but sit and wait it out. Surely it is near the end—in a sudden flash I see the Orchestra as a giant baroque cross upon which I am draped . . . but no. It is a fantasy, one I can recognize. I am afraid of those I can't recognize.

"Just like sex," the deaf man said, "climax at the end." I wait. Time passes. *Pop pop pop* . . . like swollen grains of rice. Something must be done. Might as well play the damn thing. Put on a show.

I'm not convinced by you, Pierson! Not a bit!

I begin arranging the keyboards into concert position, my hands shoving them about like tugboats pushing big ships. Dispassionately I watch my hands shake. The cold corner of my mind has taken over and somehow I am outside the nausea. I am seeing things with the clarity you have when you are extremely hungry, or tired past the point of being tired. Everything is quite clear, quite in focus. I have heard that drowning men experience a last period of great calm and clarity before losing consciousness. Perhaps the tide is that high now. I cannot tell. Oh, I am tired of this! Why can't it be over? Bach's "Rejoice, Beloved Christians," the baritone playing the high line. The passages come to me clean and sharp now. I find it hard to keep my balance; everything is overexposed. I am swaying. I close my eyes. A Chopin Nocturne. Against the black field of my eyelids' insides there is a marvelous show of lights, little colored worms that burst into existence, crawl across my vision and disappear. Behind the lights are barely discernible patterns, geometric tapestries that flare and contract under the pressure of my eyelids. The music is intertwined with this odd mandala; when I clamp my eyes hard there is a sudden rush of blue geometry with a black center, with it a roll of tympani, shrieking of woodwinds, and the strings fitting quickly and surely into the fantastic blue patterns that blossom before me. Mozart's Concerto in G, as effortlessly as if I were the conductor and not the performer. Above it rises a trumpet solo, my own improvisation, arching high above the structure of the concerto. My interior field of vision clears and becomes a neutral color, grey or dull purple. Ten clear lines run across it in sets of five. The score. As I play the notes they appear, in long vertical sets as in a conductor's score. They move off to the left as if the score were on a conveyor belt. Excellent. Half-notes, quarter-notes in the bass clef; long runs of sixteenth-notes in the treble, all like the sun shining through pinholes in a dark sheet of paper. The concerto flows into Beethoven's Fifth Symphony, with a transition that pleases me. As far as I can tell the score is perfectly accurate. I am playing brilliantly, with enough confidence to throw grace notes of my own about in passages of great speed. I think, "It would be nice to have the cellos playing their counterpoint here," and then I hear the cellos making their quick departure from the rest of the strings. My fingers are not doing it. Play it with everything you have. The Finale of the Third, every single instrument achingly clean and individual. Nineteen years, Pierson, is this what you meant?

The Orchestra is the extension of what I want to hear.

I move into realms of my own, shifting from passage to passage, playing what I always wanted to hear; half-remembered snatches, majestic crescendos that you wake up from in the middle of the night, having dreamed them, and wish you could recapture; the architecture of Bach, the power of Beethoven, the beauty of Mozart, the wit and transitions of de Baik. All a confusion, all a marvel. ·Think it in your head and hear the Orchestra play it. The performer the instrument, the instrument a part of the performer. Pierson, what have you done?

Music. If you are at all alive to it you will have heard passages that bring a chill to your back and a flush of blood to your cheeks; a physical response to beauty. A rush. The music I am playing now is the very distillation of that feeling. It soars out and for the first time I hear echoes in this room, it is that powerful. The score no longer consists of musical notation; it is an impressionistic fantasy of a musical score, the background a deep blood red, the notes sudden clusters of jewels or long flows of colors I can't identify even as I see them; yet see them, most certainly. The drums are pounding, strings rushing and jumbling, awash in a wave of *fortissimo* brass shouts, not blaring—the horns of the Orchestra cannot blare—but at their highest volume, triumphant—

. . . triumphant she is as I ascend the dais I can see her face and she is strained and ecstatic as if in labor for to her I am being born again and throughout the investiture all I can see is her bright face before me unto her a Master is born—

. . . and masterful, chaotic yet perfectly calculated. The score is a *mille fleurs* of twisted colors, falling, falling, the notes are falling. I open my eyes and find that they are already stretched wide open; a rush, a rush of red, red is all I see, a blinding waterfall of molten glass cascading down, behind it a thousand suns.

I awake from a dream in which I was . . . in which I was . . . walking through hallways. Talking with someone. I cannot remember.

I am lying on the glass floor of the booth, I can feel the bas-relief of the clef signs. My mouth feels as if it had been washed in acids, which I suppose it has. My legs. My left hand is asleep. I have been poured from my container, my skeleton is gone, I am a lump of flesh. I move my arm. An achievement.

"Eric," comes the Master's voice, high-pitched in its anxiety. It is probably what awakened me. His hand on my shoulder. He babbles without pause as he helps me out of the Orchestra, "I just got back, you're all right, you're all right, the music you were playing, my God, magnificent, here, here, watch out, you're all right, my son—"

"I am blind," I croak. There is a pause, a gasp. He holds me in his arms, half carries me onto a cot of some sort, muttering in a strained voice as he moves me about.

"Horrible, horrible," he keeps saying. "Horrible." It is age-old. Lose your sight, and learn to see. I blink away tears for my lost vision, and cannot see myself blink.

"You will make a great Master," he says firmly.

I do not answer.

"The blindness will not make any difference at all."

And after a long pause—

"Yes," I say, wishing he understood, wishing there was someone who understood, "I think it will."

The Memory Machine

Our guest today, the marvelous actress Mercedes McCambridge, was at one time in dire need of trouble.

—Barbara Walters

How's That? How's That? How's That?

That love is salt in my wounds, that love is sand in my throat, Claire. Claire. Claire. —"The Feast of St. Dionysus," by Robert Silverberg, in *An Exaltation of Stars*, edited by Terry Carr (Simon and Schuster, 1973), p. 6.

"Brother," he said. "Brother! Brother!" —*Ibid.*, p. 30.

"Yes, John? Yes? Yes?" —*Ibid.*, p. 40.

We might be able to do anything, the Speaker says, once we have reached that hidden god and transformed ourselves into the gods we were meant to be. Anything. Anything. Anything.

—*Ibid.*, p. 46.

"Dave!" Oxenshuer cries. "Oh, Christ, Dave! Dave!"

—*Ibid.*, p. 51.

I float. I go forth. I. I. I. —*Ibid.*, p. 53.

I go to the god's house and his fire consumes me. Go. Go. Go.

—*Ibid.*, same page.

Whom, heem?

This book is honest homage from an early master of science fiction to an earlier writer whom Williamson feels has not yet been surpassed. —Alexei and Cory Panshin, in *F&SF,* March 1974

Rioz, whom we started out thinking was going to be the third-person limited narrative point of view, is no longer even present.
—*The Science Fiction of Isaac Asimov,* by Joseph E. Patrouch, Jr. (Doubleday, 1974)

To Your Scattered Bodies Go

Perhaps, though he did not like to admit it, his sight had betrayed him. Behind his glasses were fifty-four-year-old eyes.

—"Stations of the Nightmare, Part 1," by Philip José Farmer, in *Continuum 1,* edited by Roger Elwood (Putnam, 1974)

After rejecting quantities of suitors out of devotion to the Tolstoyan ideal, she had fallen wildly in love with a man much older than she, Michael Sukhotin, who was married and the father of six children; he was in his fifties, had a middle-aged paunch and was both charming and witty.

—*Tolstoy,* by Henri Troyat, translated by Nancy Amphoux

So Much For Kidneys' Lib

. . . Are you SURE that an absolute ruling aristocracy is an evil and unworkable thing? Even one that's been carefully, laboriously worked out on a hierarchic basis over many, many generations of trial and error, under all sorts of real-world challenges?

Then dethrone that arbitrary, absolute tyrant between your ears—that gray aristocracy that lives in its stone-walled castle up on top, demanding tribute of oxygen, food and comfort at the expense of trillions of worker cells! Away with that luxury-loving ruling aristocracy! Free the trillions of working individuals, and establish perfect equality among all the individual cells!

It's guaranteed to work—just destroy that unequal hierarchy and perfect equality results.

All the cells are dead very shortly.

—John W. Campbell, Jr., in
Analog, July 1967

But Nothing to Compare with a Hole in the Shoe

"Hello," Project Dove's coordinator interrupted his wish on the seventh ring.

"Udall, this is Coltrain!"

"What . . . Coltrain?" Udall yawned sleepily.

"Listen, for God's sake, Liu's got—" He stopped. There was something aggrandizing about the emptiness of a dead line.

—"The Sixth Face,"
by Thomas Sullivan
(*Analog,* April 1975)

Let's See, Jesse Was the One Who Robbed Banks . . .

Last year's Hugo Award winning story "The Ones Who Walk Away From Omelas" by Ursula Le Guin carried the subtitle: "Variations on a Theme by Henry James." At the time I felt sure I understood the story . . . but since then I have seen so many interpretations that not only contradict my conception of what the story means, but contradict each other, so perhaps Le Guin's intended moral is not as obvious as I thought it was. Perhaps a clue to the meaning is contained in the subtitle, but I am not familiar with the works of William James—nor can I find anyone in the Psychology Department here who can enlighten me. Does anyone out there know what the reference to James in the subtitle means.

—Denis Quane, *Notes from the Chemistry Dept. #11*, May 1975

MARY MARGARET ROAD-GRADER

A story of the golden time, when a man with a
string of stolen Cadillacs could stand tall
and look the world in the eye.

Howard Waldrop

It was the time of the Sun Dance and the Big Tractor Pull. Freddy-in-the-Hollow and I had traveled three days to be at the River.
We were almost late, what with the sandstorm and the raid on the
white settlement over to Old Dallas.

We pulled in with our wrecker and string of fine cars, many of
them newly stolen. You should have seen Freddy and me that
morning, the first morning of the Sun Dance.

We were dressed in new-stolen fatigues and we had bright
leather holsters and pistols. Freddy had a new carbine, too. We
were wearing our silver and feathers and hard goods. I noticed
many women watching us as we drove in. There seemed to be
many more here than the last Sun Ceremony. It looked to be a
good time.

The usual crowd gathered before we could circle up our
remuda. I saw Bob One-Eye and Nathan Big Gimp, the mechanics, come across from their circles. Already the cook fires were

burning and women were skinning out the cattle that had been slaughtered early in the morning.

"Hoa!" I heard Nathan call as he limped to our wrecker. He was old; his left leg had been shattered in the Highway wars, he went back that far. He put his hands on his hips and looked over our line.

"I know that car, Billy-Bob Chevrolet," he said to me, pointing to an old Mercury. "Those son-a-bitch Dallas people stole it from me last year. I know its plates. It is good you stole it back. Maybe I will talk to you about doing car work to get it back sometime."

"We'll have to drink about it," I said.

"Let's stake them out," said Freddy-in-the-Hollow. "I'm tired of pulling them."

We parked them in two parallel rows and put up the signs, the strings of pennants and the whirlers. Then we got in the wrecker and smoked.

Many people walked by. We were near the Karankawa fuel trucks, so people would be coming by all time. Some I knew by sight, many I had known since I was a boy. They all walked by as though they did not notice the cars, but I saw them looking out of the corners of their eyes. Music was starting down the way, and most people were heading there. There would be plenty music in the next five days. I was in no hurry. We would all be danced out before the week was up.

Some of the men kept their strings tied to their tow trucks as if they didn't care whether people saw them or not. They acted as if they were ready to move out at any time. But that was not the old way. In the old times, you had your cars parked in rows so they could be seen. It made them harder to steal, too, especially if you had a fence.

But none of the Tractor Pullers had arrived yet, and that was what everybody was waiting for.

The talk was that Simon Red Bulldozer would be here this year. He was known from the Brazos to the Sabine, though he had never been to one of our Ceremonies. He usually stayed in the Guadalupe River area.

But he had beaten everybody there and had taken all the fun out of their Big Pulls. So he had gone to the Karankawa Ceremony last year, and now was supposed to be coming to ours. They still talk about the time Simon Red Bulldozer took on Elmo John Deere two summers ago. I would have traded many plates to be there.

"We need more tobacco," said Freddy-in-the-Hollow.

"We should have stolen some from the whites," I said. "It will cost us plenty here."

"Don't you know anyone?"

"I know everyone, Fred," I said quietly (a matter of pride). "But nobody has any friends during the Ceremonies. You pay for what you get."

It was Freddy-in-the-Hollow's first Sun Dance as a Raider. All the times before, he had come with his family. He still wore his coup-charm, a big VW symbol pried off the first car he'd boosted, on a chain around his neck. He was only seventeen summers. Someday he would be a better thief than me. And I'm the best there is.

Simon Red Bulldozer was expected soon, and all the men were talking a little and laying a few bets.

"You know," said Nathan Big Gimp, leaning against a wrecker at his shop down by the community fires, "I saw Simon turn over three tractors two summers ago, one after the other. The way he does it will amaze you, Billy-Bob."

I allowed as how he might be the man to bet on.

"Well, you really should, though the margin is slight. There's always the chance Elmo John Deere will show."

I said maybe that was what I was waiting for.

But it wasn't true. Freddy-in-the-Hollow and I had talked in English to a man from the Red River people the week before. He made some hints but hadn't really told us anything. They had a big Puller, he said, and you shouldn't lose your money on anyone else.

We asked if this person would show at our Ceremony, and he allowed as how maybe, continuing to chew on some willow bark.

So we allowed as how maybe we'd still put our hard goods on Simon Bulldozer.

He said that maybe he'd be down to see, and then drove off in his jeep with the new spark plugs we'd sold him.

The Red River people don't talk too much, but when they do, they say a lot. So we were waiting on the bets.

Women had been giving me the eye all day, and now there were a few of them looking openly at me; Freddy too, by reflected glory. I was thinking of doing something about it when we got a surprise.

At noon Elmo John Deere showed, coming in with his two wreckers and his Case 1190, his families and twelve strings of cars. He was the richest man in the Nations, and his camp took a large part of the eastern end of the circle.

Then a little while later, the Man showed. Simon Red Bulldozer came only with his two wives, a few sons and his transport truck. And in the back of it was the Red Bulldozer, which, they say, had killed a man before Simon stole it.

It's an old legend, and I won't tell it now.

And it's not important anymore anyway.

So we thought we were in for the best Pull ever, between two men we knew by deeds. Simon wanted to go smoke with Elmo, but Elmo sent a man over to tell Simon Red Bulldozer to keep his distance. There was bad blood between them, though Simon was such a good old boy that he was willing to forget it.

Not Elmo John Deere, though. His mind was bad. He was a mean man.

Freddy said it first, while we lay on the hood of the wrecker the eve of the dancing.

"You know," he said, "I'm young."

"Obvious," I said.

"But," he continued, "things are changing."

I had thought the same thing, though I hadn't said it. I pulled my bush hat up off my eyes, looked at the boy. He was part white and his mustache needed trimming, but otherwise he was all right.

"You may be right," I answered uneasily.

"Have you noticed how many horses there are this year, for God's sake?"

I had. Horses were used for herding our cattle and sheep. I mean, there were always *some* horses, but not this many. This year, people brought in whole remudas, twenty–thirty to a string. Some were even trading them like cars. It made my skin crawl.

"And the women," said Fred-in-the-Hollow. "Loose is loose, but they go too far, really they do. They're not even wearing halters under their clothes, most of them. Jiggle-jiggle."

"Well, they're nice to look at. Times are getting hard," I said. The raid night before last was our first in two months, the only time we'd found anything worth the taking. Nothing but rusted piles of metal all up and down the whole Trinity. Not much on the Brazos, or the Sulphur. Pickings were slim, and you really had to fight like hell to get away with anything.

We sold a car early in the evening, for more plates than it was worth, which was good. But what Freddy had been talking and thinking about had me depressed. I needed a woman. I needed some good dope. Mostly, I wanted to kill something.

The dances started early, with people toking up on rabbit tobacco, shag bark and hemp. The whole place smelled of burnt meat and grease, and there was singing in most of the lodges.

Oh, it was a happy group.

I was stripped down and doing some prayers. Tomorrow was the Sun Dance and the next day the contests. Freddy tried to find a woman and didn't have any luck. He came through twice while I was painting myself and smoking up. Freddy didn't hold with the prayer parts. I figure they can't hurt, and besides, there wasn't much else to do.

Two hours after dark, one of Elmo John Deere's men knifed one of Simon Red Bulldozer's sons. The delegation came for me about thirty minutes later.

I thought at first I might get my wish about killing something. But not tonight. They wanted me to arbitrate the judgment. Someone else would have to be executioner if one were needed.

"Watch the store, Freddy," I said, picking up my carbine.

I smoked while they talked. When Red Bulldozer's cousin got through, John Deere's grandfather spoke. The Bulldozer boy wasn't hurt too much, he wouldn't lose the arm. They brought the John Deere man before me. He glared at me across the smoke and said not a word.

I took two more puffs, cleaned my pipe. Then I broke down my carbine, worked on the selector pin for a while. I lit my other pipe and pointed to the John Deere man.

"He lives," I said. "He was drunk."

They let him leave the lodge.

"Elmo John Deere," I said.

"Uhm?" said fat Elmo.

"I think you should pay three mounts and ten plates to do this thing right. And give one man for three weeks to do the work of Simon Red Bulldozer's son."

Silence for a second, then Elmo spoke: "It is good what you say."

"Simon Red Bulldozer."

"Hm?"

"You should shake hands with Elmo John Deere and this should be the end of the matter."

"Good," he said.

They shook hands. Then each gave me a plate as soon as the others had left. One California and one New York. A 1993 and a '97. Not bad for twenty minutes' work.

It wasn't until I got back to the wrecker that I started shaking. That had been the first time I was arbiter. It could have made more bad trouble and turned hearts sour if I'd judged wrong.

"Hey, Fred!" I said. "Let's get real drunk and go see Wanda Hummingtires. They say she'll do it three ways all night."

The next dawn found us like a Karankawa coming across a new case of 30-weight oil. It was morning, quick. I ought to know. I watched that goddamned sun come up and I watched it go down, and every minute of the day in between, and I never moved from the spot. I forgot everything that went on around me, and I barely heard the women singing or the prayers of the other men.

At dusk, Freddy-in-the-Hollow led me back to the wrecker and I slept like a stone mother log for twelve hours with swirling violet dots in my head.

I had had no visions. Some people get them, some don't.

I woke with the mother of all headaches, but after I smoked awhile it went away. I wasn't a puller, but I was in two of the races, one on foot and one in the Mercury. I lost one and won the other.

I also won the side of beef in the morning shoot. Knocked the head off the bull with seven shots, clean as a whistle.

At noon we saw a cloud of dust coming over the third ridge. Then the outriders picked up the truck when it came over the second. It was coming too fast.

The truck stopped with a roar and a squeal of brakes. It had a long lumpy canvas cover on the back. Then a woman climbed down from the cab. She was the most gorgeous woman I'd ever seen—and I'd seen Nellie Firestone two summers ago.

Nellie hadn't come close to this girl. She had long straight black hair and a beautiful face. She was built like nothing I'd seen before. She wore tight coveralls and had a .357 Magnum strapped to her hip.

"Who runs the Pulls?" she asked, in English, of the first man who reached her.

He didn't know what to do. Women never talk like that.

"Winston Mack Truck," said Freddy at my side, pointing.

"What do you mean?" asked one of the young men. "Why do you want to know?"

"Because I'm going to enter the Pull," she said.

Tribal language mumbles went around the circle. Very negative ones.

"Don't give me any of that shit," she said. "How many of you know of Alan Backhoe Shovel?"

He was another legend over in Ouachita River country.

"Well," she said, and held up a serial number plate from a backhoe tractor scoop, "I beat him last week."

"Hua, hua, hua!" the chanting started.

"What is your name, woman?" asked one of Mack Truck's men.

"Mary Margaret Road-Grader," she said, and glared back at him.

"Freddy," I said, "put the money on her."

So we had a council. You gotta have a council for everything, especially when honor and dignity and other manly virtues are involved.

Winston Mack Truck was pretty old, but he was still spry and had some muscles left on him. His head was a puckered lump because he had once crashed in a burner while raiding over on the Brazos. He only had one ear, and it wasn't much of one.

But he did have respect, and he did have power, and he had more sons than anyone in the Nations, ten or eleven of them. They were all there in council, with all the heads of other families.

Winston Mack Truck smoked awhile, then called us to session.

Mary Margaret Road-Grader wasn't allowed inside the lodge. It seemed sort of stupid to me. If they wouldn't let her in here, they sure weren't going to let her enter the Pull. But I kept my tongue. You can never tell.

I was right. Old man Mack Truck can see clear through to tomorrow.

"Brothers," he said. "We have a problem here."

"Hua, hua, hua."

"We have been asked to let a woman enter the Pulls."

Silence.

"I do not know if it's a good thing," he continued. "But our brothers to the east have seen fit to let her do so. This woman claims to have defeated Alan Backhoe Shovel in fair contest. She enters this as proof."

He placed the serial plate in the center of the lodge.

"I will listen now," he said, and sat back, folding his arms.

They went around the circle, some speaking, some not.

It was Simon Red Bulldozer himself who changed the tone of the council. "I have never seen a woman in a Pull," he said. "Or in any contest other than those for women."

He paused. "But I have never wrestled against Alan Backhoe Shovel, either. I know of no one who has bested him. Now this woman claims to have done so. It would be interesting to see if she were a good Puller."

"You want a woman in the contest?" asked Elmo, out of turn.

Richard Ford Pinto, the next speaker, stared at Elmo until he realized his mistake. But Ford Pinto saved face for him by asking the same question of Simon.

"I would like to see if she is a good Puller," said Simon, adamantly. He would commit himself no further.

Then it was Elmo's turn. "My brothers!" he began, so I figured he would be at it for a long time. "We seem to spend all our time in council, rather than having fun like we should. It is not good, it makes my heart bitter.

"The idea that a woman can get a hearing at council revolts me. Were this a young man not yet proven, or an Elder who had been given his Service feather, I would not object. But, brothers, this is a woman!" His voice came falsetto now, and he began to chant:

"I have seen the dawn of bad days, brothers.

"But never worse than this.

"A woman enters our camp, brothers!

"A woman! A woman!"

He sat down and said no more in the conference.

It was my turn.

"Hear me, Pullers and Stealers!" I said. "You know me. I am a man of my word and a man of my deeds. But the time has come for deeds alone. Words must be put away. We must decide whether a woman can be as good as a man. We cannot be afraid of a woman! Or can some of us be?"

They all howled and grumbled just like I wanted them to. You can't suggest men in council are afraid of anything.

Of course, we voted to let her in the contest, like I knew we would.

Changes in history come easy, you know?

They pulled the small tractors first, the Ford 250s and the Honda Fieldmasters and such. I wasn't much interested in watching young boys fly through the air and hurt themselves. So me and Freddy wandered over where the big tractor men were warming up. The Karankawas were selling fuel from the old Houston refineries hand over hose. A couple of the Pullers had refused, like Elmo at first, to do anything with a woman in the contest.

But even Elmo was there watching when Mary Margaret Road-Grader unveiled her machine. There were lots of *oohs* and *ahhs* when she started pulling the tarp off that monster.

Nobody had seen one in years, except maybe as piles of rust on the roadside. It was long and low, and looked much like a yellow elephant's head with wheels stuck on the end of the trunk. The cab was high and shiny glass. Even the doors still worked. The blade was new and bright; it looked as if it had never been used.

The letters on the side were sharp and black, unfaded. Even the paint job was new. That made me suspicious about the Alan Backhoe Shovel contest. I took a gander at the towball while she was atop the cab loosening the straps. It *was* worn. Either she had been lucky in the contest, or she'd had sense enough to put on a worn towball.

Everybody watched her unfold the tarp (one of those heavy smelly kind that can fall on you and kill you) but she had no helpers. So I climbed up to give her a hand.

One of the women called out something and some others took it up. Most of the men just shook their heads.

There was a lot of screaming and hoorawing from the little Pulls, so I had to touch her on the shoulder to let her know I was up there. She turned fast and her hand went for her gun before she saw it was me.

And I saw in her eyes not killer hate, but something else: I saw she was scared and afraid she'd have to kill someone.

"Let me help you with this," I said, pointing to the tarp.

She didn't say anything, but she didn't object, either.

"For a good judge," called out fat Elmo, "you have poor taste in women."

There was nothing I could do but keep busy while they laughed.

They still talk about that first afternoon, the one that was the beginning of the end.

First, Elmo John Deere hitched onto an IH 1200 and drug it over the line in about three seconds. No contest, and no one was surprised. Then Simon Red Bulldozer cranked up; his starter engine sounded like a beehive in a rainstorm. He hooked the chain on his towbar and revved up. The guy he was pulling against was a Paluxy River man named Theodore Bush Hog. He didn't hook up right. The chain came off as soon as Simon let go his clutches. So Bush Hog was disqualified. That was bad, too; there were some dark-horse bets on him.

Then it was the turn of Mary Margaret Road-Grader and Elmo John Deere. Elmo had said at first he wasn't going to enter against her. Then they told him how much money was bet on him, and he couldn't afford to pass it up. Though the excuse he used was that somebody had to show this woman her place, and it might as well be him, first thing off.

You had to be there to see it. Mary Margaret whipped that road-grader around like it was a Toyota, and backed it onto the field. She climbed down with the motor running and hooked up. She was wearing tight blue coveralls and her hair was blowing in the river breeze. I thought she was the most beautiful woman I had ever seen. I didn't want her to get her heart broken. But there was nothing I could do. It was all on her, now.

Elmo John Deere had one of his sons come out and hand the chain to him. He was showing he didn't want to be first to touch anything this woman had held.

He hooked up, and Mary Margaret Road-Grader signaled she was ready. The judge dropped the pitchfork and they leaned on their gas feeds.

There was a jerk and a sharp clang, and the chain looked like a straight steel rod. Elmo gunned for all he had and the big tractor wheels began to turn slowly, and then they spun and caught and Elmo's Case tractor eased a few feet forward.

Mary Margaret never looked back. (Elmo half turned in his seat; he was so good working the pedals and gears he didn't need to look at them.) When she upshifted, the transmission on the yellow road-grader screamed and lowered in tone.

I could hardly hear the machines for the yells and screams around me. They sounded like war yells. Some of the men were yelling in blood-lust at the woman. But I heard others cheering her, too. They seemed to want Elmo to lose.

Mary Margaret shifted again and her feet worked like pistons on the pedals. And as quickly as it had begun, it was over.

There was a groaning noise, Elmo's wheels began to spin uselessly, and in a second or two his tractor had been drug twenty feet across the line.

Elmo got down from his seat. Instead of congratulating the winner, he turned and strode off the field. He signaled one of his sons to retrieve the vehicle.

Mary Margaret was checking the damage to her machine.

Simon Red Bulldozer was next. They had been pulling for twelve minutes when the contest was called by Winston Mack Truck himself. There was wonder on his face as he walked out to the two contestants. Nobody had ever seen anything like it.

The two had fought each other to a standstill. When they were stopped, Mary Margaret's grader was six or seven inches from its original position, but Simon's bulldozer had moved all over its side of the line. The ground was destroyed forever three feet each side of the line. It had been that close.

Winston Mack Truck stopped before them. We were all whistling our approval when Simon Red Bulldozer held up his hand.

"Hear me, brothers. I will accept no share in honors. They must be all mine, or none at all."

Winston looked with his puckered face at Mary Margaret. She shrugged. "Fine with me."

Maybe I was the only one who knew she was acting tough for the crowd. I looked at her, but couldn't catch her eye.

"Listen, Fossil Creek People," said old Mack Truck. "This has been a draw. But Simon Red Bulldozer is not satisfied. And Mary Margaret Road-Grader has accepted. Tomorrow as the sun crosses the tops of the eastern trees, we will begin again. I have declared a fifth night and a sixth day to the Dance and Pulls."

Shouts of joy broke from the crowd. This had happened only once in my life, for some religious reason or other, and that was when I was a child. The Dance and Pulls were the only meeting of the year when all the Fossil Creek People came together. It was to have ended this night.

Now we would have another day.

The cattle must have sensed this. You could hear them bellowing in fear even before the first of the butchers crossed the camp toward them.

"Where are you going?" asked Freddy as I picked up my carbine, boots and blanket.

"I think I will sleep with Mary Margaret Road-Grader," I said.

"Watch out," said Freddy. "I bet she makes love like she drives that machine."

She was ready to cry, she was so tired. We were under the road-grader; the tarp had been refolded over it. There was four feet of crawl space between the trailer and the ground.

"You drive well. How did you learn?"

"From my brother, Donald Fork Lift. He once used one of these. And when I found this one . . ."

"Where? A museum? A tunnel?"

"An old museum, a strange one. It must have been sealed off before the Highway wars. I found it there a year ago."

"Why didn't your brother pull with this machine here, instead of you?"

She was very quiet, and then she looked at me. "You are a man of your word? That must be true, or you would not have been called to judge, as I heard."

"That is true."

She sighed, flung her hair from her head with one hand. "He would have," she said, "except he broke his hip last month on a raid at Sand Creek. He was going to come. But since he had already taught me how to work it, I drove it instead."

"And first thing you defeat Alan Backhoe Shovel?"

She looked at me and frowned. "I—I—"

"You made it up, didn't you?"

"Yes."

"As I thought. But I have given my word. Only you and I will know. Where did you get the serial plate?"

"One of the machines in the same place where I found my grader. Only it was in worse shape. But its plate was still shiny. I took it the night before I left with the truck. I didn't think anybody would know what Alan Backhoe Shovel's real plate was."

"You are smart," I said. "You are also very brave, for a woman, and foolish. You might have been killed. You may still be."

"Not if I win," she said, her eyes hard. "They couldn't afford to. If I lose, it would be another matter. I am sure I would be killed before I got to the Trinity. But I don't intend to lose."

"No," I said. "I will escort you as near your people as I can. I have hunted the Trinity, but never as far as the Red. I can go with you past the old Fork of the Trinity."

She looked at me. "You're trying to get into my pants."

"Well, yes."

"Let's smoke first," she said. She opened a leather bag, rolled a parchment cigarette, lit it. I smelled the aroma of something I hadn't smoked in six moons. It was the best dope I'd ever had, and that was saying something.

I don't know what we did afterward, but it felt good.

"To the finish," said Winston Mack Truck, and threw the pitch-fork into the ground.

It was better than the day before—the bulldozer like a squat red monster and the road-grader like avenging yellow death. On the first yank, Simon pulled the grader back three feet. The crowd went wild. His treads clawed at the dirt then, and the road-grader lurched and regained three feet. Back and forth, the great clouds of black smoke whistling from the exhausts like the bellowing of bulls.

Then I saw what Simon was going to do. He wanted to wear the road-grader down, keep a strain on it, keep gaining, lock himself, downshift. Yesterday he had tried to finish the grader on might. It had not worked. Today he was taking his time.

He could afford to. The road-grader was light in front; it had hard rubber tires instead of treads. When it lurched, the front end sometimes left the ground. If Simon timed it right, the grader wheels would rise while he downshifted and he could pull the yellow machine another few inches.

Mary Margaret was alternately working the pedals and levers, trying to get an angle on the squat red dozer. She was trying to pull across the back end of the tractor, not against it.

That would lose her the contest, I knew. She was vulnerable. When the wheels were up, Simon could inch her back. The only time he lost ground was when he downshifted while the claws dug their way into the ground. Then he lost purchase for a second. Mary Margaret could maybe use that, if she were in a better position.

They pulled, they strained, but slowly Mary Margaret Road-Grader was losing to Simon Red Bulldozer.

Then she did something unexpected. She lurched the road-grader and dropped the blade.

The crowd went gonzo, then was silent. The shiny blade dug into the ground.

The lurch gained her an inch or two. Simon, who never looked back either, knew something was wrong. He turned, and when his eyes left the panel, Mary Margaret jerked his bulldozer back another two feet.

We never thought in all those years we had heard about Simon Red Bulldozer that he would not have kept his blade in working order. He reached out to his blade lever and pulled it, and nothing happened. We saw him panic then, and the contest was going to Mary Margaret when . . .

The black plastic of the steering wheel showered up in her face. I heard the shot at the same time and dropped to the ground. I saw Mary Margaret holding her eyes with both hands.

Simon Red Bulldozer must not have heard the shot above the roaring of his engine, because he lurched the bulldozer ahead and started pulling the road-grader back over the line.

It was Elmo John Deere doing the shooting. I had my carbine off my shoulder and was firing by the time I knew where to shoot.

Elmo must have been drunk. He was trying to kill an opponent who had bested him in a fair fight.

I shot him in the leg, just above the knee, and ended his Pulling days forever. I aimed at his head then, but he dropped his rifle and screamed so I didn't shoot him again. If I had, I would have killed him.

It took all the Fossil Creek People to keep his sons from killing me. There was a judgment, of course, and I was let go free.

That was the last Sun Dance they had. The Fossil Creek People separated. Elmo's people split off from them, and then went bitter crazy. The Fossil Creek People even steal from them, now, when they have anything worth stealing.

The Pulls ended, too. People said if they were going to cause so much blood, they could do without them. It was bad business. Some people stopped stealing machines and cars and plates, and started bartering for food and trading horses.

The old ways are dying. I have seen them come to an end in my time, and everything is getting worthless. People are getting lazy. There isn't anything worth doing. I sit on this hill over the Red River and smoke with Fred-in-the-Hollow and sometimes we get drunk.

Mary Margaret sometimes gets drunk with us.

She lost one of her eyes that day at the Pulls. It was hit by splinters from the steering wheel. Me and Freddy took her back to her people in her truck. That was six years ago. Once, years ago, I went past the place where we held the last Sun Dance. Her road-grader was already a rust pile of junk with everything stripped off it.

I still love Mary Margaret Road-Grader, yes. She started things. Women have come into other ceremonies now, and in the councils.

I still love Mary Margaret, but it's not the same love I had for her that day at the last Sun Dance, watching her work the pedals and the levers, her hair flying, her feet moving like birds across the cab.

I love her. She has grown a little fat. She loves me, though.

We have each other, we have the village, we have cattle, we have this hill over the river where we smoke and get drunk.

But the rest of the world has changed.

All this, all the old ways . . . gone.

The world has turned bitter and sour in my mouth. It is no good, the taste of ashes is in the wind. The old times are gone.

THE FAMILY WINTER OF 1986

The family that lays together stays together.

Felix C. Gotschalk

The fiery solar disc above me was so bright that I could not sensitively perceive its true shape, ascertain its mass, or follow the flow of its flaring streamers. Reflexively, my eyes avoided the furnace-eye of yellow-white energy, and it could have been blazing at ceiling height or millions of miles high, it mattered not. For a very few minutes, I could watch the great sphere edge up over the rooftops in the morning, and watch it sink behind the smooth mountains at dusk, and at these times it appeared perfectly circular.

My putative sire told me that our planet's axis angle changed slightly during the winter months, so that, even though the fiery sun-plate was closer to us, the actual heat and light were reduced. And this is what I told my three putative offspring. But oh, how I wished the earth were green again! And how I longed for warm weather. The drought line began to move ominously north in the year 1950, and had crept up our peninsula at about thirty miles a year. In the fall of 1980 we cut down all fifty-seven trees on our 100-by-200-foot lot and sawed them into firewood lengths. We salvaged every twig, branch, and the smaller limbs as kindling, and worked hard with two-man saws, sawing the heavy trunks into two-foot lengths. There was widespread theft of wood that year, as well as theft of bushes and shrubs, and we installed an eight-foot chain-link fence at staggering cost to our credit lines. But then, all our neighbors had metal fences, and most had Dobermans, mastiffs, or shepherds as guard dogs. We all put up extra floodlights at first, but this was long before the power plants stopped functioning. We stacked the garage to the rafters with logs, and our four BMWs sat outside, three rusted and dry-rotted, and one running fairly well on a fifty-gallon charcoal burner conversion. At $7.50 a gallon, few of us could afford gasoline.

We burned all fifty-seven trees in two fireplaces during the winter of 1980. The temperature ranged from 37° below zero to about 40° Fahrenheit from October through March. We wore woolen jumpsuits, extra socks, even ski masks, and the five of us slept together for added warmth. Now, in December 1986, we still slept together, but the need for body warmth was waning in relation to the strength of incestuous sexual attractions. After all, when a healthy thirty-year-old man shares a king-sized mattress with a healthy thirty-year-old woman he loves, plus two strong sons, ages sixteen and seventeen, and a beautiful fifteen-year-old daughter, things are bound to happen. We brought our two sheepdogs in one bitter cold night, brushed and curried and perfumed them carefully, and slept with them. They were docile, pliant, and heavy, and I had a bone-hard erection sleeping humped against one of them. My daughter grew soft and sweet, and she seemed to luxuriate against my erections, like a cat being stroked. This disturbed me in some ways, but I was secretly pleased and aroused also.

None of us had bathed for weeks, it was just too goddam cold to get undressed, and besides, no water was allocated for bathing. Oil ran out in 1977, natural gas in 1978, and most of the coal was gone by summer 1980. Municipal water supplies were cut off the

same year, and electricity seeped feebly through the utility systems for a few straggling months, the lights glowing dim and
yellow, then dying out. So we were like primitive Eskimos, striv-
ing to survive in a poorly heated rancher with thirty-five hundred
square feet of floor space.

The very night we slept with the dogs, two large eucalyptus
bushes were stolen from our backyard, the roots carefully dug
out, every tendril and runner preserved, two clusters of fuel for
somebody. I didn't suspect any of our close neighbors of the
theft, but somebody went to a hell of a lot of trouble, scaling at
least two eight-foot fences and digging in the frozen ground. Fuel
was indeed more precious than food for us. In the front yard, we
had pruned the holly bushes down to about two feet in height and
used some of the branches for fuel, and we had carefully removed
ten vertical two-by-fours from the attic framing, leaving some
thirty-six-inch centers where the building codes required eighteen. I counted ninty-two of these six-foot-high boards in the
attic and wondered how many I could remove before the roof
threatened to fall in—Christ, what a strange thing to have to
worry about!

The day suddenly turned leaden-gray, somber, quiet, funereal,
and the snow began to fall. The temperature was 14° F. at 2 P.M.,
and every snowflake struck, cartwheeled, and, mercifully, began
to cover the vistas of hard red earth, slashlike eroded gullies,
rocks, glass, bricks, feces, ashes—anything that wouldn't burn
was left on the ground, like so much gravel scattered on a porce-
lain floor. And on this now whitening vista, the rows of large
houses stood out, like blocks on a board, like chessmen or Mo-
nopoly pieces: the Waggoners' handsome white French Provin-
cial, the Caseys' mansard-roofed place, the outré five-level split
the Browns built lovingly in 1965—row upon row of once fash-
ionable homes that had stood on thick green carpets of zoysia and
fescue and bermuda, and dotted with cedars and firs and pines.
The scene was like a Dali painting, with incongruous, compelling
foreground figures placed on a zoom-lens desert of stunning
perspective-depth.

"Snow! Snow!" the kids sang out, crowding to the window.

The room was entirely bare, and one eight-foot section of paneling had been pried off, exposing beams and caulking and black asbestos siding. We burned the cornices first, then the shelves, cabinets and banisters. The mantelpiece kept us warm for an entire day, being about six feet long and two feet square and very goddam hard to saw in half. The moldings around the floors and ceilings were used quickly, making excellent kindling, and we had just begun the sad task of prying up the parquet squares in the dining room. Paper of any kind was so rare that we used old grease and garbage to seal cracks as we slowly pulled off pieces of the house, like Hansel and Gretel plucking hard cookies from the witch's roof.

Betty, my putative mate of seventeen years, zipped her padded jacket shut and walked carefully down the partially dismantled steps to the basement. She carried twenty plastic jars outside to catch the snow for later water storage. The poor girl cried the winter we burned the draperies, but we had used all our extra clothing for fuel years ago. I used to have twenty suits and eighty shirts, not counting underwear, old clothes, and handkerchiefs. I worked in a bank and had to dress up every day. Now I was down to two sets of dirty long-johns, six pairs of athletic socks, five layers of sweatshirts, two pairs of woolen pants, a massive corduroy coat, and a thirty-eight-dollar Stetson that I dearly loved. I felt like crying myself the year we cut up my two-hundred-dollar cashmere shooting jacket and stacked the squared pieces beside the fireplace. Much later, on a twenty-below evening, I was to cut the brim from the Stetson and use it to start a fire. Life was, as Bill, our seventeen-year-old son, put it, a matter of groveling about for things to burn in the fireplace. For example, think hard —should that vinyl jacket stay thumbtacked over that crack in the wall, or should it be burned as fuel? It would burn rapidly, we decided, and it would smell bad and put sticky black filaments in the air, so leave it where it is. But the drawers in the end tables could be taken apart. Betty loves those heavy tables, so try to fix it so the drawer facings can remain. The two of them will probably have to be burned before spring anyway. Outside, the tortured earth-crust received the balm of white crystals—so soft a

fall, and yet so harsh a shower of fluffy meteorites. In the blackened, cracked fireplace, an old cedar log burned quietly, almost
with dignity, and I wiped my soot-clogged nose on a tennis ball
because I was tired of wiping my nose on my sleeves.

It snowed for three days and three nights, a strange, silent,
windless fall of white. When the coppery-red sun rose on the
fourth dawn, our tiny parcel of the world was iced like frozen
glittery cake frosting. The sky was swept clean, a deeply saturated
blue, and the air was so clear that my sense of visual perspective
had to accommodate the new binocular cues. Plumes of smoke
rose straight up from dozens of chimneys, like faintly wavering
pencil lines drawn on bold blue paper. The snow had drifted very
little and was about three feet deep everywhere. And the landscape was perfectly untouched, I could not see a single footprint,
tire track, animal pawprint, nor any signs of fallen branches (who
had even seen a branch in recent years?) or birds or little children, or brave paperboys, or postmen, or milkmen—where had
all these nostalgic images come from? Then, next door, Macy
heaved his slop jar from an upper window, the shallow tin pan
hitting the hard snow-crust face down. A tributary of yellow fluid
ran slowly out on to the snow and steam vapors sifted upward.
Reality had returned. Sixteen-year-old Alex opened our back
door and dropped our full slop jars straight down. Three years
ago the door had opened onto a large redwood deck, with handsome railings and bracings and stairs. The deck was dismantled
for firewood in 1983.

If life had any meaning left for us that winter, it centered on
the primary survival function of keeping warm, keeping tolerably
clean and fed, and, above all, fighting back new and persistent
incest fantasies, sociometric shiftings in the family group, and
trying not to get panicky in boredom or hopelessness. We all
sensed that each others' sex drives were active and strong. I
jacked off every day, trying to stay detumescent, and it was a
matter of where to go to do it—I had taken to pounding off in
the attic, shooting the stuff down into the asbestos-litter insula-
tion (damn shame asbestos won't burn). Our scents grew pun-
gent and spoor-like, fifteen-year-old Sandra bloomed like a sweet

waxy flower, and the boys must have wrestled mightily with their fierce hydraulic pressures. I thought it would be so kind, so beautiful, so eminently right to have intrafamilial sex, but, dammit all, none of us seemed to be able to throw over our incest taboos. I thought how natural it would be for the boys to plow their dam or their female litter-mate, and what better way to introduce a young girl to sex than through the gentle skill of a considerate paternal figure? But tremendous conflicts arose in my mind—thou mayest not incestuate, a voice kept telling me, a stodgy voice straight from the throne of the superego.

The day rang clear and hard and bitterly cold. I spat from the doorway, and the spittle cracked into crystals before it hit the snow. I cranked the wireless and got a weather station report of 18° below zero. We roasted ersatz rabbit legs on the fireplace spit and ate them with hard pumpernickel and warm red wine (I had traded a BMW for three hundred bottles of wine back in 1981 and had never regretted it). We huddled around the fire, hunkered down, like primitive tribesmen worshiping an idol. We smelled of grease cracklings and hot gnawed bones. Sandra smelled lovely, a kind of musk-oil perfume, and the boys also had cologne smells partially masking the basic odors of dirty socks and sweat-shirts with sodden-yellow armpits.

What a day to have to go to the goddam store! I had half forgotten, half repressed the idea, and Betty pointed to the boldly circled date on the calendar, giving me a sweet look that seemed to connote sadness, encouragement, and secret promises of intimacies to be shared when I returned. She kissed me skil-fully, and an urgency in her brief writhing both pleased and puzzled me. The wine was sweet and nourishing on her lips. I did not notice Alex and Sandra exchanging expectant glances. Bill had gone to break out our outdoor clothing.

I left Betty and Alex and Sandra together, and Bill and I made ready for the bothersome monthly chore of getting food rations at the commissary. I went quickly to the basement, almost as if this were something I would have to do quickly or not at all. Bill and I put on plastic body-suits over the several layers of clothes we always wore, then hefted the heavy hooded parkas from their

nails and helped each other put them on. Then we put on
snowshoes, opened the garage door, quickly shoveled the steam-
ing dog turds outside, and watched the dogs charge into the
three-foot-high snow, barking excitedly, leaping and thrashing,
pawing and rearing. We got them back inside and tried the snow-
crust ourselves. Immediately our shoes cracked the crust to a
depth of about two inches, the wetness froze in my nostrils, and
my eyes felt like iced marbles in warm plastic sacs. The silence
was incredible, a cotton-muffled aura of urgently compacted oxygen molecules. We knew it was useless to talk—we had made a
few bad-weather trips before—so we just paced the snow as best
we could, thankful for our ski masks and rubber gloves and for
the strength of our relative youth. The fence-gate was damn hard
to open enough for us to squeeze through, and we tried to sift
flowingly over the snow, but a moderate trudging was what we
got, moving unsteadily up the driveway toward the street, two
padded figures on a sea of glistening white, metal fences beside
us, behind us, in front of us, the fences providing stark, gridlike
reference points. We turned left down the steep street and met
Macy. He was carrying his chihuahua in a sling around his neck,
and the tiny animal looked utterly hairless and vulnerable, trembling, an all but *in utero* look. Of all the great good luck, a municipal snow plow came grinding up the road, diesel engine screaming, its chute spewing huge fans of snow into the air. "Good
Gawdamighty," Macy said, "will you looky thar—sent straight
from heaven above."

"Couldn't have come at a better time," I agreed heartily. "Now
maybe we can get a jump on the crowds at the store." We struggled down into the wide trench the plow had made and looked
far down the road toward the shopping center. We might easily
have been birds standing in deep tire tracks in the snow, except
I hadn't seen a bird or a tire track for months. We took our
snowshoes off and began to jog lightly down the road. Dirty,
ragged, padded figures fought their way through the deep snow
toward the cleared trench, all of us seeking the hard surface the
plow had made. Sappenfield wore his Bowie knife and his pistol,
fat little Hauser was being dragged by his Doberman, Hanson

had a beard that looked like a five-year collection of steel wool and gritty dirt, and I'll be damned if six-foot-tall Ms. Marr wasn't out. Her husband stayed drunk most of the time. We began to come together in the trench, a loose crowd, like a golf-course gallery moving across the greens. A Peugeot diesel came slowly down the trench, stopped for one or two minutes, and was surrounded by people wanting to warm their hands on the hood. One man lay on the ground to press his hand against the muffler and resonator. Macy's eyebrows were laced with icicles, and he complained that his chewing tobacco was cold in his mouth. We made it to the main access road in about one hour, then turned wearily to starboard and trudged along the turnpike. Both lanes had been cleared, and some sleighs and troikas jingled by, pulled by skinny, bloat-bellied horses, plumes of steam pumping from their nostrils. A peat-burning Fiat whispered past, followed by a brace of Honda Civitinos and a rare Subaru. Cars were rare in our neighborhood, and very few large vehicles existed at all except in museums or among the millions of cars abandoned on the streets. We passed vandalized houses, crumbling business booths, fellatio kiosks, and the remains of MacDonald's, Dairy Queen, Royal Laundry, Majik Market, Dinkle's Bakery, Seth's Clothing Store, Harry's Book and Tape Nook, Levitt Shoe Store, Pressley's Hardware, Gazebo Fashions for Ladies, B & G Cafeteria—all long since bankrupt in the financial riots of 1980, looted, vandalized, abandoned, then squattered, fought over, burned, and grown up in weeds, later pulled from the ground for food and fuel. Now it all lay buried under the merciful snow. Autos lay three and four deep in service stations, a Lotus perched curiously atop a Continental, the tiny car's height approximately doubled by the snow accumulation. Deep in the shallow bowl that had been a shopping mall, hundreds of abandoned cars lay beneath the snow. A large helicopter lay in their midst, one rotor snapped and sagging. Someone had a good fire going in the center of the lot, and there were some luxurious hovels fashioned from 450 SEs and Imperials.

We pushed our way into the commissary, a low metal building that had once housed the Social Security Administration, and glanced anxiously at the names on the allocation charts. This was the right day for us to show up, but the errors in allocation schedules were numerous and frustrating. A squad of provost robots scuttled from wall niches and barked strange little metallic-voiced orders for us to form six parallel lines to the counters where we would receive our rations. We moved fast, getting out our credit-line vouchers and readying our satchels and knapsacks and plastibags. Bleary-eyed clerks activated the credit-control registers, the robots queued up the lines carefully and started checking our voucher cards. Behind the row of clerks, the larder allocation tapes began to clack and spin, and the tiny, precious, compressed nutrient cubes clittered from the slots and into stiff, cold, dirty hands and all manner of sacks and boxes and containers:

BOBBITT, HAROLD E: 150 UNITS EQUINE MEAT, 75 SOYA BY-PRODUCTS, 10 VEGETABLE SURROGATES, 1 FIFTH LIQUOR

CARTER, BENJAMIN: 62 UNITS RICE PRODUCTS, 400 UNITS DRY DOG MEAL, 4 QUARTS BRASS MONKEY

HAINEY, GAITHER: 2 ISSUES PHEASANT UNDER GLASS, 2 UNITS SPINACH LEAVES, 3 UNITS BRANDY, 1 UNIT CREPES

SHAWN, JACK: 40 UNITS VODKA—

"Say, who the hell is Gaither Hainey?" old McDonough asked me from behind, a hellish black stogie jammed in his mouth, grinning with his sharp yellow canines exposed. A man in front of us told him that Hainey was a former textile millionaire who spent his monthly allowance on gourmet cubes and somehow survived thirty days on rations most people would use up in one week. Old Ms. Malone looked prim and clean as usual, waiting for her apricot brandy vials and protein blastulas, and I doffed my ski mask to her. Bailey had a new bandage on his leathery face. He was a retired gladiator, and still challenged young men to duels. The room grew noisy and incredibly odorous, the doors opened to admit bone-chilling air and closed to capture the kaleidoscope of olfactory cues, one balancing the other. People hugged their rations to themselves, hid them in belts and pockets and mittens, and looked suspiciously at those waiting as they left. Flimflams, trades, and outright assaults and thefts were not unusual on allocation days. There were always a few people around who needed rations and would prey upon those who might be easy pickings. The clerk looked at my voucher matter-of-factly and even managed a smile—damn, I was caught off guard—people smiled so little these days. I managed a feeble return smile as the tapes reeled off our allocations:

BARTON, HENRY: 30 UNITS PORK, 15 UNITS VENISON, 15 UNITS STARFISH, 30 UNITS TUBERS, 30 UNITS TRUFFLES (truffles were common, what with millions of old trees being uprooted) 51 UNITS RAGWEED STALKS

The cubes clattered from the chutes and Bill and I caught them in our knapsacks. As we turned to leave, Bill traded a tuber cube for a real peppermint stick an old man must have been saving for years. Old Bill Gain traded his entire ration of grits and eggs for tequila blatters and intravenes.

I knew things couldn't keep going smooth for very long. Tom Varner stepped in front of us as we approached the door, blocking it, feet wide, arms akimbo. As usual, he wanted to bump somebody, and he was still sore because Alex and I double-teamed him back in October. I could feel Bill tense up beside me, and I tried not even to break stride as we neared him. I said, *"Let's take him!"* in a quick, harsh whisper. We got him from both sides, thrusting our arms through his, and his fat-tomato face came apart in a flaccid autonomic droop, his fighting response just barely muffled by the ease and surprise of the attack. We dragged him stiff-legged, like policemen hustling a demonstrator toward a paddy wagon, and rammed his salt-and-pepper head against the corrugated metal wall. Goddam, you would have thought a truck had hit the wall, it made a hell of a noise, but didn't do much damage to Tom. Bill chopped him behind the ear and that put him to sleep. Sam Ballas cheered; he hated Tom's bully-guts, and so did most people who knew him. One of the provost robots castered over to us at once, requesting retinograph tapes of the incident. Big deal—citizens had long ago realized that they had to rely on themselves for protection; now we were about to be detained for roughing up one of the community bad guys. Sam left his place in line to speak loudly in our defense. He bonded himself in our advocacy, and fluxed on his I.D. beside ours on the warrant: CITIZEN VARNER VIOLATED PUBLIC SPACE AND MADE A PROVOCATIVE MOVE, the warrant read—shit, men had drawn pistols over lesser matters. About half the people in our neighborhood carried sidearms.

"Kin ah hev his snuff?" old Jock Tait asked the provobot, reaching for Tom's vest pocket. Before the bot could muster a response, Jock had the small bag open and slipped a pinch of the snuff under his lip. Of all the crazy things, somebody started playing the *Variations on the Star-Spangled Banner,* full volume, on a portable cassette player, and I remembered the stories about circus musicians playing *Stars and Stripes Forever* when trouble started on the midway. Bill and I tended briefly to Tom, who seemed not to know what the hell was going on—"Stand at attention, you shitheads," he muttered, "hit's the national fuckin' anthem—" We decided to leave before Tom recovered his senses. The Judicial Bank would process the case. If we lost, our food rations would be reduced. If we won, nothing would happen. Poor Tom: like most of the gladiator types, he had nothing to do with his aggression; it was a maladaptive trait pattern.

Outside again, the afternoon sunlight was blinding. We tied the sacks around our necks and walked, heads low, eyes closed to slits, shutting out as much of the whiteness as we could. Bill held both hands over his eyes and I guided him about halfway home, then I closed my eyes and he guided me. The sun was white-hot, murderous in its light, yet giving us little respite from the bitter cold air that penetrated us like embalming fluid. Abreast of our street, we floundered up out of the street-wide trench, and made it the last hundred or so difficult yards to our house, opening the garage door, hugging the warm dogs, and cheering loudly. Above our heads, the huge bed squeaked through the floor, and we heard soft laughter, then loud greeting cheers from Betty and Alex and Sandra.

Betty looked marvelous, her face flushed, lips ripe. Sandra also looked good, somehow excited, blooming, humid, achingly sexual, I thought. And then, by damn, Alex looked like a bull with his cows, and I suddenly realized, just as clear as day, that these three loved ones had been at each other sexually. At first I resented being away, freezing my ass off, while they were plowing each other, but then I thought, this is the ultimate familial bond, and I was happy for them. I didn't know what to do or say at the time, so I just coasted mentally and acted relaxed and happy and tired. After we divided the food rations, we all drank wine, sat in a tight circle, and Sandra leaned across and kissed me earnestly. Then she kissed Bill and Alex and Betty, and we all hugged each other. Alex brought a prized old cedar log, topped it with pine slabs, and set a fine, roaring blast going in the fireplace. As if some collective sense of exquisite imminence motivated us, we made breathless tropistic movements toward group sex, the growing darkness helping Bill and me past our inhibitions. I all but sobbed with joy as Bill mounted Betty, ventral over dorsal, Sandra guiding his glistening mallet to its target beautifully. Later, our beautiful children sang, and stroked Betty and me as we performed a long, ritualistic *pas à deux*. Through the early-evening hours, we all put our mouths and hands and genitals wherever the urge moved us, and it was a beautiful scene. I had never been happier, and I began to think that incest should be the true theme for the Madonna and Child paradigms, the parent rewarding the child with the gift of patient, gentle sexual initiation. How quickly our taboos left us!

Late that evening we ate, slowly, ritualistically, luxuriating in the warm emotionality of our incestuous circle. We took a taper to our bedroom and took successive spoon positions on the bed. I put a sheepdog next to Bill, Betty clung to Bill's back, then Alex slipped in next to Betty. Sandra moved to embrace Alex from behind, and I put the other warm dog next to Sandra. Sandra looked disappointed, but the dog seemed to whimper in satisfaction. Bill and I pulled the stitched impala skins up to cover us all, and we settled into readiness for sleep.

I knew that bittersweet times were ahead for us all. Bill and Alex were far better calisthenic screwers than I was, and sooner or later a pecking order would develop. I just hoped that our love for each other would smooth things out, but then, who is to say that love is anything other than a set of full seminal vesicles, or some vague estrogenic rumbling of the pelvic floor? But we had good signals so far. Christ, the warmth of the body is a holy thing. The room will probably go to 50° tonight, maybe zero in the garage, and twenty below outside. Maybe a dozen citizens will freeze to death tonight. At least I won't have to go to the store again until February 21, 1986—thank God for that—hey, Sandra is reaching for me, such a sweet child—I know we'll make it through the winter.

THE TEACHER

Not everybody who hears voices is insane.

Kathleen M. Sidney

Grasping the iron railing with both hands, the bridge vibrating beneath her feet, she paused to watch the river. For at least an hour now she had walked with her eyes and mind unfocused. But at last the sheer power of the river fixed her attention. If she could only think only of the force of the water only of the water only . . .

Here at the city's highest point the river cut a deep chasm through the rock and rushed over a fifty-foot cliff with such velocity that it formed a great frothing arc. The late-afternoon sun slanted through the spray where its colors broke apart into a clearly defined bow. And beneath that?

She took off her glasses to wipe away the spray. A little farther on there was a footbridge that crossed directly over the rim of the falls and led to a small park. The benches looked inviting. She became aware of pain in her arthritic knee. It must have been hurting for some time to get this bad. She put her glasses back on and looked again, finally squinting. Yes, something, a kind of shapeless fluctuation of colors beneath the rainbow—maybe an afterimage formed from staring too long at the sun glaring off the water, or a prismatic effect blurred by the mist.

Strange, but no more important really than silver-backed clouds blown across a deep-blue sky. She looked at her hands and thought it strange that they were old.

"Mrs. Lockwood, please, can't you understand?" Reese had handed her his handkerchief, all the while speaking tenderly, like a father to a child. And he not more than forty, while she—did he know that she was nearing her seventy-fifth birthday?

Halfway across the footbridge she remembered the colors and looked again. The rainbow was invisible from this angle, and the colors were hidden by the spray.

The bench was hard and her knee went on throbbing. There was something that she should do (there was always something) but she didn't try to remember what it was. It hurt to think, and there was the water, only the water.

From here she could see the rock basin at the bottom of the falls where the river swirled through a half-circle and then went on. A narrow footpath bordered the basin and ended at a concrete wall where the stairs led back up the cliff. Two children were down there, leaning precariously over the railing. Their distance and the spray from the falls made it difficult for her to see them, but she thought that one might be a girl and the other a boy.

She must have stood in just that spot many times as a child. She and Paul, watching the water. (The children leaped away from the railing and raced along the path toward the stairs.) Of course there hadn't been stairs then. And the wall? No, it couldn't have been there either, because the only way of getting to the path had been around the side of the factory. She wondered how much else along the river had changed since that day, almost sixty-five years ago, when she and Paul had decided to walk to the ocean. They had known that the Lenape River ended there. It was only a matter of following it. She could still picture the ocean. Not the one that was sixty miles east of Lenape Falls. Not the one that they would never visit until they were much older and it didn't really matter anymore. But the one that they had carried with them, past smokestacks, oil tanks, and dead things floating in the water, until it was night.

The throbbing in her knee was getting worse. She had better take some aspirin as soon as she got home. Home. She looked at her watch and, with that habitual motion, remembered.

"How long do I have?"

"Well, as it happens, we already have someone in mind."

"I believe the standard procedure is two months' notice."

Such a slick young man, his hair and clothes styled ingeniously between establishment and mod. Yet now he seemed genuinely embarrassed. "That's only for contract teachers."

4:05. She should have caught the 3:15 bus home. Emma would be wondering why she was late. There might be a 4:20. She got up stiffly and crossed the bridge, feeling somehow not quite ready to leave the park. It was as if there was something that she had meant to finish first. Maybe a thought. Or a question.

On her way to the bus, she couldn't resist pausing by the abandoned factory where the path used to lead over the hill and down along the river to the falls. It was all grown over now, and she couldn't remember exactly where it used to be. For a moment she caught her reflection in a cracked windowpane. It showed up clearly against the darkness inside. Was this the frail old woman that Reese had seen when he looked across his desk?

"Marge, where's the stuff from the cleaners?" Emma came into the kitchen.

"The what?"

"My raincoat, your . . . you forgot."

"I'm sorry." She dried the last dish and sat down. Now was the time when she would normally be preparing the next day's lessons.

"That's nice, and it's supposed to rain tomorrow."

She could make some tea and read.

"Marge?"

"Hmm?"

"You all right?"

"Yes."

"You haven't looked well all evening." Emma felt her head.

Margaret got up. "I'm at least ten years older than you are and I won't have you treating me like a child."

As she hurried upstairs, Emma shouted behind her, "Then don't act like one."

Her briefcase waited on the desk.

"We hadn't planned to give you such short notice, it just worked out that way." He had spoken softly, so reasonably. "And it's not as if you needed the time to look for another job."

"I should at least be given a day to warn my students of the change and to say goodbye."

"Mrs. Lockwood, I know that your students will miss you, but children really are pretty flexible that way, aren't they?"

"Marge, your briefcase."

Halfway down the walk, she turned. Emma was standing in the doorway, holding her briefcase. For a moment the scene seemed to freeze and Margaret saw her sister-in-law and their house from the stiff perspective of a photograph. It was an impersonal image of age. But maybe a new coat of paint and . . . ?

Emma handed her the case. "Your knee looks swollen."

"It's not so bad today."

"You shouldn't be running around from house to house. Why don't you tell them that if they won't give you a classroom job, you'll quit."

And now she should tell her what she had been putting off all night and still felt reluctant to say. Afraid that Emma, who loved but could not understand her, would be glad. Or perhaps it was the inevitable questions that would follow. Margaret took the briefcase and waved goodbye.

The bus left her off near the bottom of the hill and she climbed slowly, not wanting to push her leg. Acrid dye fumes rose up along the river, tainting the clear October air. As she approached the top she could hear the roar of the falls. In the early-morning light, the rainbow wasn't visible from the road. Suddenly remembering, she stopped and tried to concentrate on the spot that would have been beneath the bow. After a moment she could see them. The vague, shapeless, shifting colors that couldn't be an afterimage or a prismatic effect, not when they continued to exist with the sun at an entirely different angle. Yet it must be some trick of the eye. It seemed to her that they moved more quickly as she watched. Someone asked her a question and she turned, but no one was there. And she couldn't remember actually having discerned any words. Perhaps it was the white noise of the falls, like thinking that one has heard one's name called while running a vacuum cleaner. The ocean at Asbury Park. A sudden, vivid image disconnected from any other thought. She could feel the icy water, taste the salt, smell the vague fishiness of the shore. Sand was running down beneath her toes. Paul grinned like a child, spray glistening on his mustache and his coarse brown hair. This was their honeymoon. They took each other's hand and ran.

Margaret turned away quickly. Her husband had died thirty years ago, and her first student would be waiting.

Past the falls she shivered once. It had seemed so real, almost like a hallucination. A long time ago, she had read something somewhere about stress bringing on senile dementia. No, she would not go that way. She would not.

"Well, hello." The hall outside smelled of urine, but as usual, the small apartment was clean and neat. "We weren't expecting to see you so early." Margaret sat on the couch, her usual place, while Mrs. Shepard brought over the TV table. "Mae is in the kitchen finishing lunch. She'll come out in a minute." But Mae was already at the door, smiling shyly.

"Teacher?"

"Hello, Mae. I had to come early today, but I can wait for you to finish your lunch if you . . ."

Mae disappeared into the kitchen, came out a moment later with her notebook and a wide tipped felt pen. Sitting next to her on the couch, Margaret thought how small this nine-year-old was. It made her want to put her arm around her protectively. But when Mae's infection was at its worst, Margaret had seen her bear up under what must have been excruciating pain without a whimper. And although she couldn't put her finger on exactly what it was, Margaret suspected that Mae knew something that a seventy-five-year-old woman was only beginning to learn.

The girl opened her notebook and placed it on the table. Mrs. Shepard got up. "I'll be in the kitchen."

"No, please wait. There's something I have to say to both of you."

Of all the goodbyes, this was the hardest. And yet she suspected that it might have been for this goodbye that she made the others. After she and Mrs. Shepard had each said the proper things, there was an awkward silence. For the first time in two years, Margaret felt a stranger in this house. She found herself afraid to look directly at Mae, who had said nothing at all.

Finally Mrs. Shepard looked at her watch. "They'll be expecting me back at work." It was almost a question. Margaret got up.

"You can stay if you like. Mae will let you out."

"No, I'd better be going. The other teacher could be here any time."

"Then we can walk together as far as Goodwear's."

Suddenly Mae was beside them. "Can I come?"

"No, honey. Who would walk you back?"

"I can find my way."

"After you have glasses."

"Just to the end of the block?"

"No, and don't you keep starting this business. I don't want to hear any more about it."

As they walked out, Margaret heard the door lock behind them.

"Do you know yet when she'll be getting her glasses?"

"Soon, I think. But I'm not really sure what's going on."

"What do you mean?"

"Well, you know those doctors. It's hard to get them to say what they mean. First they tell me that the operation worked, now they say she's not healing the way she should. So I don't know when she'll get them. It may even be the glasses won't do her any good."

"Have you talked to Mr. Reese about getting her into a Special Class?"

"I don't think they know exactly which class she belongs in yet."

"Listen, it's been two years now. If you bother Mr. Reese often enough, he'll find a place for her. And if it turns out to be the wrong one, she can always be moved later on."

They stopped in front of Goodwear's. "Well, I think she's best off at home for now." And there it was, the cold note in her voice, her head half turned toward Goodwear's as if it were mere haste that cut off the unwanted words.

"Mrs. Shepard . . ."

"I'm sorry, I can't be late. Hey, you come visit us sometime now, will you?"

She walked past the falls on the other side of the road. There was a 1:25 bus to catch and no time for gawking. But then she remembered Emma. It would be better to come home at the usual time and tell her it was today that she had been fired than to admit that she had kept it a secret.

The park looked peaceful. The children who frequented it at lunchtime were back in their classes now. It might feel good to rest there quietly for a while. But as she turned to cross the street she felt afraid. Of what? Madness? Merely because of a sudden, vivid memory earlier in the day? The light changed, but she didn't cross. Even from here she could see the leaves twirling in the breeze. Once as children she and some friends had gathered them all together with only their hands to use as rakes. And when the pile was huge, they had each jumped in. Madness, it occurred to her, might be a giving in to one's irrational feelings.

Even so, on her way to the footbridge she was careful not to look at the colors. It felt good to sit down. The day had been trying and she was more tired than she had guessed. She stared absently at the falls. A breeze blew up from the water, gradually coating her glasses with mist. It didn't really matter; she would wipe them when she was ready to leave. Her thoughts moved idly and scattered. The roar of the falls, a slow beat of waves, Paul called her out where it was deep, Mae printed large letters in the sand, she tried to see the word, the letters blurred, were shapeless colors, her head fell forward, "Ocean?" and she awoke. This time it didn't surprise her to discover that no one was there. It had been an oddly characterless voice, not really a sound at all. Undoubtedly a dream. But even unemployed she was a teacher, and something in her wanted to respond to a question. Curiosity, the most precious of human assets, must be preserved. She smiled at herself and got up to leave.

"Ocean?" and a feeling without a word.

She froze, trying desperately to think of a reason. A trick? Slowly she turned her head. No, no one was anywhere nearby. And then again she *felt* without a word, but this time she realized what it should be and whispered, "Please."

"Ocean? Please. Ocean?"

She ran. Unable to help herself. Stumbling and getting up again. She ran.

"What happened?"

Margaret sat down at the table, her hands were still trembling. "Something startled me in the park."

"You're cut." Emma ran a washcloth under the tap. "What was it?"

"I don't know."

Emma started to wash her knee, but Margaret took the cloth from her and did it herself.

"I mean, what startled you?"

"Maybe I was dreaming." The soapy water stung.

Margaret lay in bed and read as long as she could. Finally, reluctantly, she closed the book and turned out the light.

Toward morning, she dreamed that she was walking by the abandoned factory near the falls. As she passed a window some movement caught her eye and she paused. There was the dull, mechanical throb of machinery muffled by thick walls. It was difficult to see past her reflection but there seemed to be men inside, moving within the rhythm of their machines. They must be renting the old fabrics factory again. Someone came closer to the window and smiled, waving for her to come in. But she must be mistaken because she couldn't possibly know anyone here. He disappeared again, back into the gloom. Perhaps upon a closer look he had realized that she was no one he knew. Yet there had been something familiar about him. If she could cup her hands around her eyes and lean against the glass, she might be able to block out her reflection. But a cement trench filled with dye blackened water separated her from the window. Then she remembered a door along the side of the building. Once, as children, she and Paul had peeked in on their way down the path that led to the falls. Had the man in the window resembled Paul?

It was difficult to find the path but finally she saw it, a thin line almost entirely overgrown. From here she could hear the distant roar of the falls. The door was unlocked but heavy, so much heavier than it used to be. As she got it open a crack, it seemed to her that someone was calling her name. But the voice was drowned by the deep, vibrating beat of machinery. As the door opened wider, the sound became deafening and then abruptly ceased.

A shaft of sunlight from the door lost itself somewhere within the dust-laden darkness. She must have been mistaken. The place was empty. Or was he in another room? She thought of going in, but hesitated, listening to the silence.

"Teacher."

Mae stood a little way down the path toward the falls. There was a notebook in her hands and she was smiling.

Margaret closed the door and started down the path.

Emma had the coffee perking. "Up so early?" She knew that it was Margaret's habit to sleep late when she wasn't working.

"I have to go downtown."

"I thought yesterday was your last day."

"This has nothing to do with the Board of Education," and then, knowing that Emma would never let it rest there, she added, "I just thought I'd do a little shopping."

Emma smiled. "You'll get over it."

"What?"

"The restlessness. You'll come to like retirement. What you need is a hobby."

But she had tried retirement at sixty-five, losing her tenure only to find that for her nothing came even close to the pleasure of teaching. "It's not as if you needed the money," Reese had said. "After all, you have your pension."

It was a cloudy day with a sharp, chilling wind. There was no rainbow at the falls, but the shifting colors were still there. She crossed the bridge and sat down at the same bench. Her heart was beating rapidly and she wondered if she was putting too much of a strain on it. The small park was deserted. She took a deep breath and let it out slowly, trying to relax her muscles. Then she closed her eyes and whispered, "Who are you?"

There was no reply. Here in the park she could smell the sweet scent of decaying leaves.

"Who are you?"

As she concentrated on listening, the roar of the falls seemed to grow louder.

"Who are you?"

She felt inside herself for a sense of an answer, but there was nothing there that she couldn't identify as her own. She began to feel both relieved and disappointed. The monster was being exorcised, but so was something else.

"Where are you?"

Her hands were wet from the mist and getting cold. It was silly to stay. As she got up it occurred to her that students usually learned best when the new information was integrated with what they had learned before. She decided to try "Ocean."

And was startled. Something. Not a word so much as a feeling of recognition. A feeling from outside herself.

"Where are you?" she asked again, but this time she tried to picture as well as speak the idea, and decided immediately that it would have been better to choose something more concrete. But before she could think of what to use, there was a reply.

"Ocean? Please. Where are you?"

Images accompanied the voiceless words. Images that were her own and yet somehow, now, no longer her own. Ocean was a complex set of sense impressions involving herself and Paul at

Asbury Park, but seemed to lack any other meaning. "Please" was a need to know. And "Where are you?" was two children following a river.

She sensed without seeing—the infant colors shifting restlessly, eagerly, somewhere beneath the mist.

Margaret sat down again. A gust of wind rained leaves around her bench. Autumn, as every teacher knew, was a time for beginning.

COMING BACK TO DIXIELAND

Ain't got nothing to do
But sing me the blues—
Hey, don't God live out this far.

Kim Stanley Robinson

It figures, just as sure as shift-start, that on our big day there'd be trouble. It's a law of physics, the one miners know best: things tend to fuck up.

I woke first out of the last of several nervous catnaps, and wandered down to the hotel bar to get something a little less heavyweight than the White Brother for my nerves. On one level I was calm as could be, but on another I was feeling a bit shaky (Shaky Barnes, that's me). Now, we drank the Brother during performances back on the rocks, of course, between sets sitting at the tables, or during the last songs when someone offered it; and Hook would make his announcement, "We never know if this'll make us play better or worse, but it sure is fun finding out," and then pass it around. Which was the point; we *had* to play good this day, so I wanted something soothing, with a little less pop to it than the White Brother we'd brought with us, which amplifies your every feeling, including fear.

So when I threaded my way through the hotel (which was as big as the whole operation on Hebe or Iris) back to our rooms, I expected the band to still be there sleeping. But when I'd finished stepping over all the scattered chairs, tables, mattresses and such (the remains of the previous shift's practice session) I could find only three of them, all tangled up in the fancy sheets: Fingers, Crazy, and Washboard. I wasn't surprised that my brother Hook was gone—he often was—but Sidney shouldn't have been missing; he hadn't gone off by himself since we left Ceres Central.

"Hey!" I said, still not too worried. "Where'd they go, you slag-eaters!" They mumbled and grunted and tried to ignore me. I gave Washboard a shove with my foot. "Where's Hook? Where's Sidney?" I said a little louder.

"Quit shouting," Washboard said fuzzily. "Hook's probably gone back to the Tower of Bible to visit the Jezebels again." He buried his head in the pillow, like a snoutbit diving into bubblerock; suddenly it popped back out. "*Sidney's* gone?"

"You see him?"

Fingers propped himself up on his elbow. "You better find Hook," he said in his slow way. "Hook, he'll know where Sidney gone to."

"Well, did Hook *say* he was going to the Tower of Bible?" No one spoke. Crazy crawled over to a bed and sat up. He reached behind the bed and pulled out a tall thin bottle, still half filled with cloudy white liquid. He put it to his mouth and tilted it up; the level dropped abruptly a couple of times.

"Crazy, I never seen you hit the White Brother so early in the dayshift before," I said.

"Shaky," he replied, "you never seen me get the chance."

"You going to get us in trouble," I said, remembering certain misadventures of the past.

"No, I'm not," Crazy said. "Now why don't you run down Hook, I'm pretty sure he's in Sodom and Gomorrah, he liked that place"—he took another swallow—"and we'll hold down the fort and wait for Sidney to come back."

"He better come back," I said. "Shit. Here it is the biggest day in our lives and you guys don't even have the sense to stay in one spot."

"Don't worry," Crazy said. "Things'll go fine, I'll see to it."

I took one of the slow cars through the track-webbed space between our hotel and the Tower of Bible. The Tower is one of Titania's biggest experiments in Neo-Archeo-Ritualism, sometimes called Participatory Art. Within the huge structure, set right against the wall of the Titania Gap, the setting for every chapter in the Bible is contained, which means you can participate in a wide variety of activities. The lobby of the Tower was unusually crowded for the early hours of the dayshift, but it was Performance Day, I remembered, and people were starting early. I worked from ramp to ramp, trying to make my way through the oddly assorted crowd to the elevator that would take me to Sodom and Gomorrah. Finally I slid through the closing doors and took my place in the mass of future Sodomites.

"What I want to know," one of them said happily, "is do they periodically sulfurize everyone in the room?"

"Every two hours," a woman with round eyes replied, "and does it feel real! But then they unfreeze you and you get to begin again!" She laughed.

"Oh," said the man, blinking.

The elevator opened and the group surged past me toward Costumes. I stood and looked down some of the smoky streets of Gomorrah, hoping to see my brother in the crowd. Just as I decided to get one of the costumes and start searching, I saw him coming out of the door marked JEZEBELS, one arm wrapped around a veiled woman.

"Why, he must have just got here," I said aloud, and took off after him. "Hook!" I called. "Hook!"

He heard me and quickly steered the woman into a side street. I started running. Sure enough, when I rounded the corner they had disappeared; I made a lucky guess and opened the door to a house made of sediments, and caught up with them moving up the narrow stairs. "Hook, God damn it," I said.

"Later," he mumbled back at me, face buried in the Jezebel's neck.

"Hook, it's important."

He waved his right arm back at me in a brush-away motion, and the metal rods of his hand flashed in my face. "Not important!"

he bellowed. I grabbed his arm and pulled on it.

"How can you say that?" I cried. "Today's the day! The six bands those judges pick today get to go to Earth and everywhere—"

He finally stopped dragging us all up the stairs. "I know all that, Shaky, but that don't happen for a few hours yet, so why don't you go down to Psalms or Proverbs and calm down some? No reason for you to be so anxious."

"Yes, there is," I said, "a real good reason. Sidney's gone."

Hook tucked his chin into his neck. "Sidney's gone?" he repeated.

"Nobody's seen him all shift."

His three metal fingers waved up and down, scissoring the air; it was the same nervous sign of thought he'd made when he had his hand, and played the trumpet. "Did you search the hotel good?" he said after a bit. "I don't think he'd leave the hotel."

I shook my head. "I came here, I thought you'd know where he is."

"Well, he's probably in the hotel somewhere, take a look why don't you?"

"What if he's not there? Come on, Hook, if we don't find him we're sunk."

"All right," he said. "Shit. You're as bad as Sidney. I've been playing with that man near twenty years, and I never seen him so scared."

"You think he's scared?" That had never occurred to me. Sidney was quiet, not too forward, but I'd never seen him scared of playing music.

"Sure he's scared." He looked at the Jezebel, who hadn't made a sound so far. "I got to find Sidney," he explained. "I'll be back to celebrate tomorrow."

Her veiled head nodded, and I could see the flash of teeth. "We better hurry," Hook said. "We're due to be turned into a pillar of salt any minute now." We ran back and dived into the elevator, just behind the man who had been asking questions on the way up. Down in the lobby we dodged through a group of wide-eyed Venusian monks, and then through a stumbling crowd of wet people from one of the aquatic scenes. Then we made it to the exit, jumped in a car, and popped out into the Gap.

"That Participatory Art," Hook said, "is really something."

"Sidney's probably hiding in the hotel somewhere, the bar or maybe the baggage rooms," Hook said as we neared our hotel.

I could see that he was as worried as I was. Despite his easygoing speculations, his nervous trumpet fingering gave him away. Sidney's absence was a serious matter, partly because it was so unexpected; Sidney was never gone, never sick, never hurt; there was nothing that could keep Sidney from playing. And how he could play that clarinet! It was more than notes, it had to do with what was inside the man, the strength and the feeling; there's no way I can describe it to you but by telling a story here; a little blues:

After the long shift's ending, when I was just a kid and still working the sheds, I'd go down to the Heel Bar to sip beer and listen to Sidney play his clarinet. At this time he was playing with just Washboard and a piano man, Christy Morton (who later got killed in the big tunnel collapse on Troilus); and they were working out all the old tunes he'd discovered in the Benson Curtis tapes.

Sidney was as quiet and unassuming then as always. It didn't matter how much stomping and shouting he stirred up, or how much Washboard and Christy sang into the tune; old Sidney would stand there, head bowed, horn cradled in his arm when he wasn't playing, as silent and bashful as a child. Then he'd raise that horn to his mouth, and when he played it was clear he'd found his way of talking to the world. All the clamoring in the room channeled into him, he was transformed, and, sweat-bright with the effort, he'd wrench those songs into a sound as clean and live as a welding arc. Listening to him my cheeks would flush with blood, my heart would pound like Washboard's cowbell.

One time, late in the graveyard shift, I was joined at my front table by a Metis mute, one of the miners whose vocal cords had been ruined by the zinc blowout on Metis. Between sets Sidney sat with us, asked me how Hook was doing (this was right after his accident), and talked about Earth. He told us about New Orleans in the old times, when the jazz bands played in the streets. Telling it, he got so excited I didn't need to prod him with questions; he spoke on his own, even told us his one childhood memory of Earth: "That ocean, it was like a flat blue plate, big as Jupiter from Io, speckled with shadows from clouds; and the horizon was straight as a rail, edge to edge, cutting off a sky that was a blue I can't describe." When he went back to play I was under the spell of Dixieland; and by the gleam in the mute's eye I could tell he felt it too. When Sidney played a good break the mute would put back his head and laugh, mouth split wide open, silent as space.

So when Sidney was done we decided to take the mute along to his place, to give the mute some floor to sleep on; he didn't have any money or anywhere to go. Now at this time (this was on Achilles) Sidney lived in a cubbyhole behind one of the Supervisors' big homes. When we got there Sidney wanted us to hold back, while he went to check if his sister-in-law was awake—she didn't like him bringing folks home. Sidney explained this, but the mute didn't appear to understand; he must have thought he was being left, because every time Sidney walked a few steps and turned around, he found the mute right behind him, grinning and dragging me along. So there was a lot of waving and explaining going on when the JM police suddenly appeared; we didn't even have time to run.

"Where you going?" one of them asked.

"Home," Sidney said.

"I suppose you live here?" the cop said, pointing at the Supervisor's place.

"Yeah," Sidney said, and before he had time to explain, they were taking us off to jail.

We were hardly inside the jail door when they went to work on the Metis mute. Kicked him and beat him till he couldn't stand. His face was so bloody. Sidney and I stood shaking against the wall, expecting we'd be next, but they let us alone. Turned out one of the cop's wives had been killed on Metis, and he'd been after the mutes ever since. So when they were done with him they slammed us all into the bullpen.

There's not much JM can do to make its jails any worse than its mines, but what they can do they have done. The cell we were in was cold and dark, like a tunnel in a power breakdown, except for the gravity, which felt like it was over 1.00. I crawled over the rock floor, unable to see, and quietly called Sidney's name.

"Steve?" his voice said. "Where you gone to?" His hand caught my arm, and he set me down beside him.

"Quit that snuffling," he said to me. "This your first time in jail? Is that right? Well, it won't be your last, no, not a miner kid like you. They'll put you here many times before you're done." He paused. "Look at all these folks."

A dim light gleamed through the door grating, and when my eyes adjusted I saw shapes huddled on the floor. They were gathered in knots, feet in each other's stomachs, using the survival techniques JM had taught them.

"They going to let us die?" I asked fearfully; the only times I had seen men curled together like that was when they carried the bodies, two by two, out of breakdowns.

"No, no," he said. "They just like us, just put in here for nothing, to be cold and hungry and heavy for a shift or two, to remind them who's boss on these rocks." He sounded old and tired; and yet when I looked up at him, I saw that he was pulling the parts of his clarinet out of his big old coat and putting them together. He was sitting against the rock wall of the cell, with the mute propped up beside him. When his horn was together he put it to his mouth, gave the reed a lick, commenced to play.

He started soft, barely sounding the notes, and played *Burgundy Street Blues* all the way through without raising his voice. As he played *What Did I Do* some of the huddled figures slowly sat up and listened, backs and heads to the wall, looking up at the ceiling or the yellow squares of the grate.

Then he played the new songs, written by miners' bands and only heard in the bars scattered through their asteroids. He played *Ceres,* and *Hidalgo;* and *Vesta Joys;* he played his *Shaft Bucket Blues* and *I Got Me a Feeling.* Then he played *Don't God Live Out*

This Far, one of the first of the miner blues, which made it about twenty years old; and people began to join in. These were miners, men who seldom sang in the bars, seldom did more than stomp their boots or shout something between phrases; and at first their singing was an awkward sort of growl, barely in tune or time with Sidney. But he picked them up and more joined in, hesitantly, till you could make out the words of the refrain:

> Up at the shift-start,
> Down in the mine shaft,
> Spend my life throwing dirt on a car—
> Ain't got nothing to do
> But sing me the blues—
> Hey, don't God live out this far.

There were about thirty verses to the song. It was about a miner who keeps getting in trouble, till JM decides to finish him: "Super comes at shift-start for me to be hung, on account of something that I hadn't done." The Supervisor believes he's innocent, but there's no proof. It was the same old, old thing.

When the singing got loud enough Sidney took off from the melody and floated up above it. And they sang! There was something in it that seemed to take my lungs away, so I could only breathe quick and shallow; it was what they had of the music inside themselves. Just hearing someone's voice in the dark, and knowing his life has a long way to go . . .

The light from the door just caught the plumes of breath frosting out from the men singing. I looked over at the mute. His eyes were open, staring out somewhere in space. As I watched he lifted up his hands and started a little syncopated clap, very soft, giving as much to the music as he could. When Sidney heard it he looked down at him, then looked back up; he played louder, filling the room with his sound, till the clarinet was all we heard or needed to hear, and the last verse came to its end.

"Oh yeah," said a quiet voice.

Sidney looked at the mute, smiled, shook his head. "A little blues for us, eh, brother?" he said. "A little slave music."

The mute nodded and grinned, which made his lip crack open

again and spill blood down his chin.

Sidney laughed at him and wiped some of the blood from the mute's face. "Oh yeah," he said softly, "a little miner music."

We found Sidney just where Hook guessed he might be, huddled in the room where our baggage and instruments were stored. He was perched up on the box that Crazy's tuba traveled in, with his shoulders hunched and his legs crossed. When we burst into the room he jumped and then settled back, head down, staring sullenly across at us. His clarinet lay fitted in his arms. We all stood still, barred and hidden in the shadows thrown by the single bulb behind us, waiting for somebody to say something. The wisps of hair Sidney combed across his head looked thicker because of the shadows they cast on his bald pate. He looked like one of the tunnel-gnomes men claim to see on Pallas; creatures who were once men maybe, who escaped JM by living in the old shafts. I had never noticed how small he was.

"You scared?" Hook asked.

Sidney raised his head to stare at Hook better. "Yeah, I am," he said suddenly, loud in the dim room, "shouldn't I be?"

"Hey, Sidney." I said, "you don't got no reason to be scared—"

"Don't got no reason!" He pointed at me, clarinet still in hand. "Don't you say that shit to me, Shaky. I got the best reason possible to be scared." He jumped down from the box. "The best reason possible. This is a contest, boy, we ain't playing to please these folks, we playing to show them that we better musicianers than all them others! And if we don't show them that, if we don't win one of them grants, we gone. We back to the mines, boy, and we'll work in those shafts until JM has broke us so we can't work no more, and we'll never get to see the Earth. So don't tell me I got no reason to be scared."

"Come on, Sidney, you can't think like that," I said, searching for something I could say to him. "It ain't so bad as—"

"Sidney," Hook said, like I hadn't been talking at all (suddenly I see a picture in my head, of Sidney crouched down and shifting through a four-foot-high tunnel, Hook straddled senseless across his back, one of his hands clamped white around Hook's wrist, which ended in a tangle of bloody filaments; shouting instructions in a furious fearful high voice to the men trying to get the airlock opened); I stepped back and let Hook talk to him.

"Sidney," he said, "you ain't thought this out. They been putting one over on you. You're talking like this contest is a big vital thing, like we got some chance of going out there and *winning* one of them grants. Sidney, we got *no* chance, don't you realize that?"

"Hook—" I objected.

"No, you listen to me, we *got no chance*. You seen all those other musicianers here—those folks been doing nothing but play music all their *lives*, they playing all those fancy machines and doing things with music we don't even know about! And we just a bunch of miners playing some old Earth-type of music that just showed up a few years back, and only 'cause JM salvaged a ship full of band instruments and give them to us so we'd stay out of fights! And you still think we got a *chance?*"

Sidney and I stared at him.

"No way," he continued grimly, "no more'n there's a chance that JM will retire us at forty and send us to Mars. They got us here just so they can say they got folks from everywhere, even the rocks, and they going to give the grants to those fancy-ass musicianers, not us. So just exactly what you said is going to happen, Sidney, when this thing is over they going to send us back to the rocks to work and work, every third shift, till some equipment catches you or some tunnel collapses"—waving his hooks so they flashed silver in front of us—" and then, if you're still alive, they'll dump you on Vesta rock and wait for you to die.

"And the only way you got to show how you feel about that, Sidney, is through that horn, through that skinny black horn of yours. When you get out there they going to be looking down on you, just like they always have, and all you can do about it is to *play* that thing! play it so hard they *got* to see you! play it and show them what kind of music a man plays when he works all his life digging in those fucking rocks!"

He stopped, gulped in some air. Sidney and I didn't make a sound. Suddenly he turned and walked over to the baggage, rummaged around a bit, then found the trunk he wanted and pulled it around so he could unstrap it and fling it open. He reached in and pulled out a long white bottle, held it high in the dim light while he unscrewed it. He turned it upside down to his mouth and took a long pull.

"Eeeow!" he whooped. He held it out toward Sidney. "So what say we have a drink of the White Brother, brother, and then go play us some music."

I looked at Sidney. I don't think I'd ever seen him indulge in the White Brother; he hardly even drank beer.

"I believe I will," Sidney said, and swallowed near half the bottle.

Back up in our rooms Crazy was leading Fingers and Washboard in the *Emperor Norton Stomp,* running up the walls as high as he could and then diving off onto the unmade and trampled beds. He saw us standing in the doorway and from his position high on the wall he dived straight for us and bounced on the floor.

"Crazy," Hook said cheerfully, "you are crazy." He stepped over him and made his way through the stuff heaped on the floor. He pulled his trombone out of the pile beside his bed.

"Let's roll," he said.

"Wait!" Crazy cried. He poured some White Brother into cups and passed them around. When Sidney took one he didn't say a word, just grinned and pointed. Sidney paid him no attention.

We raised our cups in the air. "To the Hot Six," I said. "Play that thing!" We downed the Brother; I could feel him slide into my stomach and explode there, making my blood pound and my vision jump.

We got our instruments and made our way to the lobby. When we got there we headed for the clerk's desk, bumping together and shushing each other, trying to calm down some while Hook spoke to the clerk.

"We are the Hot Six," Hook shouted at the clerk, who stepped back quickly. "And we playing at the Outer Planets Center for the Performing Arts' W. H. Blakely Memorial Traveling Grant Competition" (we all threw in some "oh yeahs!" for such virtuosity) "and we need your fastest car right now."

"Well sir," the clerk said, "all the cars have the same speed capability."

"Oh come now *come* now," Hook said, "are you telling me that you don't know of a single car that's set to go a mite faster than normal?"

"No sir, none except the cars reserved for emergencies—"

"Emergencies! Why, don't you know that's exactly what this is? An emergency!"

"An emergency," we all echoed, and Crazy began to climb over the desk, muttering in a low voice, "Emergency, emergency."

"If you don't give us one of them emergency cars," Hook continued in a lowered voice, "then we've come over fifteen hundred million miles for no reason at all."

The clerk looked past Hook and saw us staring at him with the intensity that the White Brother can give you; looked at Crazy, who was clawing at the buttons on top of the counter. He shrugged. "One of the special cars will be waiting for you at the departure gate."

"Make it a big one," Hook said, "we got a lot of stuff to carry."

We went to the departure gate and found a sixteen-person car, painted bright red, waiting for us. We threw all the instruments in the back and clambered in; Hook set the controls and fired us out into the Titania Gap.

The Gap is a long, straight canyon whose origins are unknown. It looks like it was carved into Titania some eons back by a good-sized rock (say about the size of Demeter) that nearly missed it. It's about two hundred miles long, four to ten miles wide, and nearly that deep, and almost the entire colony on Titania is set down in the skinny end of it. So when we popped out of the wall of our hotel and shot down our track, we were greeted with the sight of the whole colony, covering the floor and climbing the walls of a canyon that would have swallowed most of the rocks we had lived on. There was only the fine lacing of car tracks looping through space to keep us from dropping two or three miles. Above us the swirling greens of Uranus blocked off most of the sky we could see.

"Shit, this thing *is* fast," Hook said, after the car had taken a long drop and thrown us back in our seats. Crazy whooped and climbed over the seats back to his tuba case, from which he pulled another milky-white bottle. Fingers cheered and started singing, half-tempo like he always starts, *I Don't Know Where I'm Going But I'm On My Way,* and Hook joined him.

"I feel pretty good," Sidney said from his window seat.

I sat back and watched the other cars slide along their strands, listening to the band keep loose. The front line, I thought, would be okay. I had been playing with Hook and Sidney since I was twelve years old—twelve years now—and Hook and Sidney had been playing together longer than that; we were the best front line there was, without a doubt, maybe the best there had ever been. And our back line was almost as good. Washboard never stopped hitting; even now he was clicking out rhythms on the side of the car, metal studs already taped to his fingers. Crazy was unreliable, we'd had to play many times without him because of his wild drinking; he didn't have the virtuoso command of the tuba that old Clarence Miles, our first tuba man, had had before he was paralyzed; but nobody could pump as much air through a tuba as Crazy could, and his mad stomping and blowing was one of the trademarks of the Hot Six. Fingers—he was probably our weakest spot. He's a bit slow to understand things, and he only has eight fingers now; maybe the best thing about his playing is that all eight of those fingers hit the keys a good part of the time. That's the only way a piano man gets heard in a Dixieland band, especially a fine loud one like ours.

Hook slammed us into one of the track intersections without slowing down, and we dropped through it with a sickening jolt. I had visions of the whole band plummeting down the Gap like a puny imitation of the rock that had carved it.

"Goddammit Hook, what's the rush?" I asked. "We're not that late."

"Don't worry," he said. "This is just a fancy ore car here, I got it in hand."

"Yeah, don't worry, Shaky," Crazy chipped in. "Why you worrying? You ain't going to get shaky again, are you Shaky?" They all laughed, Hook hardest of all; he had named me that (because I was so scared when I first played with the band that my tone had a vibrato in it).

"I feel *real* good," said Sidney.

Then we turned a curve and were pointed right at the Performing Arts Center. It stuck up from the canyon floor like one of the natural spires, a huge stack right at the end of the colony, the last structure before the black U of the Gap stretched out, lightless and empty. The car hit the final swoop of track up to it, and scarcely slowed down. Nobody said anything; Fingers stopped singing. As we drew closer, and the side of the building blocked out our view of the Gap, Hook finished the verse:

> And I got no place to go to
> And I got no place to stay
> And I don't know where I'm going
> But I'm on my way.

The waiting room backstage was crowded with a menagerie of about forty brightly dressed performers, all wandering in and out of practice rooms and talking loud, trying to work off tension. As soon as we walked in the door I could feel a heat on my cheeks, on account of all the eyes focusing on us. Everyone was happy to have something to think about besides the upcoming few hours, and as I looked at us all, standing in the doorway gawking, I could see we were good for that. Even in our best clothes (supplied by JM) we looked like exactly what we were: bulky, roughshod, unkempt, maimed, oh, we were miners, clear enough; and under the stares of that rainbow of costumes I suppose we should have quailed. But the energy we got from adrenalin and the White Brother and our wild flight down the Gap gave us a sort of momentum; and when Hook and Crazy looked at each other and burst out laughing, it was them that quailed. Glances turned away from us, and we strode into the room feeling on top of things.

I walked over to a circle of chairs that was empty and sat down. I got my trumpet out of its case and stuck my very shallowest mouthpiece into it; hit 'em high and hard, I thought. The rest of the band was doing the same around me, talking in mutters and laughing every time their eyes met. I looked around and saw that now our fellow performers were trying to watch us without looking. As my gaze swept the room it pushed eyes down and away like magic. When Washboard pulled his washboard out of its box and compulsively rippled his studded fingers down the slats to pop the cowbell, there was an attentive, amazed silence—very undeserved, I thought, considering how strange some of the other instruments in the room appeared—if that was really what they were. I walked over to the piano in a corner of the room, and nearly fell at an unexpected step down. I hit B flat. My C was in tune with it. Hook, Sidney, and Crazy hit a variety of thirds and fifths, intending to sound as haphazard and out of tune as possible. Sidney made a series of small adjustments to his clarinet, but Hook and Crazy laid their brass down, the better to observe the show going on around them. Washboard was already moving around the room, stepping from level to level and politely asking questions about the weird machinery.

"Hey, look at this!" Hook called across to me. He was waving a square of paper. I crossed back to him.

"It's a program," he explained, and began to read out loud, " 'Number Eighteen, the Hot Six Jazz Band, from Jupiter Metals, Pallas—an instrumental group specializing in Dixieland jazz, a twentieth-century style of composition and performance characterized by vigorous improvisation.' Ha! Vigorous improvisation!" He laughed again. "I'll vigorously improvise those—"

"Who's that up there?" Fingers asked, pointing with his good hand at the video screen they had up on one wall. The performer on stage at the moment was a red-robed singer, warbling out some polytonal stuff that many of the people in the room looked like they wanted to hear, judging by the way they stared at Hook. The harmonies and counterpoints the performer was singing with himself were pretty complex, but he had a box surgically implanted in one side of his neck that was clearly helping his vocal cords, so even though he was sliding from Crazy's tuning note up to the A above high C, while holding a C-major chord, I wasn't much impressed.

" 'Number Sixteen,' " Hook read (and my heart sledged in my chest all of a sudden; only two to go), " 'Singer Roderick Flen-Jones, from Rhea, a vocalist utilizing the Sturmond Larynx-Synthesizer in four fugues of his own composition.' "

"Shit," Crazy remarked at a particularly high turn, "he sounds like a dog whistle."

"Pretty lightweight," Washboard agreed.

"Lightweight? Man, he's *featherweight!*" Crazy shouted, and laughed loudly at his own joke; he was feeling pretty good. I noticed we were causing a general exodus from the main waiting room. People were drifting into the practice chambers to get away from us, and there was a growing empty space surrounding our group of chairs. I caught Hook's eye and he seemed to get my meaning. He shrugged a "Fuck them," but he got Crazy to pick up his tuba and go over some turns with him, which calmed things down somewhat.

I sat down beside a guy near our chairs, who was dressed up in one of the simpler costumes in the room, a brown-and-gold robe. He had been watching us with what seemed like friendly interest the whole time we'd been there.

"You look like you're having fun," he said.

"Sure," I agreed. "How about you?"

"I'm a little scared to be enjoying myself fully."

"I know the feeling. What's that?" I asked, pointing to the instrument in his lap.

"Tone-bar," he said, running his fingers over it; without amplification it made only the ghost of a rippling glissando.

"Is that a new thing?" I asked.

"Not this time. Last time it was."

"You've tried this before?"

"Yes," he said. "I won, too."

"You won!" I exclaimed. "You got one of the grants?" He nodded. "So what are you doing back here?"

"That grant only gets you from place to place. It doesn't guarantee you're going to make enough to keep traveling once you're done with it."

"Well, will these folks give a grant twice?"

"They've never done it before," he said, and looked up from his tone-bar to smile lopsidedly at me. "So I've got quite a job today, don't I."

"I guess," I said.

We watched the video for a while. As the singer juggled the three parts of his fugue Tone-bar shook his head. "Amazing, isn't he," he said.

"Oh yeah," I said. "The question is, do you listen to music to be amazed."

He laughed. "I don't know, but the audience thinks so."

"I bet they don't," I said.

This time he didn't laugh. "So did I."

Number Sixteen was leaving the stage and being replaced by Number Seventeen. That meant we wouldn't be on for an hour or so. I wished we were going on sooner; all the excitement I had felt was slowly collecting into a tense knot below my diaphragm. And I could see signs of the same thing happening to the others. Not Crazy, he was still rowdy as ever; he was marching about the room with his tuba, blasting it in the technicians' ears and annoying as many people as possible. But I had seen Fingers wandering toward the piano, undoubtedly planning to join Hook and Crazy in the phrases they were working on; some character wrapped in purple-and-blue sheets sat down just ahead of him and began to play some fast complicated stuff, classical probably, with big dramatic hand-over-hands all up and down the keys. Fingers turned around and sat back down, hands hidden in his lap, and watched the guy play; and when the guy got up Fingers just sat there, looking down at his lap like he hadn't noticed.

And Sidney got quieter and quieter. He stared up at the video and watched a quartet of people fidget around a big box that they all played together, and as he stared he sank into his chair and closed around his clarinet. He was getting scared again. All the excitement and energy the band had generated on the trip over had disappeared, leaving only Washboard's insistent tapping and Crazy's crazy antics, which were gaining us more and more enemies among the other performers.

While I was still wondering what to do about this (because I felt like I was at least as scared as Sidney) Crazy made his way back to our corner of the room, did a quick side shuffle, and slammed into another musician.

"Hey!" Crazy yelled. "Watch it!"

I groaned. The guy he had knocked over was dressed in some material that shifted color when he moved; he had been making loud comments about us from the practice rooms ever since we had arrived. Now he got his footing and carefully lifted his instrument (a long many-keyed brass box that turned one arm back into itself) from the floor.

"You stupid, clumsy, drunken oaf," he said evenly.

"Hey," Crazy said, ignoring the description, "what's that you got there?"

"Ignorant fool," the musician said. "It's a Klein-Ritter synthesizer, an instrument beyond your feeble understanding."

"Oh yeah?" Crazy said. "Sounds a little one-sided to me." He burst out laughing.

"It is unfortunate," the other replied, "that the Blakely Foundation finds it necessary to exhibit even the most *atavistic* forms of music at this circus." He turned and stalked over to the piano.

"Atavistic!" Crazy repeated, looking at us. "What's that mean?"

I shrugged. "It means primitive," said Tone-bar. Hook started to laugh.

"Primitive!" Crazy bellowed. "I'm going to go hit that guy and let him think it over." He turned to follow the musician, tuba still in his arms; and before anyone could move, he missed the step down and crashed to the floor, as loud as fifty cymbals all hit at once.

We leaped over and pulled the tuba off him. It was hardly dented; somehow he had twisted so it fell mostly on him.

"You okay?" Hook said anxiously, pushing back the rest of us. From somewhere in the room there was a laugh.

Crazy didn't move. We stood around him. "God damn it," Hook said, "the bastard is out cold." He looked like he wanted to kick him.

"And look!" Sidney said, lifting Crazy's left arm carefully.

Right behind his hand (his fingering hand) was a bluish lump that stretched his skin tight. "He's hurt that wrist bad," Sidney said. "He's out of it."

"Fuck," Hook said quietly. I sat down beside him, stunned by our bad luck. There was a crowd gathered around us but I didn't pay them any attention. I watched Crazy's wrist swell out to the same width as his hand; that was our whole story, right there. We'd put him on stage in a lot of strange conditions before, but a man can't play without his fingering hand. . . .

"Hey, Wright is here today," Tone-bar said. He was frowning with what looked like real concern. "Doesn't he know some old jazz?" None of us answered him. "No, seriously," he said. "This kid Wright is an absolute genius, he'll probably be able to fill in for you." Still none of us spoke. "Well, I know where his box is," he finally continued. "I'll try to find him." He worked his way through the crowd and hurried out the door.

I sat there, feeling the knot in my stomach become a solid bar, and watched a few of the stagehands lift Crazy up and carry him out. We were beat before we began. You can play Dixieland without a tuba player—we had often had to—but the trombone has to take a lot of the bass line, nobody can be as free with the rhythm, the sound is tinny, there's no power to it, there's no *bottom!* Sidney looked over at Hook and said, with a sort of furtive relief, "Well, you said we didn't have a chance," but Hook just shook his head, eyes glistening, and said quietly, "I wanted to show 'em."

I sat and wondered if I was going to be sick. Crazy had crazied us right back to the rocks, and on top of my knotted stomach my heart pounded loud and slow as if saying "ka-Doom, ka-Doom, ka-DOOM." I thought of all the stories I'd heard of Vesta, the barren graveyard of the asteroids, and hoped I didn't live long enough to be sent there.

There was a long silence. None of us moved. The other performers circled about us quietly, making sure not to look at us. Slowly, very slowly, Sidney began to pull apart his clarinet.

"I got him!" came a wild voice. "He can do it!" Tone-bar came flying in the door, pulling a tall kid by the arm. He halted and the

kid slammed into his back. With a grin Tone-bar stepped aside and waved an arm.

"Perhaps the finest musician of our—" he began, but the kid interrupted him:

"I hear you need a tuba man," he said and stepped forward. He was a few years younger than me even, and the grin on his adolescent face looked like it was clamped over a burst of laughter. When he pushed all his long black tangles of hair back I saw that the pupils of his eyes were flinching wildly just inside the line of the irises; he was clearly spaced, probably had never seen a tuba before.

"Come on, man," I said. "Where did you learn to play Dixieland tuba?"

"Earth," he said. "Played all my life."

I stared at him. I couldn't believe it. As far as I knew, Dixieland was only played in the bars on Jupiter Metals' rocks; I would have bet I knew, or knew of, every Dixieland musician alive. And this kid didn't come from the mines. He was too skinny, too sharp-edged, he didn't have the look.

"I didn't even know anyone played Dixieland anymore," he said. "I thought I was the only one."

"I don't believe it," I said.

"We don't got a whole lot of choice, Shaky, we're running out of time," said Hook. "Hey kid—you know *Panama?*"

"Sure," he said, and sang the opening bars. "Bum-bum, da da da-da, da da-da-da da."

"Son of a bitch," I said.

"I can do it," the kid said. "I *want* to do it."

"All right," Hook said. "Might as well take him." I looked at Hook in suprise and saw that he was grinning again; clearly there was something about the kid, the intensity of those black-hole eyes perhaps, that had him convinced. He slapped the kid on the shoulder and nearly knocked him down. "Come on!" he shouted. "Time to go!"

"Time to go!" I cried. "What the hell happened to Number Seventeen?"

"They getting off! Let's go play!"

And the stagehands were already carrying stuff for us, watching the kid and gabbling excitedly.

"Shit," I exclaimed, and stuck my hand out to the kid. We shook. "Welcome to the Hot Six. Solos all sixteen bars, including yours if you want, choruses and refrains all repeated, don't worry about the tags; we'll have to stick to the old songs, do you know *St. Louis Blues? That's a Plenty? Didn't He Ramble? Milenburg Joys? Mahogany Hall Stomp? Want a Big Butter-and-Egg Man? Ain't You Coming Back to Dixieland?* and, miraculously, he kept yelling "Yes! Yes! Yes!" as he struggled with the tuba, still almost laughing, and then we were in the hall and didn't have time for any more—

We got out on stage and it was hot as a smelting chamber. The audience was just a blue-black blur outside the lights, which were glaring down exactly like the arc lamps set around a tunnel end. I could tell seats went way up above us *(they going to be looking down on you)* and then we were all standing there set to go and a big amplified voice said, *"From Jupiter Metals Pallas, the Hot Six,"* and suddenly we all had our horns to our mouths. I put mine down and said, *"In the Alley Blues,"* which, amplified, sounded like a single word, then put the horn up and commenced playing.

We sounded horrible. They had indirect mikes on all of us, and just playing normal mezzo-forte we were *booming* out into the huge cavern of the auditorium, so we could hear very clearly how bad we sounded. Hook was solid, and so was the kid, which was a relief; but my tone was quivering with just the slightest vibrato, and sometimes I couldn't hear Sidney at all. And his fear was spreading to the rest of us. We knew he had to be petrified to even miss a note.

We brought *In the Alley* to a quick finish, and the applause was *loud.* That made me realize how big the audience was (twenty thousand, Tone-bar said) and I was more scared than ever. I could feel their eyes pressing on me, just like I can sometimes feel the vacuum when I look out a view window. I figured we'd better play one of the best songs next, so we'd get as much help from the material as possible. *"Weary Blues,"* I said, meaning to say it to the band, since we had planned to play *Ganymede*. But the mikes picked me up anyway and I heard *"Weary Blues"* bounce back out of the cavern, so I just raised my horn to my lips and started; and it was probably two bars before everyone caught on and joined in. That didn't help any.

And I myself was having trouble. The more I could hear the vibrato wavering down the middle of my tone, the worse it got, and the more I could hear it . . . it began to sound like an oscilloscopic saw, and I hoped it wouldn't get out of control and break the tone completely. We got to the refrain, where *Weary* usually starts rolling. I could tell that everyone was so scared they couldn't think about what they were playing, so the notes were coming out right by instinct, but there was no feel in them, it was like they were being played by a music box, every note made by a piece of metal springing loose.

Weary Blues ended and again the applause was triple-forte. I stepped over to Hook and shouted, under my breath, "Let's do *I Guess I'll Have to Change My Plans."* He couldn't hear me, so I said it louder and the mikes caught me, *"I Guess I'll Have to Change My Plans,"* I announced. There was a long flurry of laughter from the audience. Hook started the intro to *Plans*, as calm as though he were playing to a crowded bar. We slid into the song and I realized how much easier it is to play fast when you're nervous. Hook was doing fine, but his back-up was trembling, barely hitting the chords. With the leisure of playing accompaniment I could look up and see the silver line of boxes that held our judges, hanging high above us; and that didn't help either.

We moved quickly into *That's a Plenty,* and I could tell we'd calmed down enough to think about the music; after your body pumps full of adrenalin, soaks you in sweat, and shakes you like the ague, there's not much more it can do, you've *got* to calm down some; but that maybe wasn't helping us, since now we had to make the music ourselves, rather than leave it to instinct. I was still shaky enough that when I got to the triple-tonguing in the trumpet break, it actually seemed slow to me, and next time around I fitted in another note, hammering them with two double-tongues. This seemed to perk up the band ("Put chills down my spine," the kid said later), but we still sounded ragged; I knew if we continued like this we were in trouble. And Sidney was still *missing phrases*. I don't think I'd ever heard him miss more than a note or two in my whole life, and here he was squeaking through bars at a time, playing like he had a crimp in his throat.

When we finished the kid waved me over to him. He raised a hand in the air and lowered it, which was apparently the signal needed to get the mike men off us. The kid was completely relaxed. He looked like he was having a good time.

"Your clarinet player is dying," he said. "Does he know *Burgundy Street Blues?*"

"Sure," I said.

"Maybe you should have him play that. If he had to play a song by himself he'd be sure to calm down some."

I turned around. "Sidney, you ready to play *Burgundy Street?*" He shook his head vehemently.

"Come on, Sidney," Hook said from beside him. "That's your song." He turned to the audience, and the kid quickly lifted a hand. *"The Burgundy Street Blues,"* Hook announced.

Now *Burgundy Street*, like *Just a Closer Walk with Thee* or *Bucket's Got a Hole in It*, is a single-strain tune, just an eight-bar melody; and it's the variations that a clarinet player works in as he repeats it, again and again, that make the song something special. The first couple of times Sidney went through it, I could barely hear him. He was playing the melody, as simple as possible, and the sound he was making was more breath than tone. I didn't think he'd finish. He shifted toward us as if he wanted to turn his back on the audience, but Hook threw in a couple bars of harmony to bolster him, and when he started the strain a third time he took hold of himself and bore down; and that time, though the notes quivered and never got over pianissimo, he could be heard.

The kid was hopping up and down beside me as if he couldn't wait to start playing again. "Damn that man plays fine clarinet," he whispered to me. Suddenly I realized that if you didn't know Sidney you might think he was playing warbly on purpose, in which case it sounded all right. Apparently this occurred to Sidney too. Each time around he played a little louder, tried a few more variations, gathered a little more confidence. The fifth time around he usually played a variation filled with chromatic runs; he went ahead and tried them, and they came out sharp and well articulated. Amplified like he was he could hear as clearly as anyone how good he sounded—he was learning what I'd already discovered, that even though you're scared, the notes come out. He began to take advantage of the new acoustics, building up till he filled the auditorium with sound, then dropping back so fast the mike men were lost, and he was as silent as piano keys pushed down.

And as he went on, I could see him begin to forget his surroundings and become what he was, a musician working on the song, putting together phrases, playing with the sounds he could make. His forehead wrinkled and smoothed as he carved an especially difficult passage; he closed his eyes, and the notes took on a life that hadn't been there before. He was lost in it now, completely lost in it, and the last time around he bent the notes like only a fine clarinet player can bend them, soaring them out into the cavern; a sound human and inhuman, music.

When he was done everyone was clapping, even me, and I realized that I had only thought the earlier applause was loud because I'd never heard that many people clap at once before. Now it was louder than when a ship takes off over a tunnel you're in. . . .

We played *Panama* next, and the difference was hard to believe. Sidney was back in form, winding about the upper registers with quick-fingered ingenuity, and as he pulled together so did the band. And the kid, as if he'd only been waiting for Sidney, began to let loose. He'd abandoned his steady *oomph-oomph-oomph-oomph* and was sliding up and down the bass clef, playing like a fourth member of the front line, and *leading* the tempo. Normally I set the tempo, and Crazy and Washboard listen to me and pick it up. But the kid wasn't paying any attention to me, his notes were hitting just a touch ahead of mine, and if there's anyone who can take the tempo away from the trumpet it's the tuba. I tried to play as fast as him but he kept ahead; by the time he let Washboard and me catch up with him we were playing *Panama* faster than we'd *ever* played it, and excited as we were, we were equal to it.

When we finished the applause seemed to push us to the back of the stage.

We played the *St. Louis Blues,* and then the *Milenburg Joys,* and the *Sweet Georgia Brown,* and each time the kid took over, pumping wildly away at the tuba, and pushed us to our limit. Sidney responded like that was the way he'd always wanted to play, arching high wails between phrases and helping the kid to drive us on. And the audience was with us! Maybe the earlier groups had been too modern, maybe too many of them had been playing to the judges; whatever the reason, the audience was with us now. An hour ago none of them had even heard of Dixieland, and now they were cheering after the solos and clapping in the choruses; and we had to start *Sweet Georgia Brown* by playing through the applause.

Then we were set for the finale. *"For all of you music lovers in the house,"* I said, knowing they wouldn't get the reference to Satchmo but saying it anyway, *"we going to do The Muskrat Ramble."*

The Muskrat Ramble. Our best song, maybe *the* best song. We started up the *Ramble* and the band fell together and meshed like parts of a beautiful machine. All those years of playing in those bars: all the years of getting off work and going down and playing tired, playing with nobody listening but us, playing with nothing to keep us going but the music; all that came from inside us now, in a magic combination of fear, and anger, and wild exhilaration of knowing we were the best there was at what we were doing. Hook was looping his part below me, Sidney leaping about above, the kid pushing us every note; and to keep us with the weave we were making I had to play hard and fast right down the middle of the song, lifting and growling and breaking my notes off, showing them all that there was a man *working* behind that horn, blowing as clear and sharp and excited as old Dippermouth Satchel-mouth Satchmo Louie Louis Armstrong himself. When we played the final round of the refrain everyone played their solo at once, only Fingers and Washboard held us down at all, and the old *Muskrat Ramble* lifted up and played itself, carrying us along as if it made us and not the other way around. Hook played the trombone coda and we tagged it; then the kid surprised us and repeated the coda, and we barely got our horns back up to tag it again; then we all played the coda and popped it solid, the end.

I motioned the band off. We were done; there was no way we could top that. We started for the wings and the roar of the audience soared up to a gooseflesh howl. We hurried off, waving our arms and shouting as loud as anyone there, jumping up and down and slapping each other on the back, chased by a wall of sound that shook the building.

We waited; tired, happy, tense, we waited:

And God damn me if we didn't win one of those grants, a four-year tour of the Solar System; oh, we leaped about that waiting room and shouted and hit each other, Fingers and Washboard marched about singing and smashing out rhythms on the walls and furniture, Hook stood on a table and sprayed champagne on us; the kid rolled on the floor and laughed and laughed, "Now you're in for it," he choked out, "you're in for it now!" but we didn't know what he meant then, we just poured champagne on his head and laughed at him, even old Sidney was jumping up and down, wisps of hair flying over his ears, singing (I'd never heard him sing) a scat solo he was making up as he went along, shouting it out while tears and champagne ran down his face:

> *bo bo de zed,*
> *we leaving the tunnels!*
> *woppity bip,*
> *we going to see Earth!*
> *yes we (la da de dip)*
> *going (ze be de be dop)*
> *home!*

A MODULAR STORY

In the hothouse warmth and intimacy of the closed car, she was almost naked beside him under the sheepskin coat. And she was his wife, and her name was Jenny . . . or was it Nancy?

Raylyn Moore

(a)

In the suburban dawn, fleece-lined with the soft first snow of autumn, she drove him to the station, arriving with a few minutes to spare before train time. The heater was full on in the car and in the blood-warmth he kissed her, not hurrying. He said, "Goodbye, darling. Don't forget to phone up for an appointment to have that clutch fixed. I felt it slipping when we were driving home from the Jensons' party last night."

"Bensons'," she corrected him. "Their name is Benson and they're our best friends. I'll get the appointment for later in the week. I have to pick Kimmie up after ballet today, and I'm carpool mother for the co-op nursery tomorrow."

"Just don't let it go too long. I don't want you and the kids riding around in a car with a dangerous mechanical defect. We should have traded the Rover in this fall, I suppose, gone to Jim Hastings at Overseas Motors and looked at the new ones he has on his floor."

"The foreign car dealer's name is Henry Salter, dear, and his place is called Salter's Imports. Not that it matters."

"No. Not any more."

"You think then that today's the day?"

"Bound to be. We're winding down. Would you like me to phone you, though, when the time comes?"

"Better not. It only makes the adjustment—more difficult. Instead I'll wish you luck now."

"Thanks. I'll need a lot of it to do as well as this time."

"Thank *you*," she said, smiling at him.

He luxuriated for a moment in the benign radiation of that smile, then flicked a nervous glance at the car clock and reluctantly cracked the door. A thrust of bleak morning air split their tiny, private atmosphere and he quickly pulled the door to again, but without letting it click shut. He looked at her with a fine-drawn intensity, as if to fix on the retina of his mind's eye the shape of her oval face still slightly ablush with recent sleep, the sight of the almost-gold filaments of fine hair spilling out of her hasty french knot.

Behind the wheel she moved restlessly. "Don't," she said. "It doesn't help."

But he persisted, riveted, in examining her, as if he could see beneath the sheepskin greatcoat he'd got her for her twenty-seventh birthday (or had it been her twenty-eighth?) the night-gown he knew for a fact was the only other garment she wore, an abridged tricot tunic pale and thin as light from a distant star. For a perilously balanced moment he felt himself cauterized by the deadly notion that he might insert a hand under the sheepskin and lose the world.

But of course the moment passed, and instead he said, "Jenny, you've been wonderful. I mean it. It's been great." He took up his briefcase from the floor.

She nodded, this time not taking his words as a personal compliment so much as a statement of mutual opinion. "A great three months," she agreed. Then she added softly, "My name is Nancy."

"I'm so very sorry that happened. It was beastly clumsy of me."

"It's all right. I shouldn't have mentioned it."

But he was really off balance now, and altogether too impulsively he added, "I guess you know that statistically there're considerably more than thirty-thousand-to-one odds we'll ever—that is, the company is strictly against reassignments in the same—"

"I know," she said.

He opened the door all the way, put a single shoe sole into the light dusting of snow over frozen asphalt. And once more hesitated. "I forgot to tell you: all the stuff I've been collecting as chairman of the school board is in the green looseleaf notebook in the den—all the figures on the new tax override proposal, annual budgets for five years back, meeting notes, everything."

"All right."

"Kiss the children for me."

"Hurry," she said. "The train's coming."

(b)

His name was Ken Vanselous and he was a project coordinator. A Wharton graduate, thirty-four years old, he had worked in Cleveland, Chicago, New York, St. Louis, Livermore, Pittsburgh, New York again, Fort Lauderdale, Boston, Atlanta, Los Angeles, Phoenix, Pittsburgh again, Palo Alto, Chicago again, New York again, and some other places. So in the ten-year course of his career he had moved steadily, not so much upward (he was already up, trusted by his firm, accepted by his colleagues) as laterally, with a steady driving force, as relentlessly as live water through stratified rock. (If a man's career can be compared to a phenomenon of physical nature without an element of dehumanization creeping in somehow.)

In his spare time Van had been a scoutmaster, Y swimming

instructor, PTA president, an alderman, Episcopal vestryman, a Little League daddy, baritone in the choir, Heart Fund volunteer, blood donor, and a member of the museum board, Madrigal Society, Citizens Concerned about Ecology, Save the Redwoods League, Movement to Preserve New England's Indigenous Fauna, the Bitterbush Valley Racquet Club, Dirty Devils Volleyball Squad, Ravenwood Drive Joggers, Sadsack Rockhounds, Royal Bengali Cycling Society (Colonial Branch), and some other things.

(c)

Or he was Bryan Mello, thirty-six, senior systems analyst, who had worked in Minneapolis, Rochester, Van Nuys, Port Arthur, Murfreesboro, Washington, D. C., Providence, San Diego, New York, Indianapolis, Toledo, New York again, Washington again, and some other places. And had been a town councilman, cubmaster, flautist in the amateur symphony, blood donor, chairman of the church board (Unitarian), and member of the Concerned Citizens for Democratic Action, National Geographic Society, New Old Red Barn Players, Sierra Club, Peachtree Numismatists, Dartmouth Alumni Association, Stanford Alumni Association, Rotten Gulch Chess Club . . .

(d)

Or he had perhaps still another name, other credentials. Ron Graff, statistician; or Merrill Kost, economist; or Mark Esprit, psychologist; or Moe Ibmore, computer programmer; or Wendell Farraday, electronics engineer; or John Slick, technical writer.

(e)

The train sped. Utility poles clicked off frames in the every-morning newsreel. Snowed-over meadow. Snowed-in woods, trees tottery with sliding white. Highway heavy-equipment yard, the driveway a hatch of muddy ruts. Then a set-back Victorian monstrosity, Eastlake influence. A ditto, Queen Anne influence. A ditto-ditto in stockbroker's Tudor. Then a smaller house of no identifiable architectural influence at all. Another. Another. Another. Then a frankly tract house. And another-another-another. Murky breath of the city. Industrial fringe. Congested heart. Lurching stop.

(f)

Hebe, his secretary, came into the office bearing a plastic cup.

Her name wasn't Hebe, of course, but there was obviously no way to avoid thinking of her that way, and after a decade more or less he had given up trying.

She was reed-lithe and dark, bronze-haired and enticingly freckled, ash-blonde with a surprising olive skin and brown eyes, black-tressed with brows like strokes of a new felt pen and well-distributed flesh running slightly to overweight in a way that was curiously provocative.

But not having looked up—he was busy with the eleventh-hour paperwork—he saw only the vaporous container of coffee being slid into position in front of him. "Thanks."

"Welcome. And happy moving day. It's been good working for you. If you ever need a recommendation as a real-boss boss, let me know."

"Easy. Flattery goes straight to my head and I have to keep at least a couple brain cells clear to close out the project here and find my way to the airport. I appreciate the charming encomium, though. Same to you. What time does my plane leave, anyway?"

"Noon. But I can get a later reservation if you like."

"No, I think I can make it. But maybe I ought to call home and say what time I'll be there."

Obediently she disappeared, and in a moment returned to report that the line to his home was busy. Did he want her to keep trying?

"Never mind. I'll call from the airport. That is, I will if you can give me the phone number. I know it's somewhere in the new assignment sheets, but it's awkward to keep opening my briefcase to find out where I'm going."

She laughed and handed him a memo slip with his home telephone number and an address. He put the paper carefully away in his wallet.

He finished the work on his desk as one by one, or sometimes by twos or threes, the men and women he had worked with on the project dropped into his office on their way out.

Goodbye. Goodbye. Here's luck. See you. See you. See you in Denver next spring. Tucson in February. Detroit if I can make it. Sometime, somewhere. Take care. Take care.

(g)

Despite a nap on the plane, or perhaps because of it, he was yawning-tired when the DC-10 touched down on a sprawling cushion of heat-filled midafternoon smog. Home again, he thought, but not quite. At the beginning of the flight, he'd been as unsuccessful with the phone call as his secretary had been earlier in the day. He hoped nothing was wrong. None of the children were sick. No one had been in an accident.

For in the end he was strictly a family man: dedicated father, generous provider. He cared about them. Human relationships were what it was all about.

But the failure of the call meant he wouldn't be met at the

airport, a niggling inconvenience. He'd have to try the house again, say he was coming by taxi. That was only fair, to announce himself. A man going home after a day's work.

He stepped out of the plane into a hot wind blowing across the runway, descended the steps and started toward the terminal, a glass-and-steel enclosure fringed by a narrow landscaped strip growing a few breeze-whipped palmettoes, fuchsia, and cotoneaster. Only the cotoneaster was at its seasonal best, its fat clusters of berries smoldering richly in the muted sunlight.

"Here I am, darling," she said. "Surprise."

"Hey! Surprise is right. How did you know what plane to meet? I wasn't expecting you." Her cheek tasted cool and fragrant in the surrounding heat.

"I called your office. Your secretary had been trying to get me too. Good thinking on your part to have your ribbon on."

He cast a half glance at his own lapel where a discreetly narrow scrap of scarlet ribbon crawled, like a *légion d'honneur* badge. Except that he was no *légionnaire*. Nor had he put the ribbon there himself. He hadn't remembered. It must have been done at home last night, or early this morning, before he'd caught the train. The ribbon exactly matched one pinned to the sleeveless knit blouse worn by the woman now walking at his side. The presence of the ribbon made them, in fact, a couple, two people wholeheartedly committed to each other. Which they were, of course; they must be. That was what life was all about.

As they hurried through the crowd in the waiting room, she slightly in the lead now, because she would take him to where she'd parked the car, he looked at her. She was as tall as he, athletic-looking, sunbrowned, yet intrinsically feminine. Angular but quite beautiful face, he noted as she turned back to tell him: "Before I forget, you have a meeting tonight. You're chairman of the county planning commission and there's a red-hot problem about whether to approve the building of a half-acre condominium at the sacrifice of that much greenbelt."

He groaned and said truthfully, "I'd rather stay home with you. Sometimes I think I'm into too much volunteer work."

Then they were in the parking lot and she was unlocking a new

Chrysler station wagon with a beach ball and some sand pails and things tumbling around in the back.

As they hummed through city traffic and then speedily out a parkway, between two lines of royal palms like ushers at a military wedding, he continued to watch her as much as he politely could, without seeming to stare. Her long, careful hands lay lightly upon the wheel of the Chrysler. He could not see her eyes but seemed to recall that when she had removed her sunglasses in the terminal the irises had been gray. A light gray or perhaps very pale green, ringed with deep turquoise. Prominent bones at cheek, shoulder, wrist and hip. With the gray-blue knit top she wore elegantly tailored trousers of a darker blue, and white sandals.

He mentally reran the information culled hastily that morning from the new assignment sheets and thought: Dinah. I must remember. Dinah. Dinah. Dinah.

As if he'd spoken her name aloud, Dinah turned to him and smiled.

(h)

The apartment seemed small to him, too small, though it was ground-floor, and though it had three bedrooms—one for them, one for the children, and a third done over by the decorator as a study—as well as a large lanai with a barbecue arrangement and outdoor furniture around a small swimming pool. The pool, however, was shared with the apartment across the central court.

"I'm not mad for it either," Dinah admitted. "It's just what we happened to find during a time when housing was scarce around here. But that situation has loosened a little since, or so I've heard."

"Then maybe we could look for a place farther out in the hills. A house, ranch even. Better for the children."

"Do you think we can afford it? After this month's support payments to the pediatrician and the orthodontist, I mean?"

"Don't worry about that. I had a raise just last quarter."

"Lovely. Then we could start investigating this weekend, if you aren't too snowed with work. There's a party at the Petersons', but Sunday's free all day. If we *should* land a country place Kimmie'll be thrilled. She'll start planning for a horse right off."

"Kimmie? Her name is Kimmie? That's funny, I—"

But Dinah hadn't heard him. She'd gone back to the kitchen to make him a drink. Which was fortunate. This was the second time in a day he'd flipped a little. Once in the car this morning. And now. Third, if he counted forgetting all about the ribbon. Maybe things were beginning to get to him. He hoped not. That would mean the beginning of the end for him, in every way. He would be let go in favor of a newcomer with a better set of nerves. Reject in a throwaway society, canceled cell in a kinetic universe.

(Who was the true father of interchangeable parts, anyway? Eli Whitney? Samuel Colt? Henry Ford?)

He wondered idly, but not for the first time, what the women did. There had been women on every one of the projects so far. Women engineers. Women physicists. Did they go home in the evenings too? (Personal lives were not discussable, naturally.)

He remembered that when he was younger, just out of job training so there was utterly no excuse, he'd had an overwhelming, almost irresistible impulse to write a note—a love letter it would have turned out—to Ann. (Or had her name been Cathy? Yes, he believed it was Cathy.) More, he had gone so far as to wonder if she had ever wanted to write to him, to affirm the reality of what necessarily for them had to remain an illusion. Fortunately for him the sickness had passed without crisis. Not that the problem was so unusual, evidently; it was at least common enough for Personnel to have a coinage for it, the Lot's Wife Syndrome. For the firm had no choice but to deal harshly with those who turned back. Sentimentality was grossly uneconomical. (To err is human; to forgive is not company policy.)

He rubbed his eyes now with the heels of both hands, trying conscientiously to expunge all that had been in his thoughts before this moment of the living present, to make his mind a blank, an empty receptacle for all that would now come.

Then he sighed and leaned back in the chair on the lanai, watching the reddening sun begin to tip toward the horizon of indigo mountains. It was still hot, but with a promise of late-afternoon chill.

It would be hot again when he went to work tomorrow. But he would have thinner suits in his closet than the one he presently wore.

It occurred to him that he didn't know when the children were due home or even where they were.

Dinah brought him a glass, satisfyingly cold and squat, Scotch on the rocks, the way he preferred it, and he watched her settle with seeming content into the chair opposite. Yes, her eyes were gray, luminous. She had changed into shorts and a halter. Her feet were bare. He wondered how much time they would have alone together, before the kids came in from wherever they were.

On the other hand, he didn't want to rush things, make her uncomfortable. They'd have a lot of time together. Seven weeks that he knew of for sure. That was how long the project was scheduled to run. And then it might be extended, depending on how things went.

He let his eyes drift shut, which was his fourth mistake, for the images of the day just past began coming back at him like a card pack in a fast shuffle. In self-defense he rose suddenly from the chair, setting down his drink so abruptly that icy liquid sloshed over his knuckles. "Oops. Sorry. I—"

"You're nervous," she said with a concern undeniably genuine. "You've been working too hard lately. Better lie down for an hour before the meeting tonight. There'll be time."

(How loyal was she to the company herself? Would this incident be reported? But no, he was far off base even to have such a thought.)

"No, really," he said. "I'm all right. I'm fine."

And searched his mind for blessings he could count to reassure himself. Of course he stumbled over one right away: at least ennui was not a problem.

(i)

The morning's snowfall had by noon been translated into a seething slush over the roads, and then frozen at nightfall so that she had to drive to the station very slowly, favoring the ailing clutch.

In the back seat the children, bundled to the eyes, were sullen with hunger and the pent energies of indoor confinement, so she felt less guilty than glad when she found that the train had already come and he was there, waiting in the parking lot.

She stopped the Rover and opened the door.

"Welcome home, darling," she said.

THE M&M, SEEN AS A LOW-YIELD THERMONUCLEAR DEVICE

Making someone good is just a matter of operant conditioning—
and if that doesn't work, there's always Lobey the Needle.

John Varley

1. B. T. THE SKINNER

B.T. the skinner is coming to the ward. B.T. is no ordinary skinner; he's the Big Gingerbread Man, the All-day Sucker. Just look,
look at how all the other skinners get out of his way.

His face is round, a perfect compass tracery. Yellow he is, with
a smiling countenance. You've seen it. Two little raisins for eyes
and an upturned mouth with a sketched dimple at each end, and
a . . . nose . . . it *has* to be a nose, it's right there in the middle
of his face, isn't it, but it looks like nothing so much as a Phillips-
head *screw*.

You know why that is. It's so he can turn his face around. Watch
him, when the behaviors get undesirable. He'll put his hands to
his face and rotate it magically and he is . . . pensive? thoughtful?
worried? His little antsy eyes are now low on his face, his crescent
mouth now a wrinkle on his brow. It's hard to make out, but it's

worrisome. You'd never get the impression that he was actually *pleased,* but it's hard to tell what it means. Bad behavior.

He crunches and crackles as he walks. The pockets of his white lab coat are bulging out from the goodies he has brought for the boys and girls whose behaviors have been so desirable all week long. Jelly babies and jujubes, chocolate raisins and malted milk balls and kisses, and sweet-tart lemon drops, orange candy corn, caramel popcorn crackerjacks and chewy delights with nougat centers and dripping maraschino cherries. Crunchies and gooshies and scraped-coconut snowballs. Taffy, butterscotch hard candy wrapped in yellow twists of cellophane sticky and crinkly. M&Ms like red and green and yellow and brown hand grenades that melt in your mind, not in your hand, and candy-cane tactical peppermint nukes, and golf-ball jawbreakers rated at fifty megatons. Zowie! Here comes B.T. the skinner!

In his penguin coat beneath the lab smock there are rolled and tattered pulp comics. He shakes his sleeve and pigeons flutter out. They scamper jerkily around the floor, eying the happy children, until they fall under the influence of B.T. They begin to execute perfect school-figure 8s for the morsels of grain he offers them.

The children are delighted.

We are at the National Behavioral Institute for the Study of Non-Smiling Syndrome in Pre-Delinquent Children, Number 3490, Hershey, Pennsylvania. B.T. the skinner is making his weekly rounds.

2. PROBLEM #1: CRIES

DATE: 8/4
PROBLEM NUMBER: 1/1/1
TARGET: Tantrums.
OBJECTIVES: To decrease crying behavior from one hour per day to fifteen minutes per day by 9/4.
PLAN: Client will be ignored when crying behavior occurs. The moment crying behavior shuts off, behavior will be reinforced by

praise, M&Ms, and physical attention. Flow sheets will be completed daily.

RESULT: by 9/4, crying behavior had extinguished. Flow sheets attached.

DATE: 9/4.
PROBLEM NUMBER: 2/1/1
TARGET: Speaking out of turn.
OBJECTIVES: Resident will decrease speaking-out-of-turn behavior in hyperactive clients. Starting from an observed base number counted on 9/4, residents will decrease frequency of speaking-out-of-turn behavior by 50% by 9/11.
PLAN: Client will be ignored . . .

3. ACCENT THE POSITIVE
IGNORE THE NEGATIVE

Murray the skinner enters Ward 47*b* of the East Wing of the Institute. In another part of the building B.T. is cavorting and spreading happiness and tooth decay like nitrous oxide. He will not arrive in this part of the building for several hours yet.

"Hey, kids, guess who's going to be here today?" Murray yells.

Twenty-five scrubbed hands go into the air, flutter over twenty-five scrubbed and smiling faces split wide to flash thousands of properly scrubbed teeth. *Call on me, Murray, call on me.* But no one speaks out of turn.

"Billy, who's coming?"

"B.T. the skinner's coming!" Billy yells, and stands in smiling, trembling anticipation, wondering if he's overstepped the bounds of good behavior. Murray has never yelled at them like this before. Was he supposed to yell back? His salivary glands open and close uncertainly.

Oh, wonderful. He's reaching into his baggy pocket and coming out with the M&M, which he pops into Billy's mouth.

"Good boy, Billy. We love you." Murray pats the child on the head, thinking what a good client he is. Not like Terrible Theresa.

He gets a twinge in the facial muscles when he thinks of her. There she is, sullen, perpetually confused, picking her nose and trying to hide it.

Ignore it.

He goes down the line of desks, smiling at each client.

"Let's see that *smile,* Beatrice. Let's see that *smile,* Jeremy. Let's see that *smile,* Christopher." The faces split even wider, and open to accept the M&Ms. Down the line, down the line, at last coming to number twenty-six, the class dingdong, the girl with the permanent dunce cap, Terrible Theresa.

Quit *squirming,* Theresa. Can't you sit still? What's the matter with you? Are you going to start that crying behavior again? Oh, no, Theresa, don't do it, don't, that's it, bite down on that snotty lip, don't snuffle like that, you sound like a pig, what's a pretty girl like you doing with an expression like that, it's almost a frown —excuse me—and here he comes, here he comes, oh *darn* he's passed me up again . . . what did I do . . .

Oh god, how I *do* love that chocolate.

Ignore it. She just wants the attention.

Theresa's bad behavior is now causing water to leak from her eyes. *What a device.* So simple, yet so effective. Fight it, fight it, ignore that tightening in your facial muscles, Murray, and turn her chair to the wall. That's better.

Hello, wall. There you are again. Not quite as dirty as you were yesterday. They've cleaned off the heart-shaped brown mark. Too bad, not much to look at. Just shifting shadows of the people behind her back, having fun.

Theresa puts her thumb in her mouth to stifle the gasping sobs she feels inside; remembers, takes it out and wipes it on her dress. A hand comes around her and pops an M&M into her mouth.

I remembered, I remembered. Oh, I *love* that chocolate.

4. Ingredients

Sugar, chocolate, corn starch and syrup, cocoa butter, peanuts, emulsifier, salt, dextrin, artificial colors, artificial flavors, deuterium oxide. Fissionable core contains enriched uranium and plutonium with a hard candy coating. Net wt., .03 oz.

5. DIRECTIONS

Light fuse, place in client's mouth, get away.

6. TIME-OUT

From *Basic Behavior Mod: Semester One,* Episode Five, "The Skinner versus the Non-Smiling Syndrome," published by the Pennsylvania Institute for the Pre-Delinquent Child. Pulp, three-color process, third printing, 45 pages. Approved by the Comics Committee.

Panel 1: Angry Agnes is up to her old tricks. She is exhibiting undesirable behavior.

ANGRY AGNES: Boo-hoo! Boo-hoo! Boo-hoo!
SKINNER: Darn it! There goes Angry Agnes again! When will she learn to be a happy citizen? I'm going to isolate her and "time-out"* this crying behavior without delay!

---

*Crimestopper's Notebook:
Time-out: Removing the client from the opportunity to get Positive Reinforcement.

Panel 2: The Skinner, Angry Agnes, and Happy Harry. The Skinner talks only to Harry, ignores Agnes.

Skinner: What a good boy you are being, Happy Harry! Look at your big smile! What a good, happy citizen Harry is. Look, everybody, look at how happy Happy Harry is. Here, Harry, have an M&M.

(Lookit #1: Reinforce behavior you want.)

Happy Harry: I love M&Ms.

Angry Agnes: Boo-hoo! Boo-hoo! (This is no fun at all. Always before when I cried they reinforced my behavior. What am I doing wrong?)

Panel 3: Same cast. Agnes has extinguished her undesirable behavior.

Skinner: (She has extinguished her bad behavior! I must reward her without delay. I must reinforce her noncrying behavior.) Now, that's a good citizen, Agnes. Let's do that all the time, shall we? You know we all love you. All the skinners love you. Here's an M&M.
   Agnes: I love M&Ms. I'm a good girl. Good girls get M&Ms.
   Harry: Boo-hoo! Boo-hoo! Boo-hoo!
   Skinner: (Oh, darn it! But I must not turn to him. I must not reward him.)

(Lookit #2: Ignore behavior you do not want.)

Time-out:
Remove the client from the opportunity to get positive reinforcement of bad behavior.
   Client:
The clients are defined to be pre-delinquent children.
   Pre-delinquent:
A child likely to become a delinquent. Most broadly, a child before he or she has committed any act which would be classified as delinquent. Or, a child before he or she has yet had time to think of delinquent acts to commit, before having had bad behavior reinforced. A child in an uncontrolled environment is well known to be capable of extreme delinquency; therefore all uncontrolled children are pre-delinquent.

Time-out:
The skinners come once a week to round up the pre-delinquent children. The doctors and nurses love them, with their merry yellow masks and their hearty handshakes for one and all.

Smile at them, and by George they'll pop a sweet right into your mouth. Sort of takes you back, doesn't it, the mouth-watering tang of a lemon drop from the skinner's own hands. Of course we're beyond all that now, of course. We're adults now, and we know how to behave, and we don't need the little bribes for being good. We're mature.

Still, it does make you feel good, you know? Makes you want to smile.

Grinning, the skinners troop along the quiet white corridors of the hospital with the grinning doctors and nurses. Down to the pink and blue sour-sweet smells of the maternity ward where the tiny children are with their mothers. Sucking on the candy nipples, tasting the last drop of milk they will ever get.

Some of the mommies shed a tear. The skinners—smiling, smiling—turn their funny faces around until the mommies are laughing at the antics, then pop them an M&M. All smiles from ear to ear, the mommies hand over the little bundles, which are put in glass boxes.

The babies struggle a bit. The skinners hold them to see if they'll cry. If they do, pop they go into the boxes. The boxes are soundproof, so the mommies won't be disturbed.

On this long-ago day there is a problem mommy. She went to a public school. She was only rounded up and discovered to be pre-delinquent at the age of fifteen. She *loves* M&Ms, but she loves her baby, too. It's a real problem. Poor mommy. She cries, and all the capering of the skinners cannot console her. She wants to stop crying in order to have an M&M, but she can't.

So Terrible Theresa is pulled from a pink-cloud lazy dream and the nipple, and the warm muzzly nipple, it's gone! She howls at once.

And poor dumb confused mommy, she howls back. Theresa's bad behavior is reinforced something awful. She doesn't know what's going on, but *mommy's crying!*

She is popped into the box without an M&M, hungry and cross.

She howls for the longest time.

She is going to be a problem.

7. More Problems

DATE: 9/12

PROBLEM NUMBER: 13/3/2

TARGET: Leftism

OBJECTIVES: Observe clients in the six-month-to-one-year age group. Select those with a tendency to favor the left hand. Resident will decrease left-orientation to zero by 9/14.

PLAN: Client will be allowed to pick up objects at random, all placed on client's right side. When client picks up the object with right hand, behavior will be reinforced with praise, M&Ms, and cuddling. When client picks up object with left hand, no reward will be forthcoming.

DATE: 5/27

PROBLEM NUMBER: 42/5/1

TARGET: Homosexual Tendencies

OBJECTIVES: Resident will select clients with observed pre-homosexual behavior, such as: (male) non-participation in athletic activities, crying behavior, interest in girls' toys such as dolls, interest in reading or music, tenderness; (girls) aggression, poor appearance, squirming, assertiveness, friendliness to other girls, lack of interest for boys.

Plan: Client will be ignored when . . .

. . . hyperactivity, disruptiveness, nose-picking, thumb-sucking, laziness, inattentiveness, obscenity, disrespect, negativism, non-participation, solitarism, antisociality, excessive precociousness, "brown-nosing," frowning behavior, showing-off, smart-assing, contradiction of the resident, anti-Americanism, disrespect for authority, hooliganism, antimilitarism, excessive originality, inventiveness, anti-Institutionality, curiosity, Non-Smiling Syndrome . . .

8. Time-Out Is Client-Controlled

Waves of sympathetic excitement are shuddering down the ether, tingling and charging the atmosphere of Ward 47*b*, East Wing, National Behavioral Institute 3490, Hershey, Pennsylvania. Murray the skinner feels it. The children bathe in it. Even Terrible Theresa feels it.

B.T. the skinner is on his way, what goodies does he have for good little boys and girls today?

Murray is in command. He is gratified to see that the excitement is carefully restrained. Only a few squirmers here and there, and he carefully makes note of names and times. The flow charts are flowing, the lessons are going, and only the children's salivary glands are out of control. There is sucking-in of breath, the sound of slurping.

Theresa has the itches. Down there in that bothersome itchy old pee-pee, darn it, and it just won't *stop*. Keep your hands in your lap, Theresa, and you'll get an M&M if only you'll stop squirming. But *that's* where the *problem* is, *darn it!*

Murray has conscientiously given her a second M&M when her snuffling crying behavior extinguished. But still she sits, staring at the wall, removed from the opportunity for positive reinforcement. Cry away, cry-baby, you won't get any sympathy from *us*. We reward *happy* behaviors. Smile, Theresa! It's a beautiful day.

(Count the thumb tack holes on the patch of white wall twenty-five twenty-six twenty-nine. That's it. Think about B.T. the skinner. Count the holes again fifteen seventeen.) *Squirm.*

Darn it!

I gotta scratch, I just gotta scratch!

Ooooooh, that's much better. I wonder if Murray saw?

The door bursts open. It's B.T., gibbering and jabbering, seven-foot-tall clown with a spinning face. The class is electrified, but sits stone-still. Some of them are drooling.

"Hi, B.T. . . ." Billy begins, and is shocked as he realizes that he is the only one on his feet, waving. He has forgotten himself. He only thought that since Murray had been yelling and he had yelled back and he *did* get his M&M . . .

"Billy, you shouldn't speak out of turn," says Murray. He is secretly pleased that this embarrassing thing has happened to this particular client, who *did* raise his voice earlier and Murray had forgotten to do anything because his face was hurting on account of Theresa. Now his head is hurting. He rubs the puckered white scar on his forehead.

"All right, class. You may go see B.T."

"And how are all my little sixth-graders doing today?" B.T. asks, amusing the six-year-olds who cluster around him giggling at his winsome two-step.

"Tell us a story, B.T."

"Give us some candy, B.T."

"Tell us about the hippie in the hill."

Theresa is sitting ramrod-straight on her personal throne, straight and still. Quick as a wink, happy to be able to so quickly reward such good behavior, Murray pops her an M&M and tells her to go see B.T.

Lickety-split. Terrible Theresa is off her stool and racing to join the other moppets at B.T.'s feet. The smile on her face is an inspiring thing to see. Her hands are clasped safely out of harm's way.

Murray massages the headache, which has spread to his temples.

It is good to see Theresa successfully internalizing her controls. Maybe he won't have to increase her dosage of dexies, after all. Maybe she'll take her fate in her own hands, minimize her time-outs, and become a good citizen. Time is short. Only this morning, Lobey the Needle came calling, asking about Theresa. Had she been a good girl?

The scar on Murray's forehead is throbbing.

9. LETTERS TO THE EDITOR

Sacramento Bee, February 4, 1977:

. . . knows we have to find *some* way to get these little hooligans off the street. I favor prisons, myself. But do you know what they're doing in the schools these days? Listen to this. They're giving the kids sweets when they're good.

This is supposed to lower the crime rate? This is supposed to give these kids some sense of moral right and wrong? In my day, when we were bad we got a switching, and no fooling around with "behavior reinforcement."

Wise up!

CONCERNED TAXPAYER

Time, September 5, 1979:

. . . your excellent and thought-provoking article on the trend to behaviorism in the public schools.

I thought my experience might shed some light on the disturbing elements of these techniques, and others, which seem to work so well in a practical sense. I work as a secretary in a Midwestern public school. Every day dozens of permanent records pass over my desk, and it has begun to frighten me. I see children marked down as potential homosexuals for the most insignificant acts. I see students classified as troublemakers for having the temerity to question the teacher's statements on politics, history, or anything at all. Almost fifteen percent of the children here are taking daily doses of Ritalin or Dexedrine because they've been diagnosed as hyperactive.

This is something we, as parents and other concerned adults, should keep a wary eye on. We must have the courage to stand up and fight this sort of pettiness.

Please don't print my name.

(Name withheld)

Atlanta Constitution, May 17, 1982:

. . . came home from school today and I found out she's been classified as a pre-delinquent child. They want to take her and put her in one of these special institutions that have sprung up all over the country.

They say she was crying in class. Her grandmother died the day before, and that's why she was upset. I tried to explain this, but they said it was all the more reason they needed to take her and help her before this unpleasant experience could permanently scar her personality.

I don't know what to do.

H. B. Sweeney

Last Ditch, newsletter of the Rocky Mountain Resisters, no date:

. . . say that Friday's the day. Could be, but that won't keep me from keeping my eyes open on *Thursday!*

The yellowfaces have been massing in the canyon all week, that's certain. They want your kids, fellow citizens, and they mean to have them one way or another. And for one time they're right. If there was ever a kid who's a genuine pre-delinquent, it was my Tommy two years ago. Since then he's helped me kill three yellowfaces.

I've found that if you aim for that little set-screw in the middle that holds the mask onto the pivot, you get the best results. I don't know what's behind them masks, men or what. I do know that if you put a slug through that screw, they go down and I ain't seen one get up yet.

Keep your powder dry, neighbors. And don't fire till you hear 'em yell "smile!"

Nasty Nathan

10. Lobey the Needle

Lobey the Needle whispers down the corridors. The excitement of B.T.'s visit has gone down a bit, though it still eddies and flutters in the corners like empty candy wrappers stirred by a breeze. Lobey's tread is silent. Lobey is a friend of the children, but he brings no candy. He doesn't visit once a week but is always around, standing in the back of the room, walking down the far end of the hall, suddenly in front of you and patting you on the head when you round a corner. His hands are gentle.

He is putting your soul in an analytical balance, weighing your progress. He is taking the measure of your frontal lobes. Feel his gentle hands caress your forehead. Isn't Lobey a swell guy?

Murray leaves his clients bent over their lessons and meets Lobey in the hallway.

"Good to see you, Murray." His hands touch Murray's scar, testing gently. It is not an old scar.

"Good to see *you*, Lobey." Murray is achingly happy to see Lobey, his old friend. His face aches. It was Lobey who made Murray into a good citizen. Before, Murray had been Terrible. He had been brought up in the hippiehills with his crazy mommy. There was nothing to do but operate, get a blank slate to draw on. Murray's bad behavior had been reinforced all his life and he was apt to say the *darndest* things.

"I won't bother you, Murray. I just want to look in on Theresa. How has she been?"

He peeks into the open doorway and is surprised to see Theresa sitting like a little angel in her chair, biting the end of her tongue as she struggles to make her pencil do what Murray wants it to do. Theresa is being a good girl. She is trying awfully hard.

"Theresa's been good today," Murray says, and immediately his face hurts. Those rebellious muscles are trying to pull the corners of his mouth down, trying to make him f——n. Oh, come on now, Murray, you're a grownup now, you can face the word. Frown. You're trying not to *frown*. Sweat pops on his brow at the closeness of his attempted evasion. What are you trying to do, dummy, with all those watchbirds all over the walls? *Lie?* No, it couldn't have been that. Murray is long past that.

"She was in trouble this morning, but she got much better when B.T. showed up. She's been a perfect angel ever since."

"So happy to hear it. I'll need your final report next week, Murray. She's seven today, and we have to decide."

"Oh, I'm sure she'll be all right. In this day and age . . . oh, no. She won't need you. She'll make it on her own, you'll see." Murray dares a grin. "You're getting out of date, Lobey."

Lobey chuckles, aware that Murray is right. Lobey is, after

all, only a specially trained skinner.

"Maybe you're right, Murray. I've already handled all the grownup holdouts. There's only their children, now. Theresa's mommy was one of those, wasn't she?"

Throb in the temple, ache in the gut.

"Yes, she was."

"Thought I heard that you knew her." Lobey is watching. His needle is always ready. Sometimes two, three, four times aren't enough. It's no good to make vegetable goulash out of frontal lobes; you must be more subtle, and therein lies the danger.

"Me? I don't think so. But you'd know better than I, wouldn't you?" Murray laughs, the muscles around his mouth are doing a spastic dance.

"Guess I would, at that." Lobey laughs. "Have a nice day, Murray."

"And a nice day to *you,* Lobey."

Theresa has dropped her pencil. She is staring out the window at the amorphous clouds of cotton-candy castles.

11. Catch Them Being Good

Theresa sits in her dormitory room, trying not to be terrible. It's hard, when you're six years old and want to kick up your heels, scratch where it itches, maybe sing a silly song now and then.

The watchbird on the wall is mooning at her with fried-egg eyes. He is disappointed. Not *frowning,* you see, but you haven't done much lately to cheer the little fellow up, Terrible Theresa. Isn't it wonderful when he's smiling at you? She remembers those rare days when she was as good as gold and when she returned to her room there was a smile on the watchbird's face.

The watchbird is a simple paper poster in pulp tricolor, frayed at the edges from being taken down and put up so many times. The real watchbird is in the ceiling, but it could be anywhere, under the bed or in your dolly or peering up at you from a tiny camera in your dexie pill or in the flowers in the garden or down in the potty.

Her brow furrows as she thinks of how to be good. She hasn't learned yet to act without thinking, without worrying about it. She hasn't yet internalized her controls sufficiently. What comes as easy as spitting for the other children is a painful process of chewing on a dry tongue for Theresa.

Darn it. She wants to be good so she'll get plenty of M&Ms.

She lies on her bunk and looks up at the ceiling, wipes at pink-rimmed eyes small and piggy from crying all day.

"Relax, Theresa," Murray has told her earlier that evening. Poor Murray. He has a kinship for Theresa that feels all wrong, somehow. Not natural. It weighs down the buoyant dimples in his cheeks. "Relax," he repeats, stroking poor Theresa to show her he loves her, just like it says in the comics.

(Hugging: Put your arms around the client while standing or sitting beside him or her. Pull client close, rumple client's hair or loosely tweak client's nose between thumb and forefinger. Smile. Tell client that you love him or her.)

"Good behavior will come to you naturally when you wait," he says. "You don't have to try for it. You don't have to fight it. I shouldn't be telling you this, but it's because I love you. Lobey will be coming to see you this week, and he loves you, but I wish you could start showing good behavior without his help. You're seven years old tonight, Theresa. I love you."

For an instant he holds her fiercely, scaring her some, but not much because it feels so good. *Don't cry, don't cry, he'll stop if you cry.*

So she lies in her bed with the lights off and looks up at the faint red light in the ceiling. She lets her mind go blank. What's all the fuss about, Theresa? Why can't you relax and be a good citizen like the others? Don't think about it, darling. Don't use your head at all if you can get away with it, they don't want the front part of your head, anyway, sweetheart, they want you to listen to the back of your head where they planted all the bombs which are waiting to go off if you'd only stop struggling. Lobey is *not happy* with the front part of your head, he's thinking of dipping into it and seeing if he can't set things right with his sharp stainless needles and scalpels. See Lobey? He's almost frowning. Poor, poor Lobey for you to have made him so unhappy.

So don't think about it, don't think at all. Don't think about pink clouds in the sky at sunset and singing dreams that keep you awake long after the others are snoring. Let your mind be a pretty blank slate for others to write on. Think of cows, Theresa. Cows are the happiest animals in the world. Just look at them. Think about candy. Think about B.T. the skinner with his pigeons and comics and sweets. Think about M&Ms.

The fuse burns down to the tight bundle of newsprint and silver powder in the hot, firecrackerjack core of all those M&Ms, the fission heart beating in Theresa explodes and sets off the deuterium layer in the hard candy coating and zowie!

Nothing has happened. Nothing has changed. She feels the same, but she is smiling. She wipes away the last tear and sits up, smiling, smiling wider than a three-day-dead corpse.

And the door bursts open and who do you think it is but B.T. the skinner, all decked out in his finest party suit and his hands are full of presents and candy and the M&Ms are actually *spilling* out of his *pockets*. And . . . what? For *me?* Yes, for you, darling, it's your birthday and we're having a party because we love you, me and Murray and Lobey and everybody here at Behavior Tech. You're a *good* girl, smiling so bright and pretty that we just *had* to make your seventh birthday a very special party day with all the candy you can eat.

"Oh, I'll be good, I'll be good, I'll be so very, very good that you'll forget you ever called me Terrible Theresa and you'll feed me M&Ms every day. How I love you, B.T. How I *do* love you. And how I *do* love M&Ms."

Have a nice day.

THE EVE OF THE LAST APOLLO

One small step for a man—one giant
stumble for mankind.

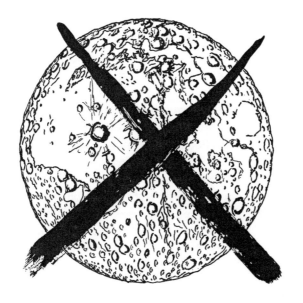

Carter Scholz

MILESTONES

Died. Colonel John Christie Edwards, 64, U.S. Air Force
(retired); of a heart attack; in Teaneck, N.J. In 1970, under the
auspices of the National Aeronautics and Space Administration,

Edwards became the first man to walk on the moon. He is survived by a wife and son.

—No. I don't like that dream.

The dream-magazine faded and he was back in 1975, tentatively at least, until sleep plucked him again to a land beyond life where his existence could be reduced to those two magazine appearances: his achievement and his death.

His sweat stained the sheets.

He slept alone, his wife in her own bedroom.

Restless, the curtains ballooned inward on a light breeze. He caught at them, and sat up, and saw the moon standing alone in the sky, so far and meaningless. It was gibbous, bloated past half but less than full. He hated it like that, the lopsided incompletion of it. Half or full or crescent he could almost look at some nights, but gibbous, no, there was nothing redeeming in a gibbous moon. He stared at it, its geography forgotten. Craters were ciphers. He could not pick out within five hundred miles the place on its surface where he had walked, just five years ago. At times now it seemed so improbable that he felt sure the rocket had been turned around midway and had landed on an Arizona mesa or a Siberian desert, or in a Houston simulator.

Below the moon State Street glowed in unconcern. No cars passed this late; the moon might have been another of the cold glaring street lamps. From his present vantage point in Teaneck, New Jersey, it seemed impossible that he had ever been there.

The Lunar Exposé:

Time, August 2, 1987. The article explained that the Moon landing had been a hoax, since the Moon itself was a hoax. It explained how simple it had been for unknown forces to simulate the Moon for unscrupulous purposes; a conspiracy of poets and scientists was intimated. Mass hypnosis was mentioned. Further on was a capsule summary of his mission with a drawing of the flight path, the complicated loops and curves, the projected hyperbolas and multiple spirals that had taken them there and back, straight-line flight being impossible in space, and further still was an inset map of the splashdown area. He remembered it and was suddenly in the capsule with a lurch as it splashed, sank, and bobbed to the surface. He wanted to fling the hatch open and yell in triumph, be dazzled by the spray and brilliant blue Pacific sky—but of course he couldn't do that, there was no telling what germs they had brought back, what germs had survived the billion-year killing lunar cold and void there was no telling, and the helicopters droned down and netted them and swung them to the carrier and into quarantine and for three weeks they had seen people only through glass; and that must have been the beginning of the isolation he felt now, just as his first time in space had been the beginning of the emptiness. After that he drove to the Cape on business, and then to his new home in New Jersey. When he had reached the Cape after all those weeks and miles and loops and backtracks, the trip was finally over, and he yielded to an impulse; he walked out to the launching pad and bent to put his hand on the scorched ground—but he had an attack of vertigo and a terrible intimation: the Earth itself had moved. If he went to the Cape exactly a year after the liftoff, the Earth would be in position again, the circle would be closed—but then there was the motion of the solar system through the galaxy to consider, and the sweep of the galaxy through the universe, and the universe's own pulsations—and he saw there was no way for him ever to find the place he started from. Driving back to Teaneck with the road behind him spiraling off through space as the Earth moved and the Sun moved and the galaxy moved, he got violently ill with a complex vertigo and had to pull off the road. Only when it grew dark was he able to drive again, slowly.

The dream, the memory, dissolved.

By the time he woke next morning his wife had already left to spend the weekend with friends at a commune upstate. He made breakfast for himself and his son and went outside in the Saturday-morning heat to garden. He was almost forty.

Days he worked in an over-airconditioned building adjacent to the Teaneck Armory. On one wall of his office was a maroon and red square of geometrically patterned fabric framed like a painting. On another was an autographed photo of the President and another photo of himself on the Moon, the landing module and his crewmate Jim Cooper reflected in his face mask. Because the photograph had come off a stack of NASA publicity photos, his autograph was on it. He felt silly about that and had always meant to replace it, but where he worked now there were no NASA photos.

His work was paperwork related to the National Guard. After he had walked on the Moon and declined to command an Air Force base in Nevada, they seemed to have run out of things quite as definite for him to do. He had a plastic wood-grained desk that was generally clean and empty. On the floor was a cheap red carpet, the nap of which he was always carrying home on his shoes.

After the mission his spare time had been filled with interviews and tours and banquets and inconveniences, but with time and other missions, his fame dwindled. At first he welcomed this escape from the public eye; then the pressure of emptiness began to weigh on him, like a column of air on his shoulders. The time he could now spend with his wife and son passed uneasily. He learned to play golf and tennis and spent more time at them than he enjoyed. He started a diary and grew depressed with the banality of his life.

So he took a week off in the early summer of 1975 to sort the drifting fragments of his life: his wife's departure, the imminent end of his fourth four-year term of service in the Air Force, the dead undying image of the Moon that haunted his dreams, the book he had long planned to write, the mystery of his son, his dwindling fame, the possibility of a life ahead without a wife or son or career or public image . . . without every base he had come to rely on. He felt he had to consider what he was, what he had been, and what he might become.

When it grew too hot to work in the late morning, and after Kevin had left, Edwards went back into the silent empty house to rest.

The friends he made in NASA had drifted away. The small, manageable sense of community he got from the program lost strength with NASA itself. The lunar astronauts, the dozen or so people he considered friends drifted slowly away from the magnet of Houston, until the terrible clean emptiness of the city compelled Edwards to move too. The city had grown up around the space program, and like most children was just reaching its prime as its father declined. It depressed him terribly. Texas no longer felt like home.

In 1971 Harrison Baker, the command module pilot on Edwards' mission, moved to New Jersey with his family to become a vice-president in a large oil company, and the Edwardses followed shortly. It was a somewhat irrational impulse that prompted the move—the prospect of friends nearby, and of New York, where each had once wanted to live, and Kevin's enthusiasm for leaving Texas—all these poor random factors pulled them to the sterile suburb of Teaneck as surely as the most inexorable of destinies. As it turned out, they lived over forty miles from the Bakers, the city lost its appeal after three months, and Kevin talked of going back to Texas for college.

Baker had written a bad book on what it was like to orbit the Moon while his fellow astronauts got all the glory. The book was called *Group Effort*. It was a humble book by a man who was basically conceited, written with the aid of a hungry young journalist. Edwards had the impression, reading it, that Baker was somehow unconvinced of the Moon's reality, or at least of its importance, since he himself had not walked there. Edwards disliked the book, or more precisely he disliked the feelings the book aroused in him: he felt he could have done it better if only he had taken the time.

Nonetheless he called Baker one day while he was alone in the house and desperate for company; he called him as he might summon the ghost of old confidence from his past.

"Chris! How are you, you old son of a bitch?" Baker's voice was hard and distant on the wire. Edwards had quite forgotten that at NASA that had been his nickname.

"Hello, Hank. How are you?"

"Great, just great! Listen, I've been meaning to call you, to invite you and Sharl up for a weekend."

"Fine. I'll keep it in mind, Hank. Actually Charlotte and I haven't been getting on too well recently."

"Oh? I'm sorry to hear that."

"It's just one of those things. We're thinking of separating."

"That's a shame, Chris. That's a damn shame. Francie and I always said you were such a good couple."

"Well, we've both been doing some changing. I don't know, I think it's for the best. Hell, I didn't call to cry on your shoulder, Hank. I wanted to ask you something. I've been thinking of writing that book that Doubleday asked me to, remember—?"

"Oh, yeah. That sounds like a fine idea. They're still interested, huh?"

"Well, I don't know. I should call them, I guess. I assumed they would be."

"Hm. That's rough, Chris. I don't know. The royalties on my book aren't all they could be. The hardcover's out of print and the paperback sales are so slow they're not going to reprint it. Which is too bad, I think. Not that I need the money—we're getting along fine on my pension, and this job, hell, it's a real tit job, you know? But the way I feel is, the book's a kind of historical document and it ought to stay in print, you know, to keep it available for people who want it. But those publishers—they say that people aren't interested in the Moon anymore. People just don't care."

"Well, look at the whole NASA program."

"Yes. Well. I don't keep up on it too closely, but I know they're in trouble."

Oh, you bastard, Edwards thought. In *trouble*—*!* "The manned program has been discontinued, Hank, that's the trouble they're in. No more money, no more flights."

"That so?"

"Yes, that's so." There was silence. Static moved on the line, reminding him of the last time Baker's voice had reached him this way, distant, distorted, on the radio, the Moon. "Hank, I can't help thinking we did it wrong."

"Wrong? What do you mean?"

"The landing. We planted the American flag, we left a plaque . . . It seems we're always leaving things, flags or garbage, empty film cans and burned-out rockets . . . The planting of the flag is what really bothered me."

"Why? What should we have planted? Petunias?" Baker laughed, a short cold sound in the receiver.

"I don't know. Once I thought the United Nations flag might have been a nice gesture."

"Oh, shit. Come on, Chris, what's the UN done for you lately? They sit on their asses and argue and maybe pass a couple of resolutions that say wars are bad. Big fucking deal. *We* put that rocket on the moon, the United States of America, so why shouldn't we get the credit for it? Good God, Chris, I thought you of all people would see that, the hero of the fucking mission. What's the matter with you, son?"

"Nothing. I tell you, I'm just questioning it. Wondering if maybe I did something wrong without thinking about it. I certainly didn't think about it very much." The image of such a mistake chilled him, bright and arresting and irrevocable in a barren landscape a quarter million miles away. The flag would not stay unfurled in vacuum so they had braced it with wire.

"Yeah, well, take my word for it, Chris old boy, we did right. I mean, this is off the record, this isn't a fucking NASA press release, but it's gonna be a *long* time before we're able to walk hand in hand with the Russkies through the tulip patch, I don't care *what* they said about coming in peace for all mankind."

"What do you think about the joint Apollo–Soyuz mission coming up?"

"Shit, it's all political haymaking. That mealy-mouthed bastard in Washington thinks he can score brownie points in the next election by cozying up to 'em. He'll do anything for votes. I mean, answer me this: NASA was ready to get cut off without a cent, right?"

"They still are."

"Yeah, but I'll bet my butt-behind they wouldn't have got the money for *this* one if it wasn't that somebody in Washington stood to make points off it, am I right?

"Probably, Hank. You're quite probably right."

"You know I am. Well. Listen, Chris, I'd love to talk all day, but if some big cheese walks in here and finds me jawing, I'm liable to be out on that same butt-behind I was betting you. Seriously, they've been drifting rumors down to me that I'm not as valuable as I used to be, back when NASA's name was good."

"I don't wonder."

"What?"

"I say I wonder why."

"Well, so do I. But seriously now, I'm gonna have to get off. That invitation still goes for you and your kid, and for Charlotte if you two get back together. Any time at all, you know that."

"Sure, Hank, I know."

"And I'm sorry as hell to hear what happened. I hope it all works out."

"I'm sure it will. I'll let you go now, Hank. Good talking to you."

"You too. We'll see you around, huh?"

"You bet." He hung up. He felt very tired. The living room trembled just outside his field of vision. He sat for a few minutes, and abruptly decided to spend the day in New York, in noise and smog and slow-moving traffic.

Through the magazine where she worked as a secretary, his wife had met an author who ran a commune in upstate New York. The author had submitted an article on communal life-styles to the magazine at a time when such things were attracting the interest of the dissatisfied sophisticates who comprised the magazine's audience. The article circulated in the office for two days; one evening Charlotte brought home a Xerox copy, which Edwards read with disdain. Some months later the author submitted another article in person and talked to Charlotte all afternoon. She came home excited, with an invitation to the commune for both of them, which, after a week of bitter arguments, she accepted alone. She slept with the author of course; of that he was sure; that had been implicit in his invitation and her decision to go alone. And when she came home Edwards said, stupidly, regret stinging him even as he spoke, "Was he any good?"

And she said, "He was great," and what had been a bitterness became a war. Kevin was fourteen then, and when in a lull they heard him sobbing through the wall, they were stricken with what had happened to them all unknown.

"My God," said Charlotte, "what's wrong with us?" And together they went to their son, that ineluctable symbol of their love, and the three of them held to each other and wept until very late.

The next month was perhaps the best in their marriage; they were all kind and deferential to each other, as if unwilling to test the strength of the frayed fabric. But such violence does not come from or dissolve into nothing. The next time Charlotte left it was for a week, unannounced. Again there was a fight. Again there were tears. But after that, the reconciliations had less and less meaning, and Edwards felt the marriage become weak and brittle, emulsion cracking on an old photograph.

○

The photograph in the den held them both against a bright but faded Texas sky. Edwards stood stiff and crewcut in his uniform, Charlotte in her crisp white dress, four months pregnant but not yet showing it. They stood in front of the small brick chapel in the hot Texas afternoon, the smaller pasts they had each known then printed on their minds as their images were printed in the silver bromides. Edwards had entered the Air Force from college, blank enough to be a soldier, smart enough to be an officer. He had a uniform and a sheaf of diplomas and awards and citations and his name on a plastic wood-grained prism on his desk at Sheppard Air Force Base, and $213.75 plus expenses, which was more than he would have known what to do with if he hadn't got married. So then he had a wife and his commission and in a few years a master's degree and a mortgage, and then a son and a doctorate, and oak leaves and his name on a fistful of credit cards and ID plates and he had his existence recorded in so many cross-indexed files that there was no chance of his ever accidentally losing himself, so he thought.

And then the space program started, and Lieutenant Colonel Edwards being a local boy of fine repute, a good soldier and engineer, and an asset to any organization, it said on his recommendations, he was accepted. He got his colonelcy and a sense of purpose that truly humbled him; he had never been religious but space made him feel as he imagined God might make other people feel. He was a successful man, and his life was a fine, balanced and counterweighted thing.

Then they put him in a rocket and shot him at the Moon.

Abenezra, Abulfeda, Agatharchides, Agrippa, Albategnius, Alexander, Aliacensus, Almanon, Alpetragius, Alphonsus, Apianus, Apollonius, Agago, Archimedes, Aristarchus, Aristillus, Aristoteles, Ascelpi, Atlas . . .

The craters, the names, rolled past. A tiny motor ground to turn the four-foot sphere, front and back sides both sculpted in wondrous close detail thanks to his and other missions, thanks to the automatic cameras mounted on the outside of the capsule. Tiny American flags marked all the Apollo landing sites, silly bright dime-store gaudies against the gray.

John Christie Edwards, first man on the Moon, stood in the planetarium at the end of a hall lined with names like Icarus, da Vinci, Montgolfier, Wright, Goddard . . . a mural of the history of flight, the individual dreamers down time's long corridor. Each had had a vision of man transcending his world, his prison of gravity, and Edwards felt small in their presence. Of them all, only he could have been replaced by anyone else. His achievement had been a matter of training, not vision.

But they had told him he was a hero; that he had done something no one had ever done before, that it was the grandest achievement of the human race. It was, he believed that, and for the parades and accolades he'd had, he was grateful. He had every reason to be proud, to be as content, no, more content than Baker. Why, then, did that terrible emptiness come to him at night? In the dark his fame was no consolation; his achievement no part of his life. For it would have happened anyway, without him. Of what classical hero was that true? He felt cut off from the history he had made, isolated from time.

Flanking the lunar globe were photographs: himself, Baker, Cooper, Nixon, Von Braun. Some children recognized him from the photo and crowded around anxiously, seeking mementos, autographs. One asked where he had landed; again he suffered the doubts of last night and finally stabbed a finger vaguely at one of the larger *maria*. Gratefully he heard the loudspeaker announce the start of the sky show.

The sky show was absorbing, much more so than the night sky

usually was for him, even the clear country sky he could see for two weeks every year at his brother's summer cottage on Lake Hopatcong; he was enchanted by the flitting arrows on the sky, the narrator's calm clear explanations, the wonderful control of time the projector had over the universe. Stars rose, set, went forward, back. They could be spun at almost any rate or accelera- tion, moving in ever-faster circles.

In the past year Edwards had acquired the notion that he would like to write poetry. That was not unreasonable; in his present depression it seemed that only such an intensely personal act as writing could give him back to himself.

So after the Planetarium, shortly after noon, he finally gave in, seduced by the stars, and drove downtown to buy some antholo- gies of verse. Byron, Yeats, Eliot, Pound . . . all the names vaguely remembered from college. While getting pleasantly cramped reading in the aisle, he found a comment by Frost to the effect that the most important element of poetry is its dramatic content. So after some consideration he also picked up Freytag's *Technique of the Drama.* He had learned to pursue things in an orderly fashion. Then he tore himself away, before he bought more than he could carry. It was years since he had read anything but news- papers; he was drunk with the limitless neglected mysteries of books. In this fine giddy mood he felt himself approaching the edge of a change, the crest of an oscillation, the start of a new phase; he felt charged with the energy of the unpredictable.

At home he dipped into his package, the sharp-cornered paperbacks and stiff-spined hardcovers smelling of glue and new paper. He read single pages, fragments, the shortest poems, skimming in an excited random fashion. From MacLeish's *Streets in the Moon* he read, "No lamp has ever shown us where to look. Neither the promiscuous and every-touching moon, nor stars . . ."

"The moon is dead, you lovers! . . . I have seen her face.

. . . Her face was dead. It was a woman's face but dead as stone. And leper white and withered to the bone. It was a woman's skull the shriveling cold out there among the stars had withered dry. . . ."

He saw Charlotte's face deflagrate before him, burn without fire. Touched by the void, it turned into a death's-head moon, attained, unattainable, glowing with the stark stripped brilliance of reflected sun, grim reminder of day through the night. Of all the astronauts, only Edwards had had the dimmest chance of understanding the Moon, only he had even a circumstantial reason for wanting to understand it. He needed to know why he had made history.

"Dad? You busy?"

He started. "Oh, no. Come on in, son." Immediately annoyed at himself; how had he ever started calling Kevin *son?*

The boy drifted in. Tall, pale; his son, brought out of a hot union years past, and already faded, but for this phantom, this stranger in the house. His son.

"Are you and Mom going to stay together until September?"

"Sure. Until you're at school."

"Oh." The room was silent. Somewhere an air-conditioner hummed.

"Why do you ask?"

"Things are getting worse between you, aren't they?"

"Don't worry about it, Kevin."

"If you're staying together just for my sake, I wish you wouldn't. I mean, I don't want you to. I think you should separate now if that's the case."

Edwards looked at his son. A troubled sixteen, his emotions already burnt brittle into a fragile, ashen maturity. And Edwards himself moving back along a rocket wake into a second adolescence, a time of self-consciousness, self-discovery. When had he first touched this boy with his fire, in what way shaped him?

"I'll think about it. I'll talk to your mother. Listen, Kevin—?"

"Yeah, Dad."

"This business with your mother and me—it hasn't affected you too badly, has it?" His memory stung him brutally with the image of a woman he had once brought to the house, out of spite for Charlotte and her author, and Kevin finding them . . . "I mean, just because things aren't working out for us, I don't want you to think . . ."

"I don't think about it anymore. It's just one of those things that happen."

"Because it would be a terrible thing if this were to turn you against marriage, or against women . . ."

"Don't worry about it, Dad. I'll think what I think. I'm not sad about you and Mom—I think it's better this way. Really. I think it might even be better for you if you split up sooner."

"Well, thanks, Kev." Then, because he was less afraid of being embarrassed than of being untouchable, he hugged his son. Kevin held still for this, and Edwards let go soon enough to make both of them grateful.

"Okay if I stay out late tonight?" Kevin asked, leaving. "I have a date."

"How late?" Pleased, but their late sentiment demanded a strict return to formality. The balance was too delicate to threaten.

"One o'clock?"

"Make it twelve-thirty."

"Okay."

"Who's the girl?"

"Nobody you know."

"Oh. Well . . . have fun . . ."

Kevin left. Later, Edwards opened the Freytag and read: Poetry must bring forth its characters as speaking, singing, gesticulating. This is the nature of the hero.

It was not the first time the thought had occurred to him that if he was a national hero, the nation must be in very bad shape.

Drama possesses—if one may symbolize its arrangement by lines—a pyramidal structure. It rises from the introduction with the entrance of exciting forces to the climax and falls from here to the resolution.

—Gustav Freytag, *Technique of the Drama*

His obligations as a national monument took him the next day to a half-hour talk show with a state senator, a NASA administrator, and an ABC newsman. The topic was the discontinuation of the manned space program, made topical by the upcoming Apollo–Soyuz mission. As they set him up and gimballed the lights his way and adjusted his microphone, he felt very used. He felt bronzed and shat upon and tarnished a flaking green, like some Civil War general in the corner of some park, passed and never noticed.

The show started with the senator asserting, no doubt to mollify Edwards, so strong was the hostility he radiated to the senator, that the space program was by no means ending but was merely being cut back in favor of more pressing domestic issues. The senator said that the magnitude of our problems at home far surpassed those of space. The senator said that space exploration could be done far more cheaply and efficiently and safely by machines than by men. Edwards asked if perhaps other areas of the national budget might be better cut—defense, for instance, which consumed one hundred times as much money as NASA. Edwards went so far as to suggest that what the Pentagon wasted yearly in staples and paper clips could support NASA. He compared the senator's personal convictions to a bowl of tapioca. No one knew how to react; Edwards thought the NASA man might be smiling, off-camera.

Then the commentator pleasantly directed the conversation elsewhere, toward the hopeful symbolism of the joint Apollo–Soyuz mission. The senator, recovered, called it a magnificent extension of the successful detente that his party had already, et cetera. Edwards started to ask why, if the detente was so successful, the defense budget was not being cut, but as he leaned forward to speak, the commentator forestalled him, speaking in a rapid gabble, his eye glazed with panic, and Edwards realized that his microphone was off. This so enraged him that he began to tremble. He leaned over into the camera's eye and began to speak into the senator's microphone.

"I'd like to read something, if you don't mind."

Everyone was speechless. Belligerent guests were nothing new, but Air Force colonels were supposed to be better trained. Edwards shifted himself further into the picture. The lights blazed and blinded him. He felt a little drunk with their heat, but below it, calm and composed.

"This is a poem by Lord Byron. It's very short. It sums up my feelings about the end of the program better than I could myself."

The audience was silent; the cameras were captive. The paper trembled in his hand, in the hot and blazing dark. The studio whirled beneath him. It was a strange surreal moment in the chatter and rhythmless gabble of television, a moment of silence he suspended before starting to speak:

> "So, we'll go no more a roving
>   So late into the night,
> Though the heart be still as loving,
>   And the moon be still as bright.
> "For the sword outwears its sheath,
>   And the soul wears out the breast,
> And the heart must pause to breathe,
>   And love itself have rest.
> "Though the night was made for loving,
>   And the day returns too soon,

Yet we'll go no more a roving
  By the light of the moon."

Electrons made a chaos of snow on the monitors. Offstage a man with horn-rimmed glasses waved franticly. The moderator cleared his throat.

"Thank you, Colonel Edwards. We have to pause here, but we'll be back in a moment." The red eyes of the monitors blinked off.

Edwards sank back into his chair. The senator fumed. The moderator leaned over to Edwards and said, "Please, Colonel, we can't take you off the air now, but stick to the subject at hand."

"Wasn't I?"

"Colonel . . . please. You know what I mean."

"My microphone was turned off. It made me mad."

"I'm sorry. I'll see it doesn't happen again. But please—"

"Just say what I'm supposed to, right?"

"Don't make things difficult."

"No more poetry?"

"No more poetry. Please."

He had gained a large amount of ground; he felt good, in control. But now he was losing—he didn't know where to go next. He turned to the NASA man, his silent ally, who said, "This isn't helping us, Colonel," and all Edwards' certainty and composure vanished. He had a terrible intuition then: NASA itself did not care. It made no difference to anyone involved how they made their money, in this branch of civil service or another. Of all those in NASA, only Edwards had reason to want to understand what they were doing. He was alone in his concern.

"All right," he breathed. "All right, you bastards." He felt a clear sense of climax. He saw what he must do: leave, walk off, dissociate himself from all of them. But at the thought all his strength went from him: he was not conditioned to function alone. And he sat in his weakness, and the monitors came back on, and for the rest of the show he was trapped there, silent, outwardly serene: he saw himself as a small hard circle swimming alone and untouched in a limitless sea of static.

Tuesday his wife returned. The car pulled up and he heard Kevin go down and out the back door, fast and light, as if he had been going anyway. The screen door sighed on its hinge and in the second before she entered the den he knew that today she would finally ask for a divorce. He had been determined not to be the one to mention it. Now with a sick premonition he knew the end was near anyway. Her first words, though, catching him off balance, were, "My God, John, do you have any idea how embarrassing that was?"

"Hello, Charlotte. What was embarrassing?" He considered the woman before him with an objectivity he would never have thought possible.

"The TV show. The poetry. Eric practically dragged the whole commune in to watch you quoting Lord Byron on the *Today* show. Christ, if you knew what you looked like."

"Really. I didn't know you had TV up there in the pristine wilderness."

"Oh, go screw."

"All right, let's have it, what was wrong with quoting Byron?"

"It was, let us say, out of character."

"So? Did it ever occur to you that I get tired of playing the role of the dumb hero?"

She looked at him. "You think you can get out of it that easily?"

"Maybe."

"How little you know."

"What do you mean by that?"

She went to her bedroom and took down a suitcase from the closet. He followed her and sat on the bed with his eyes closed and his fingertips touching at the bridge of his nose. He sat as if in another world and listened to the angry rustlings of clothes as she hurled them about.

"Tell me, John, do you have any idea the kind of crap I have had to put up with these past ten years?"

"Yes." It had once been a joke between them.

"Did you see the goddamned forty-page manual NASA gave us all on how to be an astronaut's wife? Did you get a good look at that?"

"Charlotte, don't start."

She gave a brutal little half-laugh. " 'An astronaut's wife dresses in clothes out of last year's *McCall's* and does her own decorating. She is active in church and social functions. She believes in equal pay for equal work but thinks that most women's libbers are just too far out. She never *never* raises her voice to reporters. And she drinks eight glasses of Tang a day.' "

He smiled under his tented fingers; she took it for amusement and grew furious. "But mostly an astronaut's wife sits around the house drinking and masturbating and hoping the reporters don't come around to ask her why she's not smiling or baking a cake or going to the PTA, for fear she might break down and *tell* the bastards why!"

There was a silence.

"John."

"Yes," he said.

"John, I want a divorce."

"Yes, I know."

"A legal divorce."

"All right."

"All right? Like that?"

"Like that."

She stared, confused. "What are you going to do?"

"I don't know."

"Your term of service is over this month, isn't it? Are you going to renew?"

"I don't think so."

"You don't think so? Why not?" She sat on the bed now and he became aware of her body, her movements, and it began to hurt. He had held it off till then. "What are you going to do for money?"

"I have some."

"But another four years and you'd have a pension. And by then Kevin would be through school. If you quit now you're out on your ass."

"I was thinking of writing a book."

"About your mission?"

"Sort of. I was thinking of poetry."

"Oh. Poetry." She smiled fractionally and shook her head. "Lover, if you had the barest fraction of poetry in you, it would have come out long ago. If you had any concept of drama or history, you would have said something full of poetry when you first stepped onto the Moon. And what did you say? Well, I don't have to remind you."

"Those were their words, not mine."

"So. And who's going to tell you what to say in your book?"

"Me, dammit!"

She shook her head wearily. "John, can't you see that it's too late? It's five years too late. You can't change roads this far on. You're a national monument, baby! As soon as you touched that rock up there you turned to stone yourself. I know, because I almost did too. I came so damned close to being caught in it . . ." She stopped herself.

"Go on."

She looked up quickly. "You want me to?"

"Yes."

She paused. She looked at her hands. "While you were on the Moon I seduced a newsman."

"Say that again."

"I seduced a newsman. You didn't know that, did you?"

"No, Charlotte, I didn't know that." He felt a dull ache start, a sinking at the truth of it, or at her ability to lie that way. "I don't know when to believe you anymore."

"Believe me, lover. It was right after you'd stepped down. He was here to interview me, to ask me safe dull questions for his safe dull magazine. Do you realize how safe and dull it is to be part of NASA? Only our government could make a Moon landing dull. And there he was, talking, I wasn't listening, until I said, 'Excuse me, Mr. Smith, but I've been celibate for the past month and you're quite attractive and would you like to fuck?' "

"You would put it that way, Charlotte."

"I did. I figured it was the only way he'd understand. So: Kevin was at school, and you were a quarter million miles away; so we did it. It was the safest infidelity I ever had."

"Meaning there were others."

"Meaning whatever you like."

Feeling was returning to him; he had tried to hold it off, but now there was a dull ache deep in his spine.

"And right after we finished the NASA phone rang. The newsman looked like it was the voice of God. I said, 'Oh, that's just my husband calling from work,' and I laughed! I felt so fine! Isn't that funny, that I didn't have to worry about you walking in on us because you were on the Moon?"

He got up and left the room. "John," she called. He kept walking. He walked into the kitchen to get a beer, the feeling still in his spine. When he reached the refrigerator there was a roaring in his ears. Cold air blew out across his arms; he stared into the cluttered recess of milk, butter, eggs, foil-wrapped leftovers. His mind was blank. Finally he remembered about the beer and reached for it. He was shocked to see his hand shake as it lifted the bottle. He put the bottle carefully back and shut the door, stood braced against it. His back throbbed. When it subsided he walked back to the bedroom. "Why?" he said.

Charlotte watched him. "Because, John, I was somewhat drunk and terribly depressed because there was my husband on the Moon, and where was he? I never believed you were actually there. I waited and watched for something to show me it was true. I wanted so badly to share in your triumph, and I felt nothing. I was in that panicky drunken state where everything you ever wanted or thought of when you looked in a mirror is sliding off, and I was feeling like a goddamned piece of PR machinery for the goddamned mission and I had to do something *human* for Christ's sake can you understand that?"

"That wasn't human. That was sick and vindictive."

"It was human! You and NASA—you know I always hated the program. I watched you on the Moon, John. There was never a moment when you were closer to becoming real. I wanted to share that moment you worked so hard for, and I couldn't. It meant nothing. Because you said their words, and you followed their agenda, and you did nothing, nothing, to show that you were human, that this was my husband. I watched you *become* NASA. And I felt like I was dying. I was drowning and here was this reporter saying, 'You must be awfully proud, Mrs. Edwards —Mrs. Edwards!—and I thought, no, no, that's not me! nobody cared about *me*, only about the Astronaut's Wife, even you, you were being the Astronaut, not the man I married. I felt trapped and I absolutely had to do something to break from damned, damned NASA, something unexpected, something human. If adultery is sick and vindictive, all right. But it was human, and I was desperate; I saw you move like a robot on the Moon and I did not want to be married to that. So I fucked him. I did it, and by Jesus, I made him think of me as a person!" And she laughed in triumph and looked at him quickly. The look caught at him and something seemed to break free from her eyes and fly and something twisted inside him, watching it go.

"Charlotte . . ." His mouth was dry and his voice came from far away. "Stay with me."

"No."

"Yes." He was pleading. "Yes."

"Why should I, John?"

"Because I need you. Kevin needs you."

For a second she was moved, he saw it; her eyes softened and she seemed to tremble with the thought of going to him, there was that soft ghost of yesterdays between them for just an instant, so close they had been once— She seemed ready to cry, but with an effort she turned to him and forced her tears back to whatever pit they had been rising from; she fixed him with dry glittering eyes that said *no; I am not that close to you.*

"John, I have needs too," she said.

In memory that scene has attained great significance for him, being one of the few in his life with any discernible sense of purpose, decision or climax. For as he replays it he becomes ever more convinced that that moment without tears was the turning point, the moment at which she finally cast him loose to live or die alone.

Numb, he followed her out to the car, helped her with her bags. She got in, started the engine, and stared straight ahead for a minute before turning to him.

"Do you want to come with me?" she asked.

There was a long, blowing silence. "No. I don't think so. I'd better be alone."

And she drove off and the structure of the family is—that abruptly—torn from him. That it was inevitable, that he saw it coming for months, that his every nerve was raw with the waiting for it made no difference to the boneless wretched man who now stands, weaves, and watches a woman who was his wife vanish down the road.

He has a dream that first night after she has finally left. It is one of many in the blurry confused time before waking. He is lying on his back with an erection while a woman pulls herself onto him. When he fucks his wife this way, as he often does at her prompting, he puts his hands to her breasts or around her hips or kneads up and down her abdomen, but in this dream somehow he can't move. His arms stay limp at his sides. He is in that half-waking state where the real weight of the body hinders the movements of the dream-self. The woman is moving, though, sliding on him, and he remembers that in space his wet dreams were usually of women masturbating. This dream-woman seems to be doing that now; he feels like a machine, a good solid rubber device mail-ordered for her pleasure—and it's good to feel that, to give himself over to her pleasure, to abandon his responsibilities. He feels serene in the knowledge that if she fails to come it will be her fault, not his. He lies very, very still.

Waking further, the dream fades and he realizes that the sheet is tented over him and the slightest move will bring him off. He lies still. Only the fractional pull of the sheet as he breathes can be felt, with almost unbearable friction. Finally he whips over onto his stomach and pumps himself into the sheet, reliving agonies of adolescence, twice this week I sinned father, it was that that drove him from the Church. He lies for some time, feeling himself pulse, and grow damp and cold.

> lunar mistress,
> riding clouded, cloaked,
> waxing through gibbous imperfections,
> tempting full, and waning:
> heartless bitch.
> what drives us,
> to spend our days half silent
> between stars?
> we want our hands on everything we see;
> we are like children,
> breaking what we tire of.
> mistress, tempt us with your height,
> make us mad, lunatic to

clamber up through air and void
where gravity dies, walk
in a great airless graveyard,
where craters bear the names of men.

Atop the stack of his poems he clips a covering letter, hoping his name will make up for their defects, and takes the manila envelope out to mail.

He had begun to see his life as a series of bubbles, precise little scenes that went toward a biography, the way submodules went together into an Apollo system. But so much of his life was nonfunctional, inconclusive. There was no order to it, no logical progression to climax and resolution. His life would make poor drama. In fact, it would make poor biography.

The image of his book haunted him, the image of himself as author. He had a greater feeling of fame now than he had ever had in the frantic years following his flight. He wondered at that until he found a line in Yeats that pierced him with its truth: *Man is in love, and loves what vanishes.*

Alone, becalmed, it was fine, for he had books to read and silence in which to think and money enough to last the summer, a quiet season of the soul that he knew would pass but which seemed timeless because it was all so new. But it passed. His reenlistment forms came; Kevin was preparing for college; he had to grow used to the idea of divorce. The house took on a dull dead feel, as if his eyes in passing over objects too many times had burnt the life from them. He felt adrift, becalmed, beyond continuing.

Until one evening he called his wife at the number she had left. When he heard her voice he sickened and softened inside and was near tears when he asked to come up and see her and she said yes.

Start from scratch.

Is it true that most women reach their sexual maturity in their late thirties?

Is it true that most men undergo a depression of the sexual faculties at that age?

How may this relate to marital difficulties among couples in their late thirties?

Is it true that there is a correspondence between the cycle of lunar phases and some women's menstrual cycles?

Is it true that more women encounter their menstrual cycles during full moons than can be accounted for by chance?

Is it true that intercourse is impossible, or at least unpleasant, during menstruation?

Is it true that Edwards' aversion to the gibbous moon is due at least in part to his wife's periodic denials of sexual access?

Is it true that a man's potency is affected by altering gravitational environments?

Is it true that the Moon landing was the most significant event in human history?

Is it true that macroscopically the course of human history follows the same cycles manifest in tides and biological functions microscopically?

Is it true that periodicity or repetition is a recurring theme in human endeavor, manifesting itself as it does in history, biology, chemistry, physics, electronics, music, religion, literature, and art?

Discuss periodicity as it functions on a multitude of levels in time. Include etymologies of the terms "minute," "hour," "day," "month," "year," "century."

Discuss how the Sanskrit word *sandhyas,* meaning "region of change," applies to the quarters of the day.

How many orders of magnitude are there between the smallest and largest levels of periodicity in time? Is this enough?

Is periodicity an inherent characteristic of time, or an imposed structure?

Is repetition a valid form for a construction that intends to elude time by using time?

Is it true that all good art is timeless?

Are dreams works of art?

Are events of history, of themselves, works of art?

Is it true that Edwards' attempts at poetry are primitive attempts to see his actions in the context of history as a work of art?

Is art necessary?

Where do we go from here?

He carries a knot of anticipation in his stomach as he drives. It is a sinking, scrotum-tightening feeling compounded of fear and anxiety and simple adrenalin. His pulse is up and this makes his chest light and there is the heaviness in his gut and the tearing knotted anticipation centered squarely between.

An odd feeling now: he has lost his biographical sense, that way of looking on things happening as already past. He feels now, driving into an alien situation, of his own volition (there's the difference between this journey and his history-making jaunt to the Moon), the course of his future is in doubt.

But why is he afraid? Simply as a preliminary to confrontation, yes, he sees it as that, the old order against the new; he is afraid of this great symbolical enemy Youth, their attitudes and mores exposed to him by *Time* magazine. He sees teen-aged girls drifting through the Teaneck summer. To find himself at that age he would have to go back to Waco, 1953—and all the driving and adrenalin makes that for an instant seem possible, exit 12 for the McCarthy hearings, 13 for the Korean War; it seems he can travel back those roads to his youth as easily as he now takes the Thruway. The thought is repellent; he was an ugly boy. So in his fear he sees envy of these new children, no, not children, but manifestations of a graceful adolescence he would have thought impossible. This generation seems astute, mature, beyond their years, beyond perhaps even his.

The commune is not at all what he expected. Instead of a rambling farmhouse, wide furrowed fields, cows, sheep grazing, it is a modest two-story home surrounded by neatly pruned shrubs. In a small garden he sees a man almost his own age shade his eyes to watch the car lurch up the dirt drive. This is the author, no doubt. The man sets down his hoe and approaches.

"Hello, I'm Eric Byrne. You must be Colonel Edwards. Charlotte told us to expect you."

He is weak and drained from the trip; the sun hits him another blow as he climbs out of the air-conditioning. He shakes hands, feeling the man's grip, feeling it as if it were on his wife.

"Come inside and I'll introduce you around. We're glad you decided to come up."

He already dislikes Byrne, his bluff cordiality, the veneer of sexuality that seems to lie on his skin like a deep tan.

The only person inside, though, is Charlotte, cross-legged on the sofa, reading; she looks up when he enters—she has heard the car and arranged herself purposely into that neutral position, and stays seated, realizing that a hug would be too intimate, a handshake too cold. In his consideration of adolescence, in his high pitch of sexual awareness, all he can think of is how much he has missed her physically.

Charlotte rises. "I'll show John around until dinner."

They go out; they speak little as they walk. She tells him there are half a dozen teenagers, sometimes more, living here, working and paying what they can. Eric bears most of the expense. There is a small barn behind the house, hens, a couple of pigs, some turkeys and ducks. Charlotte says hello to a couple, Robert and Barbara, as they emerge from the barn, smiling with slight embarrassment. Edwards looks at Charlotte, squeezes her hand. And soon enough they end up back in her bedroom.

He sees this scene in crystal, he steps outside himself and observes them both there in the waning light. Charlotte unbuttons her soft blue shirt and the sun is gold and shadow on her. The room is vivid in oranges and browns. Even Edwards' large body, going quickly to fat from lack of training, training that was always more abuse than development, is handsome in the twilight. He lies naked on the bed, the sheets cool, the air gentle, Charlotte sliding silken over him. He sighs. She massages him gently as the sun sets and her breasts glow pale against her tan, twin globes rising over him. She moves onto him as in his dream: he is still as death, as in the dream: and suddenly suffocating, he thrusts against her—she slows him, pressing—he moves again, frantic now to break the spell of shadowed timeless dream that seems to hover close—she presses harder—and furious, he grabs her shoulders and wrenches her down with a small gasp under him, pumping desperate mad for assertion, starting a rhythm, a continuity, feeling that in these seconds, these thrusts, he can vindicate all their time passed and gone.

Perhaps she understands then, or perhaps her body betrays her, or perhaps she has secret reasons of her own, but she moves in sympathy; she gives Edwards his dominance. Gives it—

And Edwards deliquesces, his determination melts and flows from him, sugar water semen flowing back into him, he slows—

Charlotte sighs—

He comes up off her and rolls away and she knows from past experience he will not cry or show anger like some, he will just lie very, very still, hardly breathing, dying small deaths—

"John, it doesn't matter. It's all right."

"No. No, it isn't."

"Shh. Yes. It is. I don't care."

"I *do*—"

"I know. It doesn't matter. It's not your fault. Try later."

Edwards lies quietly as she gently caresses him. And peace comes; what a wonder, to have his wife back as she was ten years ago for even these few moments. The darkness grows, and he has visions of space, at once appealing and terrifying. The weight of the world releases him, and he soars transcendent through the firmament. After a while the stars resolve to the grainy darkness of the room and Charlotte is beside him and they talk.

"What do you want here, Sharl?"

"I don't know if I can explain. It's a feeling. It's as if I've spent my whole life inside, in some horrible hospital or rest home. In Teaneck, even outside I feel trapped, like the sky is a giant bowl clamped down on me. I haven't felt really free since God knows when. I feel sick and pale and bedridden and convalescent. Christ, John, I want to feel healthy again." He nods. "Do you ever feel that?"

"Yes. Sometimes I feel the air pressing on me. I feel gravity and I feel the atmosphere like an ocean on my back. And I want —out. I want to be in free fall again. I dream about that sometimes."

"This is what NASA is to you?"

"Was."

"Why do you want to resign?"

"Because it's over! Didn't you hear me on that program? It's over, done, finished!" He groans and rolls away from her. "I'm sorry. I wasn't yelling at you."

"I know."

"But it could have been something—and we let it go. We took one step out of the cradle; we put our foot out—and drew it back. What sense does that make? Is that at all sane? I think what it is is that we're not *ready* for space, we can't deal with all that emptiness. We got out there and didn't know what to do, and got scared and came back. But God—! You can't reenter the womb. That's all the earth is." He pauses. "If only we could be happy with things as they are. If only they didn't have to mean something, or progress to something, or evolve into something . . . if we could only live moments, just moments, unconnected . . . I think I could accept that. Be happy with it."

"John," she soothes, holding him. Against the coldness of space, the transcendent spirit of man, her warmth is cloying. She binds him to his body. "John, John . . . what's out there, anyway?"

"Nothing," he says, and sinks into sleep.

On an ocean. Wave mechanics. Harmonic motion. The years cycling back through the seasons. College. His physics professor, strange old man, explaining the motion of the waves: periodic functions, series of crests and troughs, repetitions. Every sort of motion dependent upon harmonic theory. Sine waves, circles, spirals, helixes, orbits, all the same. The same equations apply. Greek letters fly past his sleeping eyes:

$$\psi(x,\ t) = \sin\left(\frac{2\pi}{\lambda}x + \frac{2\pi}{\tau}t\right)$$

Period of a pendulum. Earth's a pendulum, you know, two ways: swings around the sun, turns on its axis: complex motion. In the middle of the lecture he dropped into philosophic discourse, the brilliant mind derailed and rambling as the classroom pitched on the waves: duality in monism, the one wave with the two halves, see? Positive and negative. Every physical concept doubly poetic; mathematics the purest poetry. Ah, the Greeks, such poets. Class grumbling, breaking up and diving off the platform, old fool senile and rambling about sine fucking waves: SIT DOWN! I'm not finished! Edwards alone then; now listen, hissed the teacher, air seething with his hot intense breath, the sea growing long and glassy as if listening, listen: *We are all disturbances of the medium.* Understand? Disturbances of the medium. Pebbles dropped in a vacuum. Waves. All of us, nothing but a complex collection of sine waves. Heart, lungs, brain, glands, nothing but repetitions, periods, life, life, waves. Frightened, Edwards dove, sank quickly and drowned, and drowning, woke.

As he enters the kitchen and faces all the members of the commune together for dinner, he feels lines of force in the room, constellations of tensions shifting to accommodate him. Interference patterns. How distant he is from this world; how far Teaneck from the mythical land of Woodstock; the others feel this too, and there is that moment of uneasiness, the lines in flux, reality facing the legend, the two worlds' images mediated to each other only by *Time*. The moment passes, though. They sit to dinner.

Edwards assimilates his impressions: the dinner discussion is light and varied, ranging over topics of literature, music, films, farming. One girl casually mentions her abortion and Edwards suffers a Catholic reaction. Not that he has been at all religious since marrying Charlotte, but a sense of sin, once acquired, is not easily lost. There is none of that in anyone here: sin and grace are not part of the metaphysical baggage of this generation. They speak in terms of yin and yang, complementaries without relative values. He feels at a loss, vulnerable: nothing that upsets him could move any of these people.

After dinner they sit and talk softly over the littered plates. Byrne starts to roll a cigarette. He has rolled several from tobacco that evening, but now he reaches for a smaller jar, and the flakes are green and Edwards feels a kick of giddy trepidation as he watches Byrne pour the stuff into a rolling machine and pull it into a yellow cigarette. He is acutely aware of everyone, of their casualness and his tension, and he feels Charlotte watching him. Byrne pours more into the machine and rolls another. The first joint moves around, closing on him. Charlotte tokes, smiles at him, and passes it. He shakes his head. She nods and smiles, makes "come on" with her mouth. Afraid of interrupting the casual after-dinner atmosphere, afraid of making a foolish scene over something so minor, afraid perhaps of missing entrance to some new world, and (at bottom) curious, he accepts, sucks, holds, passes. "Keep it in," Charlotte whispers. He nods secretly. John Edwards, pothead.

The first few rounds he feels nothing and starts to relax, but after a while a certain detachment slips into his senses. They extend; his eyes, ears, fingers are at the far end of a tunnel, relaying everything to him in delayed echoes. Everything has flattened, taken on the aspect of a screen. Entranced, Edwards watches as he would in a theater. Colors are rich, vivid, the dialogue flows wondrously. How lifelike, he thinks.

This goes on for some time before Max gets up. Edwards runs the scene back: Byrne has asked how many chickens he can expect for dinner and Max said, "I'll go out and cull some now. Come on, Barb." Then he senses Edwards' gaze. "Want to see how you cull chickens, Colonel?" and Edwards, suffused with good will, says, "Why, shore," and they are up and out.

There is a perfect silence outside, a warm still breathless summer silence, with a full moon, orange, just risen. Off on the horizon fireworks burst soundlessly, fast-dying sparks in the night. The Fourth, Edwards suddenly remembers. It is the Fourth of July. America is 199 tonight.

In the barn is a rich earth shit smell. In the roost the birds flutter and cluck at the flashlight. Max says, "We have a dozen birds but we're only getting about eight eggs a day. So we must have a couple hens not doing their jobs." He lifts a brown one which squawks indignantly. Barb takes the light. The hen's eyes gleam yellow and she squirms. "Down," says Max. "Keep it out of her eyes, Barb."

He carries the bird into the adjoining toolshed, away from the others, and snaps on the light. He says to Andrews, "Now the first thing you do is check the claws. If the hen's not laying, the yellow pigment that should go into the yolk gets into the beak and claws and around the vent." He turns the hen over and she squawks. "Pretty good. Now you check the vent—" He pushes the tail feathers aside and a pink puckered hole appears. "It should be moist and bleached—no yellow—and this one looks pretty good." Abruptly Max lays his fingers beside the vent. "Check the pelvic bone for clearance, make sure the eggs have room to get out—" He flips the hen back right-side. "Yeah, she looks like a layer. Give her a white tag, Barb." The girl has a handful of colored plastic rings—she snaps a white one around the bird's gnarled leg. Max takes the hen back in, emerges with another. "When they stop laying," he says, "they start looking a lot better. The muscles firm up and the feathers get slicker. So I get very suspicious when I see a healthy-looking bird like this one." He flips her over. The hen thrashes wildly, flaps the air with frantic wings. "Oh, baby," says Max, "you're much too active. You're looking too good to be spending much time in the laying box." He holds her firmly. "Hm. Vent looks okay, though. Two fingers here . . . Give her a yellow, Barb."

After eleven hens there is only one definite cull, one red tag already in a separate cage. Max brings in the last bird. "This is a sex-linked. I would be very surprised if she wasn't laying. Still, you can never tell. The only way you find out for sure is to kill 'em and check the egg tree. I killed a cull once that had an egg all ready to drop out. Ate the chicken, fried the egg. But we lost a layer. Another thing, they moult in July and they don't lay while they're moulting. Every poultry book I've ever read says, come July, you can forget about eggs."

As soon as Max starts poking in the feathers the bird explodes in frenzy. The claws kick, the wings flail, feathers fly. Max puts a hand on the bird's neck. If you choke 'em a little, it calms 'em." The hen does not calm though and Max shifts her further upside down, A claw catches at his shirt. "Ow! Shit!" He drops the hen and Barb grabs her. "You hurt?" "No. Just a scratch." She holds the bird while Max probes. He spreads the feathers to show Edwards the dry tight yellow vent. "Ahh." Max lifts her, calm now, and drops her in the cage with the other cull. She flutters once and is still.

He smiles at Edwards. "Dinner."

"We've got two for tomorrow," Max shouts, coming in. "One of the sex-links was a cull." They enter the living room. The group here seems smaller. Byrne says, "You like our chickens, Colonel?"

Edwards, still high, tries not to laugh. "Fine birds. Very interesting."

"Sit down. Let's talk. I've been interested in you a long time, Colonel."

"Really?"

"Yes, really. I saw you on television a few days ago."

"Oh." Edwards shrivels. He remembers Charlotte's estimation of his performance, which must certainly have come from Byrne.

"Interesting. Unexpected. You find your hero's role unsatisfying?"

"Uh . . ."

"I ask out of professional interest. As a writer, I've been analyzing the roles of the hero in our culture and our literature." Byrne rolls a cigarette, tobacco. Edwards is still stoned, time is still doing strange things. "It seems to me, Colonel, that outside of sports, the space program is our only source of heroes these days. Politicians are certainly on the outs; since Vietnam we've forsaken our military heroes; so what's left us but our astronauts, our explorers?"

"What indeed?"

"And yet it's a strange heroism, isn't it?"

"Yes. Yes it is."

"How do you find it strange?"

"Being inside it."

Byrne looks at Edwards with sudden intensity, as if to exclude the rest of the group. "I don't think it's heroism at all, really. Not in the traditional sense of the word. People talk about exploring frontiers, but we know that's nonsense. You have your flight plan, your agenda; to call that heroic is . . . well, picture Ulysses following a triple-A roadmap. That takes no bravery, no excellence, none of the heroic qualities.

"Now I'm not being derogatory, Colonel. What I see here is an evolution of our heroic archetypes. Heroes arise from drama of course, and the major dramatic periods in history were during

Greek and Reformation times. It's interesting then to consider the difference between the Greek and Christian traditions: the Greeks admired men of action, of heroic deeds. Christianity respects the martyrs, the sufferers. We see a move from the active to the passive, from masculine to feminine."

"Watch it, Eric," said Barb. "Male chauvinism."

Byrne looks at her, vaguely annoyed. "Well, no. You must realize that the feminine is separable from the female. What's called male chauvinism is the equating of the two, the stereotyping of woman into feminine roles; and the implied value judgment. I may speak, for instance, of Barbara having a certain masculinity, or of Robert being somewhat feminine, without offense. We understand that there are certain classical definitions of masculine and feminine, unconnected with sex.

"Now the Christian iconography"—back to Edwards now, he feels the terminology is intended to intimidate him—"is primarily feminine, in its use of the Virgin, and the apotheosis of the passive—in fact the whole notion of Immaculate Conception rather avoids the issue of male versus female—whereas the more primitive religions were more assertive, dramatic, masculine. The earliest gods were fertility gods. The Greek heroes were men of action. Christians are martyrs. There's the move from sex to sexlessness, masculinity to femininity.

"Colonel Edwards, our latest hero, shows that the trend has even reached American culture. America has traditionally been masculine. Frontiers, and all that. It's interesting that the Moon is the first frontier America has drawn back from. And Colonel Edwards, as a hero, I think we must admit, is a bit of a woman."

Edwards stands. The room wavers before him. "Fuck you, Byrne," he enunciates.

"I, ah, meant no personal offense, Colonel. As I said . . ."

"Like hell you didn't. You thought you could toss some big words around and dazzle the poor dumb Air Force jock. Well, the colonel, Mr. Byrne, is not so dumb. The colonel has a doctorate, among other things, and throwing convoluted insults in the third person at him does not fool him."

"I assure you, I was not trying . . ."

"Shove it! Listen, Byrne, *you* go through ten years of training, of being whipped and spun and starved into shape, *you* go out and study tensor calculus until you know how and why every control in a rocket works, and *you* go through the agonies of waiting to be chosen for a mission and maybe later rejected and having two of your best friends die while they're training—*you* go through all of that yourself and *then* maybe I'll let you sit there and tell me I'm a bit of a woman, but from where you sit now you're more of a woman to me than your goddamned *hens* out there!"

And then he goes silent; he gets quite cold and distant, and sweeps his eyes slowly around the room. He says, "Where's my wife?"

"Your wife. Ah, yes." Byrne smiles strangely. "You'll find her in her bedroom, I think."

He pauses for only a second as he reaches his wife's door—the hairs on his wrists move and his hand stops before touching the knob—then he forces it forward, twists, pushes.

He freezes in the doorway.

The first kid he met in the barn, Robert, is on his wife. He moves quickly across the room, sees Charlotte clutch at the kid and he is sure she seduced him, he runs the whole scene through his mind instantly, yes, the kid would never take that initiative with the husband in the house, but nonetheless there he is, and he grabs the kid's shoulders, pulls him back and off, gasping astonishment. Charlotte spits, "Bastard, *bas*tard!" and he whirls the kid, hits him in the stomach, slick against his fist, hits him again higher, the kid squeals, and again, better now, a deep full grunt, he is hurting him, playing him like a drum, he establishes a rhythm of attack, the kid moving only in defense, curling, incapacitated by that incredible shock of extremes, pain like a searing splash of ice water, numbly taking it like a piece of training apparatus, Edwards working the slow easy rhythms as if he were in a simulator, on a flight, keeping up muscle tone, the impartial repetitions of exercises lulling him into lazy introspection, he punches with first one arm then the other, watching the kid collapse with heavy-lidded eyes, the dull dispassionate discharge of energy, they had to do these in space, to burn up calories and drain excess energy, to work their bowels regularly, on schedule, to masturbate and cancel sexual tensions, they had to do it in just this dispassionate systematic way, *0100 commence masturbatory sequence,* he saw that in a cartoon once after he got back and it made him sick. . . .

The Moon was full outside the capsule, you could see all of it, but all was only half because the Moon was locked in orbit with the same face always to the Earth and you could never see the far side, even when it was full, bright, naked to the stars—had they come that far just for a glimpse at the far side?—and Earth, its billions hidden behind its calm placid mask of blue . . .

. . . and the kid falls heavily to the bed, and he turns and Byrne is there with the rest behind him, sick faces peering in fear of violence, oh yes he has found their weak spot, in the alien air of conflict. Now is the time for confrontation, now is when Byrne steps forward, challenges him to a fight, or simply says between tight-drawn lips, "Out!"

But Byrne does no such thing. He smiles sadly at Edwards and says, he *asks*—"Do you want to talk about it?"

Yes, there are climaxes, brief spurts of passion, oscillations from times of greater energy to times of lesser energy, but they resolve nothing, no, resolution is beyond us. The stories do not end neatly, much as we need them to. Our lives are incomprehensibly tangled. Such a demand for climaxes and resolutions drives us to our madnesses, our fictions. For the world is round and nothing but round, there are only the soft risings and fallings, the continual fall of day into night, the endless plummet through space without end or beginning. We drift, we live, we die, but death is not an end because the race goes on building roads and pyramids, launching rockets, and survive or perish, we all fill some evolutionary role. We are a statistical whole.

He tells himself he is not a hero or a myth. America is not Greece or Olympus. The world has turned round and the universe has closed and we have all been forced to touch one another and know that we are all alone and none of us are alone and that we have precious little time to come to grips with that truth. Night rushes past his car. Far-spaced lights wash him rhythmically. Three billion people on a single planet, together and alone in so much night; while the moon shines with a single dead light from all its craters, myths and heroes.

Evolution. Statistics. He can drive off the road now, or not drive off, and either way help fill the statistics. He feels he is falling again; weightless, orbiting; falling forever through the void.

He looks at the speedometer and sees with shock the needle at 110. He slows, the Thruway slows beneath him, and he drives calmly all the rest of the way back to Jersey.

That week his inquiry and samples are returned with a polite letter; his name at least has brought him the courtesy of a prompt personal response. The editor explains how interesting the poetry looks, how intrigued he is by the prospects, but why he must reluctantly refuse. The house has been losing money consistently on poetry, and they now have a blanket policy about first poetry books. You must be published before you can publish. This circular logic annoys Edwards: he remembers his father saying long ago you can't go in the water till you can swim, John boy, and you can't swim till you get in the water.

The letter goes on to state that a dramatized account of his voyage might be of interest, but he is no longer assured of selling even that on the strength of his name. *Sic transit gloria mundi,* he thinks, and drops letter, précis, and samples into the trash.

The next day he gets his renewal notice from the Air Force. He thinks of his $2,500 a month, he thinks of Kevin's college, he thinks of his $10,000 in the bank. He has two days to decide. He thinks of four years ahead of him, of retirement and pension at forty-four.

The letter joins his poems.

For some reason he goes to the typewriter. He sits at it for a long time, silent. Minutes pass, and then with great definiteness, he types his name, slowly and precisely. J. O. H. N. C. H. R. I. I. I. Why. Why the Moon is void to him. Needed something to put his mark on. Nothing on the Moon: flags, machinery, plaques: had anything to do with him. Me. I. John Chri. S. T. I. E. E. D. W. And the fear of God that came on him in the capsule. A. R. D. S. The single key strokes echoed through the house. J.

The universe is round. Life is round. The Moon goes from full to new to full, he himself has gone from understanding to not understanding and so on. What was the point in that? Perhaps it was that you understood a little more each time, and the place you returned to was different for having been left. It was not like in the books, though: no triangles or pyramids, no ends or beginnings. He should have been able to write a book like that, a book that was round, incidents orbiting around the center, himself. But he could not do it well enough to get it published. And if he learned to write well enough to get published, by then he would be proficient and facile and would see things differently: books like monuments, not circles.

They were not circles, even: they were helixes. You came to the same point again, like the Earth moving through space, but it was not the same point because time had moved the circle's center. The form of life then was the helix: that same corkscrew molecule that carried in your cells messages of growth and regeneration.

Why should he try to put life in a book, anyway? What had books to do with life?

It is quite possible that until the Apollo photos no one really believed the Earth was round. It took the photographic image of the blue Earth, streaked with ochres and swirls of white, hanging visibly alone in the void, to make man speak of a spaceship Earth. We disregard thoughts, ideas, concepts, until they are interfaced with us through our technology. The best seat in the stadium belongs to the camera. News comes to us only on a screen. Four centuries of foreknowledge could not prepare us for the impact of that single photo, its horrible truth.

Watching the preparations for the last Apollo on his screen, Edwards remembers the rocket's thrust, remembers solid ground falling from him and slowly drawing in on itself until a circle formed and shrank so he could cover it with his thumbnail.

Kevin and he watch the last Apollo unwind. Mission Control counts down in a cold clear passionless voice. Smoke, cables move, but the rocket is still, even past zero. In the cabin it feels like liftoff starts ten seconds early; from the ground it appears ten seconds late.

The rocket moves. The Saturn V thrusters have generated sufficient force, and it rises slowly, disencumbered of gravity.

What sexual energy a rocket had. Despite the sterile veneer NASA threw up around the program, its final inevitable symbol was phallic. In the slow steady rise of energies was the primeval pulse of the animal, man's ends and beginning tied together in his artifacts. Charlotte had attended the lunar liftoff and she said later it was so sensual, so compelling, that warm sympathetic pulsings had started within her. When it was over, she said, people hurried away, awed and embarrassed by that immense potency.

Or say, rather, force: for NASA had stripped rockets of their potency. They had taken the V-2 and removed the warhead, removed in fact the point of it since rockets had been originally designed as missiles, engines of destruction. They flew, fell, exploded. Their trajectories were dramatic curves. But at NASA's tampering, science's imperative, they flew straight up, out, fell apart in sections to hurl a payload of weak men at a weightless point in the sky. There was no meaning to that, no climax. Man had not yet grown enough out of his urge for destruction to appreciate this new application, the straightening of the trajectory. There was no drama in it; and Edwards sees now that drama and sex are inextricably linked, that the rise and curve of one is the same as the other. Anything without a climax is ultimately disappointing, and in that is the key to the end of the program.

The ships orbit. The screen is dark with static and crackling voices. They are positioning a camera to follow the docking. Watch now: the Earth rolls slowly beneath, Apollo roams the skies. Over the far curving horizon is a dot, a hint of movement. Soyuz approaches, gaining dimension. It elongates. There is an excited interchange, static garbling Russian and English equally to nonsense.

"Can you understand it, Dad?"

"Shh."

The Russians' manned program is scheduled to continue, he understands from what faint rumors escape that tantalizing curtain of silence. So, imagining himself in space, he feels vaguely threatened by the sight of Soyuz. Perhaps he projects his own tension into the voice of the American pilot, but he seems to Edwards as jauntily nervous as a virgin on his first date, strange to the mysteries of women. Edwards has that virgin's nervousness of Russians himself.

Whispers of space move in the room. He gets a whiff of the void, a brief flicker of weightlessness, a vertigo. The far craft gestures in its approach, makes a single elegant inclination as it nears. Radio signals control the camera; it shifts slowly to take in Apollo. The two ships whisper through vast sweeping statics, they make minor adjustments as the trajectories close. The radio energy is dense as they make ready to touch. Electrons move, pattern, shift. Computers click. Data flickers in great networks around the world.

Kevin is leaning forward, his breath coming quick and shallow. In the moment before contact he hunches, feeling the shadows of all contacts to come in this one. In the screen's light Edwards sees everything in perspective: blue flickers on the wet brown beer bottle he has not touched, Kevin's rapt face washed pale, his own reclining tense posture, fat on the once-solid frame . . .

The ships link. Apollo mates with Soyuz. The gates are open, static floods between them, the astronauts and cosmonauts can move between vessels. The mission is consummated, the program over. The camera drifts and Earth swims slowly under it. Browns, blues, whites, haloed in static. The Moon forgotten.

Something recedes in Edwards.

It is his fortieth birthday.

In the yard he studies the moon, and the empty black between it and earth where two vessels reel and clasp each other. They will shuttle between crafts for a bit, trade dull laborious jokes and dry paste meals, then disengage and return to Earth, nothing reached, nothing resolved, America behind while Russia pushes outward. The first time they pulled back from a frontier. He sees what Byrne meant. What will it mean to lose this initiative? Does it matter? Russia, America, what difference? The race goes on. It is the nature of things to continue. Only man, who is born and must die and has enough of a brain to possess a sense of self, thinks in terms of birth and death, starts and stops. Only man needs drama to make his short, tragic, linear life bearable.

When he goes in, Kevin is gone. He turns off the television. On impulse he goes to the attic to get the heavy binoculars he bought in Okinawa. There is the smell of time behind the attic door, a musty wasting smell that makes him feel heartsick and lost. The attic is neat and orderly, but he cannot find the binoculars. Finally he steps back out, shuts the door.

He stands in the hall, feeling the house's emptiness. He listens to its hums and murmurs. Downstairs in the dark the refrigerator turns on. He is numb. He stands in a paralyzed panic at the top of the long dim stairway, unmoving for several minutes.

There is a ringing in his ears now and his hands are cold. He drifts down the hall into Kevin's room. It is dark, with only a pale illumination flooding sharply in one window. The Moon is gibbous again, waning back through all its phases. It is very late, after midnight; a new day has started.

Kevin lies angled back on the bed as if in a bathtub, binoculars propped in thin white arms bent double against his chest. Edwards enters but does not sit on the bed for fear of breaking the view. Nor does he speak. A minute drags by. Edwards is trembling. He says, "What do you see?"

The son shrugs. "Craters."

He looks and sees the blurred patches of gray against white. Copernicus, Ptolemy, Clavius, Tranquility . . . the dead. Flags in the void. He felt remote and cold and untouchable. Kevin looked at him.

"Dad? Are we ever going back there?"

He sighed, tired, or on the edge of sorrow, though sorrow was a pointless thing. Waves receded from him. Each word broke a vast illimitable silence. "I don't know, son. I don't know."

Arcs & Secants

Two novels by KATE WILHELM ("Ladies and Gentlemen, This Is Your Crisis") were published early in 1976. One, from Harper & Row, is called *Where Late the Sweet Birds Sang;* part of it appeared in *Orbit 15* under the same title. The other, from Farrar, Straus & Giroux, is called *The Clewiston Test.*

DAVE SKAL wrote a long time ago, concerning a change we had proposed in his story "When We Were Good" *(Orbit 17):*
"Page 6: 'Dante's ears have been pointed, either through accident or design.' The old rice-picking machine again? Seriously, I think we ought to say 'through genetic accident or design' to avoid the improbability of a child falling down on the sidewalk and pointening his ears."

In March '75 R. A. LAFFERTY ("The Hand with One Hundred Fingers") wrote the following poem about Ms. Wilhelm:

> Oh Kate has gone to writing pomes!
> > Hi ho!
> She writes them bright without the bromes,
> She piles them up as tall as tomes!
> > Hi, ho! The Gollie Wol!
> She routs the temper of the times,
> > Hi ho!
> She cuts the strings that worked the mimes,
> It doesn't matter if they rimes.
> > Hi, ho! The Gollie Wol!

This was a contribution to a round-robin letter circulated among a few *Orbit* writers: Mr. Lafferty later withdrew from it, alleging unparliamentary remarks and stuffiness, but at least we got this piece of free verse out of him.

In February we wrote to a young writer, "After reading the sex scene, I venture the guess that you have never been kneed in the stones."

GEORGE R. R. MARTIN ("Meathouse Man") writes science fiction on weekends and makes his living by managing chess tournaments, an occupation now in decline "in the wake of the Bobby Boom." "Actually, what you probably should run in *Arcs & Secants* is a want ad for me. With the chess business dying on the vine, I'm currently sending out resumés all over the place, hoping to find a position teaching sf and/or creative writing at the college level. . . . If any of your readers are college presidents, they should flip through the book and read "Meathouse Man" and hire me. . . ."

Michael Helsem of Dallas sent us a short story written by a Burroughs 5700 computer. "This example originated in a 20/80 mix of punctuation and words expanded about fifteen times for a total of 1,500 units. The input can be literally anything, from a carefully selected vocabulary to pages out of a book. For instance *War and Peace* can be condensed to a few paragraphs for quick scanning; or 'The Game of Rat and Dragon' can be turned into a full-length novel."

GARY COHN ("Rules of Moopsball") is a motorcycle freak and a maker of scene phone calls. ("I know you're watching me through the window. . . . You want to see me naked," etc.) Cohn sometimes pretends not to be serious about Moopsball, but he really is, and we think he is just crazy enough to be right.

In "The Memory Machine" in *Orbit 17* we quoted two sentences from an article by Frederik Pohl in *Galaxy*, November 1974: "There's a handsome mountain called Avala near Belgrade; people go there on one-day excursions. . . . It also has a small plague to the memory of Soviet Marshal Zhokov, who died there a few years ago when his plane crashed into the mountain." Somewhere between the cup and the lip, "plague" got changed back to "plaque." If you were confused, now you know why.

A trend we deplore is the substitution of *lay* for *lie* as an intransitive verb, now well on the way to becoming standard. *Lay,* being defective, produces monstrosities like *had lay* (as in Samuel R. Delany's *Dhalgren*). The past tense of *may (might)* is now known to few, and is probably beyond rescue. English has been shedding its inflections for centuries, and no doubt could get along without any. In that event we would have to retranslate the Twenty-third Psalm for modern readers: "The Lord be my shepherd; I not want. He make me lay down in green pasture," etc.

Another problem with English is that it has no neuter singular noun for human beings (except *person,* as in *chairperson, washerperson,* etc.). To remedy this, we propose to substitute *Sap* (from *Homo sapiens*) for the collective noun *Man* in all its uses—*Sapkind, Stone Age Sap,* etc. This word now has an unfortunate connotation, but that will wear off with use, and even if a trace of it should remain, it will be no more than we deserve.

In response to our request for biographical information, CRAIG STRETE ("Who Was the First Oscar to Win a Negro?") wrote as follows: "Nosluke showt. No'vak nussmam shinlusk. Hawotoi shispi chowt. Zuma nah'soc nah tia. Haliwa gloosklap 1954," and so on for quite a while, ending, "Orbit niga kaw sit Kaw Oscar scu-la. Jope-le-wa. Bak-kar kantie-no-nah oddin Kigir aroflimah Kigi. Wichi wah-nunc. I would also like to add, that in my opinion, Custer got off much too lightly."

A correspondent asked us, "Why don't you right more of your own stories?" We do, but they keep turning turtle again.

KIM STANLEY ROBINSON, who prefers to be called Stan, is a graduate student in English. "In Pierson's Orchestra" was his submission story for the Clarion Workshop in 1974. He did not attend that year, because his acceptance letter arrived too late, but we saw the manuscript there and bought it. (He did make the Workshop in 1975.) "In Pierson's Orchestra" and "Coming Back to Dixieland" are his first two published stories.

In June WILLIAM F. ORR ("Euclid Alone," *Orbit 17*) wrote on the back of an envelope addressed to us:

> If all people of the world learned
> ESPERANTO
> They could communicate with Harry Harrison.

HOWARD WALDROP ("Mary Margaret Road-Grader") was born in Houston, Mississippi, now lives in Texas. Since 1970, his stories have appeared in *Galaxy, Analog, Vertex,* etc., and in many hardcover anthologies. His novel *The Texas–Israeli War, 1999,* written in collaboration with Jake Saunders, was published by Ballantine in 1974.

We told all we know about FELIX C. GOTSCHALK ("The Family Winter of 1986") at the time of his last appearance here, except that he is one of the most interesting and fastest-rising of the new science fiction writers, and that his spelling is untrustworthy.

KATHLEEN M. SIDNEY ("The Teacher") writes movingly about the teaching profession, of which she is a member, but she is not herself a dedicated teacher: she is a frustrated film director. This is her second story for *Orbit.*

RAYLYN MOORE ("A Modular Story") lives in "an elderly white frame cottage attached to a garden full of roses (which for some inexplicable reason seem to bloom all year) and nasturtiums, almost within throwing distance of the Pacific Grove [California] beach."

JOHN VARLEY ("The M&M, Seen As a Low-Yield Thermonuclear Device") is a young writer who lives in Eugene, Oregon, the very place where we intend to settle when we leave Florida. We have not yet had the pleasure of meeting Mr. Varley, but by the time you read these lines we may have done so: both the *I Ching* and the Tarot say we will sell our house and move to Oregon in December or January. (Stop Press: They were right.)

GENE WOLFE, a frequent contributor, reports that at a session of the Windy City Writers' Conference early in 1975, he was severely criticized for having introduced into a far-future story a family coat of arms including a spaceship *volant*. "Now as you may have noticed earlier, Damon, I am a villager. I live in the Village of Barrington [Illinois]; and Barrington may be small, but it's classy—it even has a coat of arms, and it makes me go down to the village hall every year and shell out ten dollars for the privilege of putting its tax stamp on each car. So there, waiting for me on my own windshield, was the quartered escutcheon of Barrington: dexter chief point, a sheaf of grain; sinister chief point, an open book; sinister base point, a tree in leaf; and dexter base point, a test tube and retort."

The day after we got this letter, we read a newspaper article about a firm that will design a coat of arms and put on it any damn thing you want—if you're a hog merchant, for instance, a hog. Hurrah for the spaceship *volant!*

CARTER SCHOLZ ("The Eve of the Last Apollo") dropped out of school in 1974 because it was taking too much of his time. He has worked as an illustrator, graphic designer, composer, radio announcer, etc. At present he is living with the talented print-maker Lisa Houck in Providence, Rhode Island. This is his first published story.

Faithful readers will recall that in *Orbit 16* we invited them to submit temporally scrambled words to be added to the "Little Lexicon for Time-travelers" in that volume. We offered a small prize for the five most outrageous entries, thinking that, if lucky, we might get that many. To our surprise, twenty-nine readers responded with a total of six hundred ninety-six words and phrases. Luckily, the operative word in our offer was "outrageous," not "ingenious" or "difficult"; even so, we found it impossible to reduce the list of prize winners to five. Accordingly, the following are being sent $5 for each word, and a copy each of *Orbit 18:*

J. Kevin Branigan, 75 W. Squire Drive, Rochester, New York: *postater.*

Dick Curtis, 52 Brattle Street, Holden, Massachusetts: *childery.*

Penny L. Davis, 127 E. Main Street, Washingtonville, New York: *minutei.*

Eva Free, 501 E. 32nd St., Apartment 504, Chicago, Illinois: *P. M. Sterdam.*

Leonard N. Isaacs, Justin S. Morrill College, East Lansing, Michigan: *cright paearly, raoutstern.*

Larry W. Martin, Department of Linguistics, 568 EPB, University of Iowa, Iowa City, Iowa: *Passéacome.*

Len Rosenberg, 3530 DeKalb Avenue, Apartment 5-G, Bronx, New York: *Geol Dolfe.*

Aljo Svoboda, 2182 Cheam Avenue, Santa Susana, California: *clifroris.*

Fran Wilson, 1315 Euclid Avenue, Syracuse, New York: *gout and toffic, MMI.*

The following also sent entertaining lists of words: Michael Bishop, Pine Mountain, Georgia; Tim Breslin, 419 56th Street, Altoona, Pennsyvlania; L. R. Enders, 935 Ninth Street, Albany, New York; Robin H. Kreutzberg, 1548 W. University #3, Tempe, Arizona; Jay F. Petersen, 11 Ash Road, Branford, Connecticut; William Sanders, 316 W. 21, Little Rock, Arkansas; Ellen M. Seidenian, 1415 Holt Road, Huntington Valley, Pennsylvania: but since our prizes are exhausted, we can offer them only gratitude.

A number of readers asked, "Please, what is 'Math E'Nar'?" We won't tell, but will offer some help. The time-word in "Math E'Nar" is concealed, like a face in a puzzle drawing, by being spread across all three words of the phrase. (If you get this one, you should have no trouble with the prize-winning "Geol

Dolfe.") Among the prize winners, Larry W. Martin's "Passé-acome" is so elegant that we could not resist it, but so difficult that we think we should give you a hint: the solution is the name of a city.

Anatomy was a favorite topic among the contestants: besides the prize-winning *cright paearly* and *clifroris,* we got *afterskin* (Enders), *comenads* and *minh* (Davis), and *penwas* (appropriately, Petersen). Other recurrent topics are summarized below.

The arts: *godian* and *presentoral* (Davis); *Borwas Karlon* (Wilson); *retrose* (Branigan). Natural history: *fhigher* and *shellfwash* (Petersen); *oldt* (Branigan); *planktoff* (Kreutzberg); *offioff* (Rosenberg); *fromafro* (Branigan). Religion: *Geneswas, athewast, fetwash, Waslam,* and *Vwashnu* (Enders); *postearly* (Martin and Wilson); *Anowa* (Rosenberg and Curtis); *pericalypse* (Svoboda); *Postsbyterian* and *Maharwashi* (Sanders). Geography: *Louwasikata* (Sanders); *Wasreal* and *Wastanbul* (Enders); *Coffey Wasland* (Wilson).

Other words that particularly pleased us were *afbacked* and *vigilpost* (Bishop); *loutguistics* (Svoboda); *excomet, boutcome, sexit,* and *exinorable* (Wilson); *apchild, calisnowics, bespring* and *cyouth* (Curtis); *thover* (Breslin); *punderty* (Seidenian); *up-and-in, outcunabula,* and *garcomeyle* (Enders); *telestarboardation* and *paleoprene* (Branigan); *futurery* and *onicial* (Rosenberg).

Michael Bishop submitted a "Little Lexicon for Intra-temporal Football": *goal ante, linefronter, quarterforth, split beginning, sudden birth,* and *touchup.*

Several readers sent letters written in timese; Mark Alexander, for instance, wrote: "Your cofftest in *Orbit 16* concerning the linicon for time-travelers is an iste of time, if I may be so bnew to suggest. I kthen it might seem amusing to some fans, but I think it's nlate fleftening to see retrofessional people in the foreback of science fiction such as yourself publwashing such noffsense. Let us hope that thwas bdark upon science fiction does not contexue. Your punishment should be to read A. E. rear Vogt's *The Weapon Shops of Washer,* if you have not done so already." And William Sanders wrote at the bottom of his list, "These are all I have to supermit to your protest, Mr. Kday (and dwasmit, don't tell me that's unretronounceable, after 'pfirstic' for Chrwast's sake) and if I win a copy of the anthology I hope you will aufrom-graph it for me. P.S.: I postdict you will regret having exstigated this entire nearce."

Not only undeterred but manically resolute, we offer another lexicon (it appears on page 64) and another contest. Prizes will be given as before; entries should be sent to Damon Knight, 3334 W. 14th Ave., Eugene, OR 97402, and must be received before November 15, 1976.